FOR LILA, FOREVER

WINTER RENSHAW

COPYRIGHT

DESCRIPTION

The words "For Lila, forever" adorned the front of the envelope in blue ink, the handwriting all too familiar, but it didn't matter what it said. I didn't have the heart to open it.

We couldn't be together.

Not after everything...

Leaving Rose Crossing, Maine was one of the most painful moments of my life—or at least it was until the day I came face-to-face with Thayer Ainsworth again.

After a decade of searching, he's found me, and he wants to know why I quit my housemaid job and left his family's island estate without so much as a goodbye. But I'm bound by a devastating secret much bigger than the two of us, and telling him the truth has consequences.

Looking into the eyes of the only man I've ever loved, I tell him the only thing I'm allowed to: never contact me again. And when he's gone, I sit down and finally open his letter.

Only it isn't a letter at all.

And it changes everything.

PROLOGUE

MAY **2010**

THAYER

"*WHERE ... ARE ... THEY?*" My lungs burn after sprinting from The Lila Cottage to my grandfather's house where I stormed into his study, a man on a mission.

"Thayer." He rises from his leather chair, a cordial smile on his face as he dog-ears his Architectural Digest magazine and rests it on a coffee table. "What a pleasant surprise. Wasn't expecting you until tomorrow. Come on in. Have a seat."

He waves me over, but I remain planted. I won't rest, I won't make myself at home until I know why the Hilliards are nowhere to be found.

The boat dropped me off at the dock a half hour ago, and as

I made my way to the main house, I couldn't help but notice from a distance that The Hilliard Cottage looked ... off. And then I realized there were no flowers. Junie always plants flowers at the end of April, and it's the middle of May. Also there were weeds growing out of the old flower beds. Ed never would've allowed that to happen. Curious—and concerned—I made my way to their cottage, only to find the front door unlocked and the place looking different from the last time I was there.

I made my way from room to room, and it only took me a minute to realize all the family photos that Ed and Junie had were gone. In their place were the faces of smiling and posing strangers. I went to the main bedroom next, only to find the closet half-filled with women's clothes, not so much as a hint of anything a man would wear. When I went to Lila's old room next, I found it stripped to the bones. Not a picture. Not a book. Not a single article of clothing on the dresser.

The Hilliards were gone.

I left their cottage and sprinted to the abandoned cottage. I know Lila—she wouldn't have left without an explanation. I was positive I'd find a note somewhere in the house, and I tore the place up looking for it only to come up empty handed—except for the notes I'd written and hidden for her before I left.

She didn't find a single one, never had a chance to read them.

Granddad rises from his chair, the corners of his lips turning down. "I'm not sure why that's any of your business." And then he chuckles. "Or why you're so visibly upset." Walking toward me, he places a hand on my shoulder. "Let's head to the kitchen. I'll have Bernice prepare a snack for you. I'm sure you're hungry after your travels."

"Bernice?"

He ushers me out of his study. "The new help."

"Where are the Hilliards?" I ask as we walk.

He chuffs through his nose, taking his time answering. "They retired, Thayer. That's what people do when they reach a certain age."

I exhale, the tension in my shoulders dissipating in small increments. Retirement makes sense. They were in their early sixties last I knew, and they'd been caring for the family's island off the coast of Maine since before I was born. Junie did the cooking and the cleaning and Ed tended the garden, maintained the landscaping, combed the private beaches, and kept up the boats and three main houses all twelve months of the year.

"They moved to the mainland then?" I ask.

"I haven't the slightest. I sent them on their way last fall and haven't heard from them since. For all I know they're living their golden years in sunny Florida, or perhaps they made their way to Arizona. I believe Junie has a sister there. Either way, they're having themselves a time, I'm sure of it."

His nonchalance is nothing short of concerning.

Ed and Junie were like family. They'd been around for decades. I can't imagine they wouldn't stay in touch—or that my know-it-all grandfather wouldn't have so much as a clue as to where they went. That coupled with the fact that Lila didn't so much as leave a goodbye letter tells me that he's not giving me all the facts.

I follow him to the kitchen where a middle-aged woman with gray-brown hair stands at the sink, washing dishes by hand. She's shorter and thinner than Junie, her hair straight and cut blunt at her shoulders. There's a permanent scowl etched on her face. She doesn't light the room like Junie did.

"Bernice, this is my eldest grandson, Thayer," Grandfather says.

The woman glances over her shoulder, offering a blink-and-you'll-miss-it half-smile and a nod, her yellow-gloved hands still deep in the dirty dishwater.

"Very nice to meet you," she says, her back toward us. "I've heard so much about you. Your grandfather tells me you're pre-law at Yale?"

"Yes, ma'am," I say.

"Just finished his second year." Grandfather beams from ear to ear. It thrills him to no end that I've chosen to follow in his collegiate footsteps. "Anyway, he's made quite the jaunt today and my boy is starving. Would you mind preparing him a sandwich?"

"It's fine. I'm not hungry," I say.

"Don't be ridiculous." He puffs his chest and follows with a pompous chuff. "You just drove several hours and then you ferried in."

He's right.

I drove four straight hours from New Haven, not stopping once, because all I could think about was getting here—to

Lila, Ed and Junie's granddaughter. And then I waited two hours for a ferry that took three hours to get me here because of all the other island stops we made.

Mile after mile, the thought of seeing Lila kept me going. The sheer excitement and anticipation of being together again was all the distraction I needed.

I daydreamed about sneaking up behind her and wrapping my arms around her waist.

I pictured her sweet smile and her sparkling amber-green eyes.

I felt her hands on my face and her hair between my fingers as I stole her away and claimed her pink lips with a kiss behind the boathouse.

"How can I find them?" I ask my grandfather.

His thick brows knit. "Who, Thayer? I'm afraid you're going to have to be a bit more specific."

He's playing dumb. I know better than to buy into his act.

"The Hilliards," I say, without naming Lila specifically.

"And what reason on God's green earth would you have to contact them?" my grandfather asks. "They're *retired*. I'm sure we're the last people they want to hear from."

"They were a big part of my childhood. I considered them family," I say. "It'd just be nice to be able to keep in touch is all. Would've been nice to know the last time I saw them was going to be … the last time."

Granddad hooks a hand on my shoulder and gives it a squeeze.

"You're too sentimental, boy. Just like your mother. Speaking of which, she'll be here in two days. The rest of the crew should be here by the weekend. Say, I was going to get the ol' ketch out and go for a sail this afternoon. You'll join me." In true Howard Bertram fashion, he isn't asking.

"If you don't mind, I think I'm going to pass. Not in a sailing mood today."

His cheery disposition fades and he studies me for a moment. "This isn't about the Hilliards, is it? If you'd like to write them a letter, I'd be happy to have my attorney work on locating them and sending it on."

I consider his offer. "And how long do you think that would take?"

He squints. "Is this an urgent matter? I was under the assumption you were simply wanting to keep in touch."

Yes, it's urgent.

The woman I love—the only woman I've ever loved and will ever love—is out there somewhere and I haven't the slightest idea as to where she is, how to contact her ...

... or why she would've left without saying goodbye.

Lila had my address at school—before I left, I gave it to her for emergency purposes as well as my number and email address. She could've written me a letter. The Hilliards didn't own a personal computer of any kind, but there was a lab at the public library in Rose Crossing—she could've easily looked me up and emailed me.

The last thing I told Lila when I left here last August was that I loved her more than anything in the world. She kissed me hard as the ocean breeze played with her sun-bleached waves, and then she whispered, "Two hundred and sixty-three days…"

We didn't do the long-distance relationship thing. Not in the traditional sense. During the school year I focused on studies and extra-curriculars, and she planned to stick around Rose Crossing Island and help her grandparents whittle away at their never-ending To-Do List. When I left, we agreed that we didn't have to spend hours on the phone talking about nothing to keep that flame flickering. We agreed we didn't have to wait by mailboxes for hand-written letters every week as proof that our unwavering devotion was still received and reciprocated. Not that either of those things were options, but we both just knew. We knew that the other was always going to be there no matter what.

Waiting.

Trusting.

Missing.

Loving.

I believe that the Hilliards retired, but I don't believe that Lila would have left here without so much as leaving a letter in the cottage.

Something isn't adding up here.

"Thayer." My grandfather clears his throat. "I'm speaking to you. Are you all right?"

I realize now that I'm sitting at the base of the grand stair-case in my grandfather's foyer. I don't remember walking here. I don't remember sitting down and placing my hands in my hair, tugging until my scalp throbs.

Coming to, I pull in a deep breath and force myself to stand. "I'm fine. Think I just need to lie down for a bit."

His mouth flattens. He's disappointed I won't be sailing with him this afternoon, but he's not going to push it. The summer is young, I'm sure he's thinking.

"All right. I'll have Bernice get you the key to Ainsworth," he says. "We weren't expecting you home this early, but everything should be in order. If it isn't, let me know. This is her first time opening the island for the summer."

Opening the island ...

He opened the island the way other people open their pools for the summer: with checklists and procedures and quiet fanfare. "Opening the island" was always his expression for this time of year, when our entire extended family would abandon their modern lives, their work and school in favor of sun, sand, and sailing off the coast of a New England island hideaway. It was always Ed and Junie who would prepare for our arrivals. All the linens would be freshly washed, beds made. Junie used to fold our towels into little animal shapes, like we were at some resort, and Ed would shine up the boats and hose off the dock. Junie would place freshly picked and trimmed flowers in vases in every living room, kitchen, bathroom, and bedroom—that alone must have taken her hours if not days considering each home had at least five bedrooms and six baths. But she always loved to go the extra mile to make our annual homecoming a splendid affair.

My grandfather disappears into the kitchen, returning with

a set of keys to my family's designated house just a few hundred yards down the drive.

"Dinner will be at six," he says, dropping the key ring in my hand. "Get some rest, but don't be late. We have much catching up to do."

As soon as he's gone, I realize I'm squeezing the set so hard, the metal teeth are leaving indentations in my palm. Relaxing, I show myself out and head down the path to Ainsworth, gaze locked on the cedar shake siding that covers the backside. Last summer, I stole a kiss from Lila next to the white peony bushes on the north side of the house.

The bushes are lackluster now, appearing as if they hardly intend to bloom this year.

Once I get to the house, I unlock a side door and head in. My lungs fill with stuffy, slightly damp air. Apparently Bernice didn't air out the house the way Junie always did in anticipation of our arrival, but I know she's new so I won't fault her for it.

Passing down the hall, I make my way to the living room before cutting through the foyer to get to the kitchen. There's no bowl of fresh fruit waiting on the counter. Not a single vase filled with picked hydrangeas or lilacs as per tradition.

A moment later, I climb the stairs to the second floor and find my room at the end of the hall.

No folded swan towels.

No welcome note in Junie's whimsical handwriting.

No secret welcome note from Lila tucked into my pillowcase.

I head to the windows first, sliding up the sashes and letting some much needed fresh air fill the space.

Collapsing on the bed next, I slide my hands under my neck and stare at the lifeless ceiling fan above. Everything ... and I mean everything ... has taken on an empty quality.

The island.

The house.

Me.

It's like a substantial part of me is missing—and that part of me is her.

Squeezing my eyes shut, I try to rest despite knowing damn well my head isn't going to stop spinning long enough to make that possible. But I need to calm down so I can come up with a game plan.

There's no internet access on the island—my grandfather contacted the local phone company once, and they were told there was not enough infrastructure to support running cable or DSL lines to Rose Crossing at the time, and then they said that running those lines to the island would've been humanly impossible. The only options he was given were satellite or dial up. My grandfather made the executive decision to forgo both—deciding that the island was better off with as minimal technology as possible because family time was too priceless to sacrifice for *"computers and video games and the like."*

I grab my cell from my pocket and check the service. It's

always been spotty out here, even at the highest point, which happens to be the attic of my grandparents' house, so I don't hold my breath.

One bar.

One bar is enough to make phone calls if you're okay with the sound cutting in and out, but it makes any internet capabilities virtually useless.

I try to refresh my email inbox as a test ... my point proven in under two minutes when the app times out before it has a chance to load.

I'll have to try and sneak away to town in the next day and use the computers at the library.

I'm sure a quick online search will tell me exactly where she is ...

Placing my phone aside, I close my eyes once more and listen to the crash of the ocean outside my windows.

It doesn't sound the same without her here.

And it sure as hell doesn't feel the same.

I close my eyes and try to get some rest.

I'll look for Lila forever if I have to.

I'll start first thing tomorrow, and I won't stop until I find her.

PART ONE [PAST]

MAY 2009

CHAPTER 1

THAYER

SHE ARRIVES at the island on the mail plane the Tuesday after Mother's Day.

"Do we know her name?" I ask Granddad as we watch Ed and Junie, the estate's caretakers, make their way up the cliffside to greet her.

"Lila, I believe it is," he says. "Anyway." His massive hand grips my shoulder and he turns away. "Good day for a sail, don't you think?"

"Shouldn't we say hi?" I ask.

Granddad huffs, his barrel chest inflating. "Welcome her? Thayer, the poor girl just lost her mother and got shipped three thousand miles from the only home she's ever known. Give her a chance to get acclimated before you unleash your one-man welcome committee."

For as long as I can remember, the family's poked fun at my penchant for never knowing a stranger. In preschool, my nickname was Mr. Personality. In high school, I was elected class president all four years.

Granddad has never said it, but I think he views my inclusive nature and inherent friendliness as a weakness. That or he resents the fact that I'm not more closed off—like him.

In his older years—and since losing the love of his life back in '93, the man has become an island himself. It used to be he would only summer at Rose Crossing Island. But now my grandfather spends the entirety of the year here, biding his time until his daughters and grandchildren join him for three months of sun, sand, and sailing.

"Why hasn't she been here before?" I ask, staying put as I try to get a closer look at the girl. From here, all I see is sun-kissed legs as she rises on her toes and California sun-bleached hair cascading down her back and shoulders as she wraps her arms around Junie's shoulders. I find it odd that the Hilliards have worked for my grandparents' since before I could walk, but not once has their one and only grand-daughter ever paid them a visit.

"Why would she want to hang out with her grandparents while they work?" he asks, hooking his arm over my shoulders and leading me back toward the main house. "Speaking of which, she's going to be working for us this summer, mostly helping Junie in the kitchen and with the laundry and housekeeping."

"Okay ..."

He leans in as we walk. "I'm telling you this for a reason, Thayer."

He stops. I stop.

"I won't have you distracting that young woman from her work," he says. "Nor will I have you creating any ... liabilities for me."

"What are you talking about?"

"You're a charming young man, Thayer. And the two of you are only here for the summer," he says. "I won't have you creating any liabilities, do you understand? She's staff. She's not to be some summer fling."

I lift my palms. "All right."

"There's no limit to what a woman will do—or say—once her heart has been broken," he adds as he begins to climb the steps toward the front door of the massive cedar-shingled home he once shared with my grandmother. Stopping, he turns back to me. "Have I made myself clear?"

"Yes." I lean against the porch railing, letting the spring wind rustle through my hair and the salty air fill my lungs.

"I'm going to see if any of the others want to join us for our sail," he says before disappearing inside.

The screen door opens and slams, but a second later it swings wide.

"Hey." My cousin, Westley, steps out, adjusting his Red Sox cap, wavy tufts of auburn hair sticking out from beneath the blue canvas material. "You going on the boat with us?"

Squinting back toward the cliffs, I watch Ed, Junie, and their granddaughter make their way down the stony, weather-beaten path that leads to their cottage.

Westley tracks my gaze before hopping down the steps. "Ah, the mysterious granddaughter has arrived."

"Be prepared for Granddad to make it abundantly clear to you that she's *just the help* and there's to be *no fraternizing.*"

Westley rolls his eyes. "Come on. He can't expect us to ignore her all summer. It'd be cruel not to ask her to hang out."

"Who's to say she'd even want to hang out?" I watch Ed struggle to lift her giant suitcase, and I get the urge to jog over there to help, but before I have a chance, they're already heading inside. "Her mom died, I guess."

"Yeah, that's what I heard."

"I doubt she wants to be here," I say. Rose Crossing isn't for everyone. In fact, that's exactly how my grandfather wanted it to be when he originally purchased this private island. It was meant to be a summer getaway for his wife and two daughters. A place where they could escape a sticky hot Manhattan for three months and unwind and recharge before life started over again in September. But over the years, it became so much more than that. A haven. A heaven. Another world entirely.

Granddad Bertram had the main house built first: a massive, eight-bedroom cedar-and-white monstrosity with a million-dollar view, gourmet kitchen, and antique-filled library. Next was the Ainsworth house, built for my mother after she married my father in the nineties. When her sister married Ari Caldecott around the same time, Granddad gifted them with a house as well.

Now we refer to the homes by their family names: The

Bertram, The Ainsworth, and The Caldecott. The Hilliard Cottage looks like a shack next to the other houses, but Junie insists it's the nicest house she's ever lived in and the way Ed prunes the hedges around the front makes the place worthy of a magazine cover in the right light.

One big happy family.

The screen door swings open again, and my mother steps out, her sandy hair wrapped in a Pucci scarf and oversized sunglasses covering her face.

We've all been here a handful of days so far and this is already the fourth sailing trip Granddad has insisted upon.

As a child, sailing enthralled me.

As an extroverted nineteen-year-old who just finished his first year of pre-law, all I can think about are all the things I'm missing out on back home.

Granddad steps out of the house, grinning wide, his favorite white visor over his salt-and-pepper head of hair, and he slaps his hands together. He gets like this every time we're about to hit the water, all Christmas-morning smiles and childlike wonder in his eyes.

Aunt Lorelai steps out next, an oversized Breton-striped bag hoisted on her shoulder, followed by Uncle Ari and Westley's twin sister, Whitley. If my father wasn't on a business trip in Shanghai until next week, the whole gang would be here.

One by one, we file down the wide steps, to the stone path that leads to the boathouse.

We're halfway there when I catch the Hilliards coming out

of their cottage maybe twenty yards away. Lila stops on the front stoop, gathering her hair in her hands and securing it at the top of her head. Almost as if she can feel me watching her, her eyes flick to mine.

It's the craziest thing, but in an instant, I can't breathe, like the wind is sucked from my lungs. And while our eyes hold for maybe a second or two, it feels like an eternity.

"Thayer." My grandfather's voice booms in my ear, and I jerk my attention away from the beautiful girl in the distance. "Did you hear what I said?"

He knows damn well I didn't.

"Strong winds out of the north," he says as we walk. "Might have to be a short excursion today."

I don't tell him I'm fine with that.

Just like I don't tell him I'm going to invite Lila to the bonfire Westley and Whitley planned for Friday night.

CHAPTER 2

Lila

IT'S THE STRANGEST THING: my grandparents have called this island home for as long as I can remember, but it takes the untimely passing of my mother for them to let me actually visit.

My entire life, they always came to us. Mom would pick them up at LAX and we'd drive up the Pacific Coast Highway with the top down on her vintage BMW, showing off the agreeable weather and abundance of sunshine. I always thought it was Mom's way of trying to convince them to move west because she hated the East Coast—and that says a lot because Mom didn't have a hateful bone in her body.

I stand in the middle of a bedroom in the house my grandma simply refers to as *The Ainsworth*. It's the last cleaning stop of the day. The weekends are mostly for cooking and food prep, but come Monday, we'll have the joy of scrubbing the entirety of *The Caldecott* from floor to ceiling. *The Bertram*, I'm told, is a three-day job.

If you look up "pretentious" in the dictionary, I'm sure you'll find a picture of Howard Bertram surrounded by his spawn—all of them in canvas boat shoes.

I giggle at the thought as I dust the nightstand beside a freshly-made bed. I'm not good at this cleaning business yet. As a child, I had chores. Sure. But out here, there's a certain way things need to be done. The corners of the bed linens have to be tucked a certain way. The pillows fluffed and arranged in the right order. The floors are always last—I made that mistake the first day and I won't make it again.

These people take themselves way too seriously. Their wallpapered and wainscoted halls are lined in black-and-white family photos spanning generations. They keep antiques in every corner of every room. They wear boat shoes like they're the only shoes in existence. And their dinners could give places like The Ivy and Spago a run for their money. But at the end of the day, it's almost kind of nice living on this alien planet with these strange people and their unfamiliar ways. It's a distraction. And I'm not constantly reminded of Mom.

I lift a framed photo off a desk and wipe the non-existent dust beneath. Before I place it back, I examine the picture. It's two boys—Howard's grandsons I think. The one with the auburn hair and goofy grin has his arm around the one with the bronze tan and sandy blond hair and an attention-demanding Yale sweatshirt.

I don't know their names yet.

Or wait, I don't remember them.

Grandma told me what they were in passing, but I was only half listening and now all I remember is that they were old-money names—the kinds of names that sound like they should be last names and not first names.

In L.A., we had names like Ocean and Sea and Skye and Plum and Pilot. Nouns. Here it's like people pluck surnames from their family trees and call it good.

I return the picture frame to its home next to the shiny blue lamp and make my way to the en suite bathroom. Dragging in a breath of sea salt air, I tug on a pair of yellow latex gloves, grab a scrub brush, and drop to my knees. Months ago, I thought for sure I'd be spending my summer at the pool between putting in hours at the fro-yo shop, but here I am, on an island with no internet polishing some rich asshole's toilet.

But in all fairness, I don't know if the sandy blond Yale guy is an asshole. It probably isn't fair of me to make assumptions like that, but anyone who summers on an island and sails seven days a week and has a name like Remington or Bexley or Ellington or ... THAYER.

His name is Thayer.

That's right.

Anyway, anyone who summers on an island and sails seven days a week and has a name like *Thayer* ... and has a disgustingly wealthy grandfather and attends Yale statistically isn't the most down-to-earth, relatable kind of person. At least not in my experience.

Not to mention the fact that I've caught him staring at me a few times now—the first time was shortly after I'd arrived.

The second time was when I was helping Grandma wash breakfast dishes and Thayer came in to grab a green apple from the fruit bowl (which I swear was nothing more than an excuse to be in the room) and locked gazes with me the entire time.

I'm not sure what his end game is, but I'll have no problem informing him that he's not my type—if it comes to that.

My hand throbs from gripping the handle of the scrub brush too tight, so I stop and rest for a second. Sweeping my hair out of my eyes, I take a look around at all the marble and penny tile and shiny silver hardware that surrounds me.

It's beautiful and timeless, and I hope these people know how lucky they are to have a place like this as a *second* home.

"Oh. My bad," a guy's voice sends my heart ricocheting into my throat, and I glance up to find Mr. Yale Sweatshirt himself standing in the doorway of the bathroom.

Shirtless.

Glistening with sweat.

Like he's just gone for a run or a hike or whatever the hell people can do to work out on a rock-and-cliff-covered island.

I've been here four days now and he's yet to say a single word to me. He simply stares at me with those stormy sapphire blues that I'm sure make all the campus girls swoon.

The burn of bleach cleaner stings my eyes. "I'm almost done. Give me two more minutes."

I don't know if I'm allowed to tell him to wait or what the

rules are in this kind of scenario. Grandpa said something about how we're supposed to be seen and not heard and we're never to argue with any of them or refuse a single request, but it seems ridiculous to be so formal with him given the fact that we're practically the same age.

"No problem." He grabs a towel within arm's reach and dabs at his damp forehead, messing up his hair in the process. I have an urge to finger comb it back into place for him, but I'm pretty sure touching these people in any capacity goes against the house rules too. "I can wait."

I don't tell him he could alternatively use one of the other dozens of bathrooms in this place.

Thayer lingers, watching me as I get back to scrubbing the marble penny tile floor of his bedroom-sized bathroom. I'm pretty sure you could fit an entire studio apartment in here. Maybe two if we're talking Manhattan-style.

I wipe the rest of the bathroom down in a hurry and snap off my gloves, returning all the supplies to my plastic caddy, and then I squeeze past him.

"Lila, right?" he asks when I'm halfway across the room. I stop, pivoting toward him.

I realize now that we haven't been properly introduced, nor have we been alone in the same room together. The only introduction I've received so far was on my first day on the job when I was pouring coffee in the dining room as Mr. Bertram went around the table spouting out names I had no intention of memorizing, and then he asked me to grab the creamer from the kitchen.

"Yeah," I say, trying to keep my eyes on his when all they

want to do is pore over the length of his perfectly-chiseled torso.

He might not be my type, but it doesn't mean I can't find him attractive.

I mean, honestly, you'd have to be dead or blind not to see how ridiculously, unfairly, and disgustingly hot this guy is.

"Thayer," he says.

"I know."

He lingers, leaning against the doorway, the sweaty towel still in his hands.

"You, uh, you like it so far out here?" he asks.

No.

But I can't tell him that.

"It's beautiful here," I say. "I look forward to my stay here this summer."

His full mouth inches up at one side and my heart revs in my chest.

"You're lying," he says with the cutest smirk I've ever seen in my life.

"Excuse me?"

He takes a step closer.

Then another.

What is he doing?

"It's lonely here. It's isolating. We're an hour's boat ride from the mainland. We get the mail and groceries once a week. There's no internet. You don't have to say you're looking forward to your summer here," he says.

"All right. Fine." I straighten my shoulders and clear my throat. "But the place is beautiful. I meant that part."

His smirk morphs into a full-on smile that literally makes me weak in the knees, and he drags his hand through his mussed-up hair.

"I've summered here for as long as I can remember," he says. I hate that he's using 'summered' as a verb, but I let it slide. "If my family wasn't freakishly close knit, I'd never come here by choice."

I don't know why he's telling me this, but I smile and nod like the good little housemaid I'm trying to be.

"The twins are having a bonfire tonight," he says, his dark brows arching as he pauses. "It's on the other side of the east cliffs, just after the sun sets. You should come hang out with us. There's this little alcove right off the water, and—"

"—I can't," I interrupt him.

His eyes search mine, and then he squints as if he thinks he misheard me. But from the moment I set foot on this island, my grandparents made it abundantly clear that I'm not to hang out with Mr. Bertram's grandchildren. They told me I'm here to work and not to play, that it was imperative that we remain professional at all times, and that any trouble I might find myself in would reflect poorly on them—potentially costing them their jobs.

"Thanks for the invite though." I turn to leave.

"You can't? Or you don't want to?" he asks.

I stop again, but this time I keep my back to him. I appreciate his kindness, but this is for the best.

"I can't," I say. "I'm sorry."

I close his door behind me on my way out and all but sprint down the stairs. Turning the corner, I nearly run into his mother on my way to the back door.

"Excuse me. I'm so sorry," I say.

"Everything okay, lovey?" she calls as I slip my shoes on. I can't remember her name—only that she's nice and she calls everyone 'lovey.'

"Yep, everything's fine," I call back. "Thanks."

"Have you seen Thayer, by chance?" she asks.

"He's upstairs, I believe." I tie the laces on my Chucks, and then I'm gone, out the door, heading back to my grandparents' cottage, which is ironically bigger than the average American house. There's nothing quaint about it, though I guess when you put it next to *The Bertram, The Ainsworth,* and *The Caldecott*, it gives off cottage vibes.

When I get inside, I kick off my shoes and trek to the kitchen to pour a glass of my grandma's famous Earl Grey iced tea, and then I collapse on the plaid sofa, watching the wind make the curtains dance and listening to the seagulls and crash of the ocean waves.

The muscles of my upper back burn, and my knees are on fire. Cleaning all day every day is no joke—and my grandma's been doing this for decades.

I think she likes this sort of thing though, being a house-keeper. She likes structure and order and cleanliness and being needed.

The sound of a chainsaw in the distance is more than likely my grandpa doing one of the zillions of outdoor projects Bertram has him working on. I think this morning over breakfast he mentioned cutting down some dead trees for firewood—aaaaand now I'm thinking about that bonfire.

I'd be lying to myself if I said I didn't want to go.

Of course I want to go.

There are three other people on this island who are my age, and I'd much rather hang out with them on a Friday night than hole up in my new room getting firsthand experience of how people lived before the internet was born.

Sitting up, I rest my arm on the back of the couch and stare out the window toward Thayer's house. I can't quite get a read on him yet given the fact that we've had one conversation in the history of ever, but if he was nice enough to try to include me in his plans tonight, he can't be all that bad.

But still, I've been here less than a week. I can't rock the boat. I can't flirt with rebellion. If there's anything the last several weeks has taught me, it's that life can get real in a matter of seconds.

All it takes is one moment and your entire life can change.

Just like that.

CHAPTER 3

THAYER

"THAYER, you want to take over once I get us turned around?" Granddad steers us portside as Westley tightens the flapping sheets in the second mast of the ketch. It's just us three this afternoon on the water. Junie packed us a picnic basket filled with enough food to feed an army, and Rat Pack music plays from the tinny speakers of a portable radio.

I'm lying on my back, hands behind my head and the sun warm on my face.

"You need me to?" I ask, sitting up.

Granddad's smile fades, and I realize he was only asking because he takes pride in watching me follow in his footsteps in any capacity. He never had a son—but the way he treats Westley and I, you'd think we were his.

"I got it," I say, motioning for him to get out of the way as I take over steering duties.

He moves to the windward side, taking a seat and grabbing the handrail for balance. There's a look on his face, the one he gets when there's something he wants to talk about, so I brace myself.

"So." Granddad clears his throat. "That girl. That ... Lila."

"What about her?" I adjust my sunglasses. I've done my best this week to avoid being overly friendly, but I couldn't help talking to her when I came back from my hike and she was in my room. It would've been rude not to make small talk when we were in such close quarters, and I refuse to ignore her, to treat her like she's beneath me just because she's a housemaid.

Granddad chuckles. "Don't play dumb with me, boy. Wasn't born yesterday. I know what it means when a young man looks at a young lady a certain way ..."

"I have no idea what you're talking about."

He leans forward, elbows on his tanned knees. "She's a beautiful girl, and I remember what it was like to be nineteen. That said, I just want to make sure you remember our conversation the other day."

Westley finishes tightening the sheet and glances back at us, removing his hat and replacing it as he tries to determine if he should join us or not.

"Granddad, I can assure you I would never create a liability for you," I say.

"You're a good kid, Thayer," he says, and I cringe at the fact that he still views me as some knobby-kneed, freckle-faced child running around the island. "But you're young. And you're naïve. And there's a lot of life you haven't experienced yet. All I'm saying is if you're smart, and I know you are, you won't waste your time on some meaningless fling. She might be beautiful, but beauty fades and summer always ends."

"All due respect, I'm not sure why you're telling me this."

He leans back, almost grinning at the water like he's lost in his own thoughts for a second.

"Because as different as we are, I still see so much of myself in you," he says. "And I see a whole future for you that won't happen if you lose yourself in someone else at your age."

"I'll never lose myself in anyone."

He turns back to me, removing his sea-misted aviators. "That's what I always said too. And then I met your grandmother."

He draws in a long breath between parted lips before slipping his glasses back over his nose, and then he lets it go, shoulders sagging. He always gets like this whenever she's mentioned—contemplative, melancholic. And I get it. She was the love of his life. She was his person, his everything, his soulmate.

A part of him died along with her, and he's never been the same since. At least that's what my mother says. I was only four when Gram passed. I don't remember much of what he was like before that, but I do have pictures of him bouncing us on his knees, playing "horsey" and letting us try on his skipper hats.

I know he means well, he's just trying to protect me from the hurt and the pain he's been suffering since losing her, so I let the conversation go.

The gruff old man with the hard outer shell turns his face from mine, and from the corner of my eye, I watch him wipe a single tear from his eye.

"May I ask if Westley got the same warning or does this only apply to me?" I ask in partial jest, though I'm curious to know just the same.

"I've already had this talk with Westley on three separate occasions," Granddad snips back, his tone a wordless reminder that it's none of my business. "Anyway, should we check the lobster traps?" he asks a second later, as if the last two minutes never happened. "Yes. I think we should. And we will. Westley ..."

The two of them adjust the mainsheet and boom, and I steer us toward one of Granddad's lobster traps.

The rest of the afternoon is spent in contemplative silence, Granddad likely thinking of better times with Gran and Westley probably thinking about lacrosse.

By the time we get back, the sun's just beginning to set over the water, and once the ketch is stowed away and we head back up to Granddad's, it's almost dark and there's a chill in the air.

The Twins will be starting the bonfire soon over at the alcove, and I can't help but wonder if Lila might change her mind about coming and show up.

I can't say I'd be disappointed.

Quite the contrary.

Granddad can lay down all the laws he wants, but it doesn't make me any less curious about her. Despite the fact that we've spent all of maybe ten minutes around one another total, I can already tell she's unlike anyone else I've ever met.

On the outside, she's the quintessential sun-kissed, bleached-blonde Californian, but there's nothing warm or laidback about her. She's guarded and distant, but I know there's something more beneath all of that. All the times she's caught me staring at her, she's stared right back—and I don't even know if she realizes it. And earlier? In my suite? I clearly made her nervous. She couldn't get out of there fast enough.

All I know is she's a cocktail of contradictions and I find her utterly fascinating.

CHAPTER 4

Lila

I HAVE a couple of hours to myself after breakfast clean-up Saturday morning, so I take it upon myself to do a little exploring.

There's another cottage, practically a carbon copy of the one my grandparents live in, just over one of the cliffs and down the hill. I noticed it the day I arrived and my grandma mentioned it had once belonged to the nurse who was hired to care for Mrs. Bertram some fifteen years ago when she was ill, but once Mrs. Bertram passed, the nurse's job was done and no one has set foot in there since.

I traipse through a grassy path filled with wild flowers that hide the stones that once made a proper path, and when I get to the front door, I peek in the window, fully expecting to find nothing but dusty dilapidation. But to my surprise, the place is fully furnished, complete with books and magazines littering the coffee table in the living room. Almost as if someone was here just yesterday and picked up and left.

Just for the hell of it, I twist the doorknob, but once again I'm shocked to find the place completely unlocked. Then again, on an island inhabited by nothing but family and two caretakers, there's not much reason to lock doors around here.

Showing myself in, I close the door behind me and step across the small foyer. There's a dining room to my right, filled with a farmhouse-style table and white wooden Windsor chairs. To my left is a living room which holds a hunter green and burgundy floral sofa, a worn leather recliner, and a boxy TV resting on a wooden TV stand.

I reach down and grab one of the magazines—People, May 17, 2004. It appears to be an issue dedicated to what's real and what's fake in the world of reality television. I put the magazine back and find a stack of books, mostly Danielle Steele and Nora Roberts novels, beside it.

Moving on to the kitchen, I poke and prod my way through drawers and cupboards, all of which are empty, but there's an adorable farmhouse-style sink with a window above it that overlooks a small bay on the west side of the island.

When I'm finished there, I head down a hall, poking my head into two bedrooms and a bathroom before meandering into the biggest bedroom, which also happens to have breathtaking ocean views.

It's a shame this place sits here alone, unused. I'm sure my grandparents would love these views, but Mr. Bertram probably demands that they live in the closest cottage to his estate.

I take a seat on the bed in the center of the biggest room and let the silence swallow me for a moment, soaking in as much of the present as I can.

The burn in my chest is followed by the hot sting of tears in my eyes. Ever since Mom passed, I've been going back and forth between feeling nothing and feeling everything. And I swear all week my grandparents have been constantly watching me from the corner of their eyes to make sure I'm okay, whispering amongst themselves in their bed at night, as if I can't hear them through the paper-thin walls that separate us.

But here, alone with my thoughts, away from prying eyes, I can miss her in peace.

Crawling up to the head of the bed, I lie on my side and bury my face against the musty white pillow beneath me and allow myself to cry, really cry, for the first time in over a week.

I'm not sure how much time passes when I hear the creak and gentle closing of the front door, followed by footsteps too heavy and fast to belong to my grandparents.

"Hello?" a voice calls.

Sitting up, I wipe the tears from my cheeks and brush the hair from my face, knowing damn well there's no hiding my current state.

The footsteps grow louder by the second until the door to the bedroom swings open and Thayer's muscled frame fills the doorway.

"What are you doing in here?" he asks.

I rise from the bed and slide my hands in the back pockets of my cutoff shorts. "I just needed a minute to myself."

He studies me.

"There are just so many people ... everywhere ..." I continue.

"Are you okay?" he asks.

I shrug. "I ... don't know how to answer that."

"I'm sorry." He lifts a hand. "That's a horrible question and I shouldn't have asked. Obviously you're not okay. I mean. You're okay. But you've been through a lot. And ... I'm going to shut up now."

He smiles his perfect, straight, bright white smile and it instantly makes me reciprocate, almost like I have no control over my facial expressions. But it doesn't stick for long.

"How did you know I was here?" I ask.

"I saw you heading west after breakfast this morning. There's really nothing on this side of the island except this cottage."

"Oh. So you came looking for me? Like on purpose?"

He laughs under his breath, an easy, relaxed sort of chuff, like he finds my question adorable.

"I guess so," he says. "Yeah. Guess I wanted to make sure you didn't get lost or anything."

"Appreciate it." I don't buy it for one second. "I should probably get back. It's almost time to prep lunch."

I squeeze through the doorway and make my way down the

hall when I hear him say my name. Nothing else. Just ... Lila. Turning back, I see he's standing still, feet planted, in no rush to go anywhere.

"Yes?" I ask.

"If you ever want to talk ..." he clears his throat. "I'm sure you miss your friends. And I know you're going through a lot right now ..."

There's a gentleness about him, an easiness that I didn't anticipate. It's in the smoothness of his voice, the way his eyes crinkle when he smiles. He never talks about himself—even during meals. He's always asking everyone else what they're doing or what's going on in their lives. And it's plain to see he's the clear favorite among the three grandchildren. He's the apple of Howard Bertram's eye.

And I get it.

So far ... he seems like a nice guy—a good person.

I almost wish he wasn't.

I almost wish he fulfilled every stereotype I conjured up about someone with his name and his background and his family and his privileges.

But now all I feel is guilt and an onset of extreme self-awareness, suddenly second-guessing the placement of my hands or the puffiness of my eyes.

"Does this house have a name?" I ask, changing the subject because I feel another wave of emotions about to wash over me when I think too hard about his unexpected kindness.

"What?"

"You know. Like your house is The Ainsworth," I say. "And Grandma and Grandpa's house is The Hilliard. What do you call this one?"

Thayer shrugs before shaking his head. "Nothing. I guess we mostly pretend it doesn't exist."

"That's kind of ... sad. Is it weird that I feel sorry for this place?" I half-laugh.

He smirks. "Yeah."

His on-the-spot honesty makes me respect him that much more.

"Back home, my mom had this friend, and she was always talking about how everything had a soul. People, animals, plants, even inanimate objects. Mom said even if that isn't true, it doesn't hurt to treat everything with respect, like it has feelings. I thought they were out of their minds, but I guess a little bit of them rubbed off on me."

"You think the house's feelings are hurt?" He scratches at his temple.

"Maybe. Sort of. So what if I do?" I bite my lower lip for a flash of a second. I'm teasing, flirting, and I shouldn't be.

He doesn't say anything, which makes this moment as awkward and nerve-wracking as possible. I swear I hear my heart beating in my ears—that, or it's the whoosh and crash of the ocean outside. I'm too distracted right now to differentiate.

My mom's crazy friend always talked about auras. I never saw them, never believed in them, but she claimed mine was dark red, which meant I was self-sufficient and able to persevere anything.

She also told me that at my mother's funeral, so she might have simply been trying to comfort me.

If Thayer had an aura, I bet it would be light blue. The color of the sky. Serene and calm.

"You want to name the house?" he asks.

"What?"

"This cottage." He glances up at the ceiling. "Give it a name. It can be your house. What's your last name?"

"Hilliard." My mother gave me her last name on account of my father abandoning us early into her pregnancy. I never knew his name. Never saw a picture. Only heard a few details, like he was smart and charismatic and successful, but also self-centered and narcissistic. "So obviously there can't be two Hilliard Cottages."

"All right. Then we'll just call it The Lila Cottage."

I snicker. "That doesn't quite have the same ring to it as *The Ainsworth or The Caldecott*."

"You think?" he asks. "Nah. It sounds fine to me."

"Would your grandfather be okay with you naming this place without his permission? I'm getting major control-freak vibes from him."

Shit.

I need to shut my mouth before I get myself in trouble.

Sure, Thayer's easy to talk to and he seems like a reasonable person, but I literally just insulted his grandfather —my boss.

My cheeks flush with a burning warmth and I glance down for a moment.

"He is *absolutely* a control freak, and we don't have to tell him. It can just be our thing."

Our thing.

So now we have a thing.

"I used to hide out in here when I was a kid," he says, looking around. "Westley was always so clingy. Like a shadow. And Whitley was always whining about this or that. And sometimes I just needed space."

"This is quite the hideaway for a kid. A whole house."

"Yeah," he says. "Anyway, if you need a hideaway of your own, you've found a good one. But I can't say I won't be using it too."

"We should probably come up with a custody agreement of some kind." I'm flirting. Again. But I can't help myself. He's so damn cute. "Maybe I get weekends? You can have holidays because I'll likely be working those, so ..."

He laughs at me and our gazes lock until our respective smiles fade. There's a glimmer of something in his eyes ... fascination maybe? Curiosity? I don't know him well enough to tell, but he looks at me in a way that no one else ever has before.

Perhaps I'm a novelty to him.

Or maybe this is what he does. Charms you. Works you

until you're putty in his hands so he can use you until you're all used up, and then he moves on to the next girl.

"I should probably get back to The Bertram," I say. "I'm sure Grandma's wondering where I am."

"We're going to watch a movie tonight," he says. "At Westley and Whitley's."

AKA *The Caldecott.*

"You should come by," he says.

Yesterday it was the bonfire.

Tonight it's a movie.

I head to the door, the wood floorboards creaking beneath my quick, soft steps, but before I leave, I turn back to him. "You should probably stop inviting me to hang out."

I don't wait for him to respond ... I just go, heading back to the main house where my grandma is waiting for me with a five-pound bag of potatoes and a peeler.

She doesn't ask where I've been and I don't volunteer it.

Getting to work, I promise myself I won't think about him. I convince myself I don't like bonfires or movies or hanging out with people my own age. And I assure myself that no good can come out of flirting with Bertram's favorite grandson.

CHAPTER 5

THAYER

LILA MAKES her way around the dining room table, dishing out tongs of corn on the cob and boiled crab, her chin tucked low and eyes averted.

I've attempted to make eye contact with her every chance I get, but she refuses to reciprocate.

I'm not sure what happened. I thought we were having a nice talk in the abandoned cottage and I felt like I was getting to know her in snippets, like she might have been letting her guard down and opening up the tiniest bit. Pretty sure she was flirting with me too. And then the second I invited her to hang out tonight, she bolted like Cinderella at the stroke of twelve.

Despite the fact that Granddad had made his expectations clear, I see no harm in asking her to hang out. She's just suffered an incredible loss, and the last thing she needs is to feel even more alone.

Lila disappears into the kitchen, and I glance at my plate to find that she's given me an overly generous serving. I'm not sure if that's her way of apologizing or if she was trying to be funny—I can't quite put my finger on her and honestly, it's beginning to drive me wild.

I reach for my claw cracker when I feel the sharp jab of an elbow against my ribs.

"Dude," Westley whispers, leaning close. "Can you make it any more obvious?"

"What?" I play dumb, glancing up to ensure Granddad isn't tuned into what's going on at our end of the table.

"You won't stop staring." He grabs his crab mallet. "Honestly, you're just torturing yourself. You can't have her. And let's be real, she probably doesn't want you."

His sister, Whitley, leans in to add her two cents. "She seems nice, but, like, what if things go south and you have to spend the rest of the summer avoiding each other? I don't know about you guys, but I will *not* have my summer stained with awkward moments all because Thayer wants a piece of the pretty maid. Why don't you just—"

The cacophonous tinkle of shattering glass cuts through the dinner conversations, and Whitley's eyes flick up to the space behind me. When I follow her gaze, I find Lila falling to her knees, gathering up bits of broken wine goblets.

Westley looks away.

Whitley reaches for her iced tea, turning her face away.

I have no idea how much she heard, if anything but obviously she heard something.

"Oh, lovey, you're bleeding," my mother says to Lila. "Can someone locate the first aid kit for this poor thing?"

Granddad and my father pause their conversation and glance our way but I pay them no mind.

Without giving it a second thought, I scoot my chair out and I'm on it. Heading to the hall bath, I grab Band-Aids, cotton, and antiseptic from the medicine cabinet and when I return, I find her in the kitchen, rinsing the cut on her finger beneath the faucet.

"Here," I say, placing everything on the counter. "Let me see."

"No, thank you."

"Lila."

Her pale hair curtains her face, but I don't have to see her expression to know she probably heard everything Whitley said.

Blood continues to spill from the slice on her finger, but she holds it under the water.

"You need to put pressure on it," I say.

"I'm good."

I stand beside her, not willing to leave yet.

"Your food's probably getting cold," she says under her breath.

"Then you should probably let me fix you up so I can get back to dinner." It's my lame attempt at flirting, trying to add some lightheartedness into the moment. But it goes over like a lead balloon because I get no response from her. "Seriously. Just let me look at it and make sure you don't need stitches."

She sucks in a long, hard breath, her lithe shoulders rising and falling, and then she shuts off the faucet with her good hand.

"Had no idea you were a doctor," she says, extending her hand to me. "Lucky me."

"Smart ass." I examine the cut on her finger, which is still bleeding, and I dab at the blood with some cotton before putting pressure on it.

"But wait. Wouldn't a real doctor be wearing gloves when he does this?" she asks.

"Good to see your sense of humor is still intact."

I get the bleeding to subside enough to clean the cut with antiseptic, and then I place a flesh-colored Band-Aid over the small wound.

"There," I say, admiring my work. "It's like it never even happened."

Lila places her hand over her heart and stares up into my eyes. "You saved my life, doctor. How could I ever repay you?"

I laugh through my nose. She's so damn cute. "You could repay me by stopping by later and hanging out with us."

"Not a chance." Her tone is flat, the sparkle in her eyes

gone. Turning back to the sink, she grips the edge and stares out the window.

"Why?"

Lila scoffs, shooting me a look. "Why? You're asking me why?"

I shrug. "I'm just asking you to hang out."

"Yeah, well, I know how your type operates."

"My type?"

"Cute. Charming. Nice," she says. "Too nice."

"Since when is it a crime to be a decent human being?"

She fills the left side of the sink with warm soapy water and begins dunking dirty dishes, frantically washing and scrubbing and rinsing, like she's all worked up.

"I heard what your cousin said," she finally speaks. "About you wanting a piece of the pretty maid or whatever."

I roll my eyes. "Don't listen to her."

"Just so you know, it's not going to happen."

"Got it."

"There's no chance," she adds before looking at me. "Zero. *None*."

For a second, I stop and entertain the possibility that she has a boyfriend back home. Or maybe she's into other girls. But I know she was flirting with me earlier. I didn't make that up. I didn't imagine it. I'm not that dense.

"Understood," I say. "So does that mean you'll hang out later?"

"No. But just out of curiosity, what movie are you guys watching?"

"Mystic River."

She's quiet for a second, rinsing off a fork as she sighs. "I really want to see that, too."

"Okay, then come. We'll probably start it around nine."

Lila grabs a striped dish rag and begins drying dishes and silverware that are already dry. "I'll think about it."

"Okay. You think about it and I'll plan on seeing you around nine." I head toward the doorway, back to the dining room.

"Don't get your hopes up," she calls out.

"Nine o'clock."

I enter the dining room with a smile on my face, one that disappears the instant I lock eyes with Granddad.

CHAPTER 6

Lila

I SHOW up at 9:04—not to be rude but to prove a point (though I'm not entirely sure what point that is if I'm being honest). And also because I had to make sure my grandparents were in bed.

The Hilliard Cottage isn't very soundproof. The windows are older than dirt and single-paned, the glass paper thin. The ocean and seagulls and boats motoring by tend to create a white noise of sorts at night, which is an unexpected bonus.

There's only one interior light on in The Caldecott and it's around the back of the house, just off the wraparound porch. When I peer inside the window, I find the three cousins sprawled out on different cushions of a leather sectional. Westley fusses with the DVD player remote. Whitley pages through a glossy magazine.

Thayer checks his watch. I bet he's wondering where I am, if I'm going to show.

I wait another minute on principle and then dragging in a hard breath, I rap three times on the glass until I get his attention.

He pops up from the couch in an instant, his face lit. Or maybe I'm imagining it. I'm kind of in a daze right now because I tried my hardest to talk myself out of coming but in the end, it's like I was drawn like a moth to a flame for reasons I can't fully comprehend.

All I know is I want to be here.

With him.

Even if every atom in my body, every particle in my soul knows I shouldn't.

Whitley's words earlier today echoed in my mind all afternoon. I so badly want to believe Thayer's a regular, nice person and not a Douche Charming with ulterior motives.

"You came," he says when he gets the back door.

"Only because I've been dying to see Mystic River." It's true.

Thayer moves back and I step inside and remove my shoes. The place is set up like a makeshift home theater slash family room. Movie posters on the wall. A popcorn maker standing in the corner. A bookshelf filled with an impressive collection of DVDs.

"Hey, hey," Whitley says, giving a wave without looking up from her magazine.

"Aaaand there we go." Westley presses a button on the DVD remote and the main menu fills the screen.

"Sit anywhere you like," Thayer tells me as he dims the lights.

I choose the corner seat of the sectional, and when I sit down, my body melts into the downy cushions until it's practically enveloped in luxurious softness. This might be the nicest sofa I've ever sat on in my life. My mind wanders to the logistics of how this sofa got here—how everything got here, actually... Were the houses built on site? Built off-site and ferried over? Grandma said the mail plane comes once a week (usually Tuesdays or Thursdays)—weather permitting. And another boat drops boxes of groceries off at the end of the dock on Mondays.

This sort of life would never be my cup of tea, but I have to admit it's fascinating.

"Is this okay?" Thayer asks, voice low as the credits roll.

He takes the spot next to me, but in his defense, the only other option was sitting between the twins, and I don't blame him for not wanting to be sandwiched between them.

I want to tell him to stop being so damn nice, but part of me secretly appreciates his refreshing politeness—genuine or not.

"Yes, now shhh," I whisper, pointing to the TV.

The movie begins and I try my hardest to concentrate as I've waited months to see this and I've heard nothing but amazing things, but every few seconds, I can't help but find myself watching Thayer from the corner of my eye.

The light from the TV screen flickers against him, painting his face in all sorts of colors, illuminating and highlighting his perfect features: chiseled jaw, full lips, straight nose, broad shoulders straining through his white Yale t-shirt ...

It's so weird how we're all sitting here actually watching a movie. Or at least I'm watching for the most part. Pretty sure the other three are fully invested already. It's the strangest thing to actually sit with a group of people my age who aren't attached to their phones like life support.

For a moment, I think about my friends back home. I've been trying not to think of them all week because whenever I do, I miss them too much and then I get wrapped up in wondering about all the things I'm missing in addition to missing them ...

I thought about sending letters since I don't have a cell phone out here, but with all the chaos and commotion of the past couple of weeks, I didn't think to ask for any of their addresses and seeing how we don't have so much as a cell tower or internet connection here, I'm sort of screwed. Grandma said I could use their phone, but I'd have to buy a calling card from the store on the mainland. One of these days I'll get around to it, I'm sure.

I try and focus on the movie again but my gaze wanders to Thayer for a couple of seconds. He looks good from this angle.

Who am I kidding, he looks good from every angle ...

His hands are folded across his lap as his legs stretch across the rest of his side of the sectional. He's so close I can smell his cologne ... something like cedar and citrus and definitely top shelf. He was out on the dock earlier, helping his grandfather with something. I'm guessing he came back and took a shower after, which explains why he smells like a million bucks.

"This movie is boring." Whitley sighs, sitting up and reaching for her Seventeen magazine.

"It's been five freaking minutes, Whit." Her brother huffs before reaching across and yanking the magazine from her hands and tossing it back on the table.

"Hey," she says.

"Watch." He points at the TV before readjusting his baseball cap, which I'm beginning to realize never leaves his head. And I'm not sure why because he's an attractive guy with a full head of tousled auburn waves. I guess everyone has their thing ...

Thayer turns to give me a wink, as if to say he agrees that these two are annoying as hell. Or maybe I'm assuming that's what he's implying. It's too soon to think we're on mind-reading levels.

Once again, I turn my attention back to the show. I'm a little lost, but I'm sure I'll catch up.

We're twenty minutes in when a chill runs through me. I'm realizing it gets cold here at night and once the temperature drops, it drops fast. Also, I'm realizing that although Bertram is richer than the devil, he's also a frugal bastard, opting not to heat the three gigantic houses at night because "blankets are cheaper."

I run my hands along my bare arms, my fingertips tracing the gooseflesh, and then I draw my knees against my chest.

It only takes Thayer a few seconds to turn his attention to me.

"You cold?" he whispers.

I nod.

Without hesitation, he pops up and heads to a sea grass bench by the window, lifting the lid and pulling out a thick plaid blanket lined with fleece.

"Here," he says, covering me up.

Again with the niceties ...

"Thanks," I whisper.

From the corner of my eye, I can tell Westley's watching. Whitley is shockingly oblivious. Guess she's into the movie after all.

As soon as my shivers subside, I get back into the movie—sucked back in actually. In fact, I'm so into it I completely lose track of time. It's like I blinked and it was over.

Westley stops the movie and Whitley gets the lights and I head to the door to grab my shoes.

"Thanks for the hang tonight, guys," I say, stepping into my leather sandals.

The twins mutter tired responses.

Thayer makes his way across the room. "I'll walk you home."

"You don't have to." I reach for the doorknob but he gets it first, and then he follows me outside.

I stick my hands in the pockets of my cut-off shorts and hightail it toward my grandparents' cottage in the frigid, ocean-scented wind.

"Hey, wait up," he jogs to catch up with me and when he does, I stop in my tracks.

"Why?" I ask, hands on my hips as the wind whips my hair in my face. "Why do you keep ... why are you so ... what is your end game here?"

Lines cross his forehead as he peers down at me, and I fully realize now how tall he is and how the top of my head would fit perfectly beneath his chin.

But I snap myself out of it.

"End game?" he asks.

"You obviously want something or you wouldn't be bending over backwards to treat me like some guest of honor when I'm just the girl who scrubs your freaking toilet."

"Jesus, Lila." He rests on hand on his hip, the other rakes through his hair, and then he looks away. "Is that what you think? That I want something from you?"

I lift my brows, a silent, "Obviously."

"Lila ..." he sighs. "You've been through one of the worst things anyone could ever possibly go through. And then you were ripped from your home and your friends and your life and flown all the way across the country and forced to live on an island with a bunch of strangers. I look at you ... and I see that you're hurting. Even when you're running that smart mouth of yours. And yeah. You're beautiful. You're gorgeous in this warm, exotic way that makes you stick out like a sore thumb in a state like Maine. You also confuse me. And intrigue me. But I would never prey on you. I would never show you kindness just so I could take advantage of you ..."

My heart knocks around in my chest as I listen to him ramble on. There's no gentleness to his tone like earlier, there's an edge to it. Like I got him worked up. Like I offended him by thinking he was anything other than what he's claiming to be.

"That's not who I am," he says. "And it's not who I'll ever be."

"What about what your cousin said?" I ask. "About you wanting to get a piece?"

"She's an idiot." His hands hook at his hips and his head is tilted and my lips burn at the thought of what his mouth might taste like. "She's my cousin and I love her, but she's an idiot."

A pause rests between us.

I don't know what to say.

Honestly, I kind of just want to go home, lie in bed, and let his words replay in my head until I fall asleep. It's like I need to digest them and let them sink in before I can determine how I feel about this.

"I'm sorry," I say.

"Lila, don't apologize." I love the way he says my name, like he's taking his time and letting it linger on his tongue.

"Thanks for the movie. I should get going before my grandparents wake up and realize I'm gone."

His nose wrinkles. "Would they be mad if they knew you hung out with us tonight?"

I bite my lower lip and contemplate my answer. I don't want to get them in trouble.

"I didn't exactly tell them I was going, and I left after they were in bed, so yeah," I say. "I think they'd be kind of pissed if they woke up and I was gone."

He studies me.

I wish I knew what he was thinking.

I wish I didn't care what he was thinking ...

"Goodnight, Thayer," I say as my body begins to shiver from the cold. I couldn't feel it before when he had my full attention and was rambling on about his sympathies for me, but damn, do I feel it now.

"Goodnight, Lila."

I head back to the house in the pitch dark, under a starless sky, the wind at my back, and I manage to make it inside unheard and unseen. Changing into pajamas and washing up, I climb into bed with un-kissed lips, flushed skin, and a heart that won't stop hammering.

Every time I close my eyes, I see him.

And when I see him, I try and picture the two of us together, side by side.

In my mind's eye, we look ridiculous together ... him a blue-blooded American prince attending an Ivy League school with preppy good looks and intelligence to match.

And me ... a California daughter who grew up with a working-class single mom. No college prospects. No idea what she's doing with her future.

He's sweet and kind and handsome and thoughtful, the kind of guy you read about in the engagement section of the New York Times, and I'm a broken, cynical nobody.

If anything comes of this, odds are he'll break my heart—that is, if I don't break his first.

CHAPTER 7

THAYER

I FIND Lila sitting at the end of the dock Sunday afternoon, her bare toes skimming the top of the water as she pages through a book in her lap.

She's in a strappy tank top and white shorts that showcase her long legs, and she's completely oblivious.

I didn't see her at breakfast this morning, and when my grandfather asked Junie where Lila was, she said Lila wasn't feeling well and she requested the morning off.

"Hey," I take a seat beside her and she does a little jump, sucking in a quick breath. "Didn't mean to sneak up on you."

She dog-ears her chapter and closes the book.

"You okay?" I ask. "Your grandma said—"

"I'm fine. I just needed some time to myself." She stares

across the water, shoulders slouched, looking like she's lost in thought for a moment.

"Good, good. I was worried after last night, maybe I said something that upset you."

"Not everything's about you, Thayer ..." There's the tiniest hint of a tease in her voice, but it's not enough to cover up the fact that something's bothering her.

"Obviously," I say, nudging her.

She's quiet. I'm quiet. And a boat motors by in the distance.

I almost ask if she's ever been sailing before, but then I stop myself. I doubt Granddad would let me take her out on the boat because that's the sort of thing you do with a girl you like and he'll assume I'm being defiant, and there's nothing that Granddad hates more than when someone goes against his orders.

As far as I'm concerned, there's nothing wrong with spending time with her in an innocent, platonic capacity—despite the fact that I might sneak glances at her every chance I get and daydream about what her skin would feel like beneath my hands, the softness of her mouth on mine, the way her body would feel beneath me, the heat of her breath in my ear ...

"Any plans for the afternoon?" I ask.

She splays a palm across the book in her lap before peering across the sea. "You're looking at it."

I wish so badly that I could take her into town tomorrow. We could hitch a ride with the grocery boat and find some local to bring us back later. I could show her it's not so bad in Rose Crossing, that it's quaint and the people are nice and welcoming and there are shops and a library and cafes and a laidback sort of beachy vibe that might feel somewhat familiar to her since she's from the West Coast.

"How about you?" she asks.

I shrug. "Aunt Lorelai wants to do a clam dig. Promised Granddad a game of chess on the porch later. Pretty exciting stuff ..."

"Then you shouldn't keep them waiting." She opens her book, resting her fingers against the bound center. "Thanks for checking on me."

I push myself to a standing position. "See you around."

I don't say "See you later" because she doesn't need to be reminded that the next time we see each other, she'll be serving me dinner. I want her to know she has a friend in me, that I don't see her as some housemaid.

Growing up, my father has always instilled in me the importance of treating everyone like an equal. He grew up middle class, the son of a third-grade teacher and a city planner. And then he met my mom and was whisked into her world of privilege and opportunity, and he was determined not to let the spoils of the Bertram estate ruin me.

I won't deny the perks that come with being in this family.

But I also won't let them determine my fate.

CHAPTER 8

Lila

"YOU'LL NEED to set an extra place at the table today," my grandma tells me as we prep Monday's lunch. "We have a visitor."

I grab a linen placemat from the drawer followed by two forks, a spoon, and a butter knife before locating an extra plate and water goblet. With full arms, I head out through the swinging doors and into the dining room where some of the family members are already filing in.

I'm almost done setting the extra place when I hear a squeal from another room.

"Lovey, would you mind grabbing the lavender napkins from the hall closet? We've been using the same old boring white ones since last week and I'm in the mood for a bit of color," Thayer's mother says.

"Of course." I exit the dining room and make my way down

to the linen closet in the hall, but on my way, I pass the parlor where Westley, Whitley, Thayer, and an unidentified girl stand in a circle chit-chatting.

The girl, whose back is to me, has long dark hair that stops in the middle of her back. She's talking a mile a minute, her hands waving wildly as she rocks back and forth on her Chanel flats.

Thayer spots me from where he stands, and I glance away, trying to mind my own business. I locate the lavender napkins in the hall closet a minute later and bring them back to the dining room.

"Perfection, Lovey. Thank you," Thayer's mom says as I fold them into little tents and place them in the middle of each white plate.

The cousins and their special guest file into the dining room as soon as I'm finished with the last one, and I duck back into the kitchen.

"Oh, Lila. There you are," Grandma says as she fills a glass pitcher with iced tea and mint leaves.

"They wanted lavender napkins," I say to explain why it took me so long to come back.

"Grab something, will you?" she asks as she heads to the swinging doors.

I grab as many salad plates from the marble island as I can carry and follow.

The entire time I serve them, I feel the weight of Thayer's stare, but I've yet to make eye contact with him. That girl, the squealer, is sitting between Thayer and Whitley. I don't know yet if she's a friend of Whitley's or a girlfriend of Thayer's.

I also don't know why I'm letting it bother me, because it shouldn't matter. It's a moot point. And honestly, it's none of my business.

The girl with the long dark hair is yapping away to Mr. Bertram and he's in rare form—smiling—as he eats up her every word and laughs at everything she says.

We're almost finished with cleanup an hour later when Gram tells me to head to The Caldecott.

"Prepare the guest suite on the third level in the turret," she says. "The bed will need fresh linens, and make sure there are more than enough towels in the bathroom."

I sneak out the back door of the kitchen and make my way next door to the twins' house to prepare the guest room. The whole way there, I try to determine if they're putting her up in The Caldecott because she's a friend of Whitley's or if they're putting her over there because she's Thayer's girlfriend and it wouldn't be "appropriate" to have them sleeping under the same roof. Knowing Bertram and his rules, the latter wouldn't surprise me.

The house is quiet when I get inside, all except for the chiming of the grandfather clock in the hall and the roll and crash of ocean waves through dozens of open windows.

I stop at the linen closet on the second level before climbing another flight of stairs to the guest room in the turret.

The room is enormous, complete with 180-degree views of the water and a white four-poster bed covered in a million pillows.

I crack the windows to let some fresh air in and to clear the warm stuffiness that lingers in this unused room, and then I strip the bed.

I'm almost finished with everything when the door swings open and footsteps indicate I'm no longer alone.

"Hello?" I call before exiting the Pottery Barn catalog-looking en suite.

"Hello ..." an unfamiliar voice calls back.

I step out and find the girl standing in the middle of the room, an overstuffed Louis Vuitton duffel bag over her shoulder.

"I was just dropping off some towels," I say, pointing behind me.

"I'm Ashlan," she says, extending her hand.

Her formality catches me off guard, but I return her gesture. "Lila."

"They told me you're Ed and Junie's granddaughter."

"I am." How the hell is she on a first-name basis with my grandparents?

"They're the sweetest," she says with a nostalgic smile. "So what do you think of the island so far? Big change from ... L.A. is it?"

I nod. "I grew up mostly in Santa Monica. And yeah, it's a big change, but so far so good ..."

Ashlan takes a seat on the bed, running her hands along the white quilt. "I've been coming here for years. Practically my whole life. Rose Crossing's like a second home to me."

"Oh, yeah? Are you a friend of Whitley's?" I have to ask.

She crosses her legs, her ankle bouncing a little. "I'm a friend of everyone's. My mom grew up with Thayer's mom and the twins' mom. We were all born literally in the same season of the same year so we've been friends since before we could talk." She laughs. "They always used to call us the quadruplets because we were inseparable and we were all the same size."

I can't help but think she's trying to establish her place under the guise of sharing quaint stories with me. If I were to read between the lines here, I'm pretty sure she'd be saying, "I was here first, so don't even think about taking my place."

"That's adorable," I say, heading to the door. "Let me know if you need anything else, okay? It was nice meeting you."

I leave The Caldecott and head to my grandparents' cottage, where I find my grandma relaxing in her recliner as she pages through a Better Homes and Gardens magazine.

"Ashlan's room is good to go," I say as I step out of my shoes.

"Lovely girl," Grandma says without looking up.

"She seems to think highly of you guys." I take a seat on the yellow velvet sofa that must be at least thirty years old and tuck a throw pillow under my arm. "How long is she staying, do you know?"

"From what I understand, she'll take the mail plane back to the mainland on Thursday. She's doing a summer semester at Yale so she needs to get back. In the past, she'd stay at least until the Fourth of July."

"She goes to Yale?"

Grandma flicks to a new page. "She does. From what I hear, she and Thayer are both studying pre-law."

Half of me wants to ask if the two of them ever dated, but I know better than to raise any suspicions. If my line of questioning isn't obvious enough, a question like that will seal the deal.

I kick my feet up on the sofa and sink into the worn cushions, staring at the bead board ceiling above and the wobbly bronze ceiling fan.

"Don't get too comfortable, Lila. We're polishing the silver at The Ainsworth this afternoon and your grandfather could use your help getting the groceries off the dock after four."

The thought of possibly running into Thayer at his house makes my skin heat and my breath catch until I mentally shrug it off.

Ashlan is the epitome of the kind of girl Thayer would match perfectly with. She wears the same preppy clothes as him. Their mothers are best friends. They go to school together and even study the same subject. They have inside jokes, I'm sure, and summers upon summers of memories.

I can't compete with any of that.

But again, it's a moot point because nothing's going to happen between us no matter how kind he is to me, no matter how hard I melt when he does something sweet, no matter how many times I think about kissing him ...

It can't and it won't and that's all there is to it.

————

THE AINSWORTH WAS quiet this afternoon. Apparently Mr. Bertram took all the "kids" out for a sail, and the sisters and their husbands are having an afternoon at the private beach.

It's just Grandma and me and a quiet old house that smells faintly of flowers and ocean musk and bends and creaks in the wind.

"Lila, why don't you go find your grandfather? It's almost time for the grocery drop off," my grandma says, a shiny fork in her hand. "I'll finish up here and then I'll meet you at The Bertram after. You can help me put everything away just before dinner."

I rise and close the cap on the bottle of polish in front of me.

"And Lila?" she asks as I get up from the table and push my chair in.

"Yes?"

"Are you doing okay?" Her forehead is creased and her eyes are soft.

"Of course."

"You're just so ... quiet," she says. "And you never used to be. You used to chat my ear off every time we'd come out.

Talking about movies and boys and friends and books and concerts and anything and everything."

Her mouth twitches into a quick, bittersweet kind of smile.

"I ... I hope you don't think we're pretending like nothing happened. It's hard for us, too, you know?" She pauses. "I don't ask you how you're doing every five seconds because I don't want to annoy you. But I think about it all the time. The things that must be going through your head. The way you must be feeling. If you ever want to talk ..."

"Thank you. I know. I know I can tell you anything," I say. "I'm just taking things one day at a time."

She places a butter knife on the cloth before her, dragging in a long breath. "You remind me so much of her, Lila. Every day. The way you talk. The way you walk. Your expressions. Your strength ... it's all her."

My eyes fill with tears, but I blink them away.

I don't want to cry.

Not here, not now.

"In a way ... she lives on. Through you," Grandma continues. "And while I know this isn't exactly the kind of place a girl your age would want to live for the summer, just know that having you here has been a blessing for your grandfather and me." Rising, she walks to me, cupping my face in her hands. "We'll get through this together."

"I know."

She smirks, her eyes glassy. "All right. Now get going."

I hurry out the back door and trek through the lush green

lawn toward the dock, passing The Bertram along the way, where a trail of younger-sounding voices in the wind tell me they must be back from sailing.

Keeping my eyes forward and my head down, I keep walking, focused and undeterred.

"Lila!" a voice calls for me. "Lila, hey, wait up!"

I glance back and spot Thayer jogging down the porch steps and toward me. His hair is wind-swept and the bridge of his nose is a shade darker than it was at lunchtime. He's wearing dusty red chino shorts and a white polo and belongs on the cover of a Lands' End catalog.

"Hi," I say.

His eyes hold mine. "What are you doing?"

"Working."

For a split second, I glance over his shoulder, toward The Bertram's porch, and catch Ashlan watching us like a hawk as she twirls her dark hair around one finger.

"What are you doing ... later?" he smiles.

"I really have to go." I turn and take a few more steps, only a couple of seconds later, his arm hooks the bend of my elbow and he leads me behind the little white machine shed, out of sight from any prying eyes.

"We're having another bonfire tonight," he says. "Ashlan brought a bottle of Grey Goose. Could be fun ..."

For a moment, I try to imagine myself sitting around a fire with the four of them ... but I can't.

I'd rather wash my hair, I think.

"You don't have to drink. You can just sit around and watch Westley make a fool of himself if you want ..." he winks.

"I'll pass. But thank you. And I reallllly need to go."

"You didn't look at me once at breakfast," he says. "And I tried to say hi to you at lunch and you wouldn't give me the time of day."

"I was working ..."

"No. It wasn't that. It's something else."

I scoff. "And you know that because you're psychic?"

"We had a nice talk last night. Or at least I thought we did. And then you went all cold on me today. I don't know what's up or down with you, Lila. I have no idea what you think of me." His jaw flexes and his eyes flash intense as he leans in. "And it drives me insane ..."

His breath is warm against my ear, sending a wave of tingles down my back.

Clearing my throat and straightening my shoulders, I glance into his eyes and say, "That makes two of us, because I don't know what I think of you either."

Neither of us says a word. I don't think I could if I tried.

Everything is racing: my mind, my heart, the goosebumps traveling across my skin.

I fight like hell to compose myself so I can tell him for the third time that I need to get going—but the second my lips part, they're claimed by his.

Full and soft, his mouth covers mine as his hand cups the side of my face and his fingers hook around the back of my neck. I'm pressed up against the side of the shed now, my body melting and knees threatening to give out. When our tongues meet, I taste sweet spearmint and when I breathe him in, my lungs fill with his cedar cologne and a mix of fresh salt air.

I let him kiss me.

I let myself have this moment.

I let myself go a few endless moments without worrying, without overthinking, without second-guessing.

And then it's over.

Thayer removes his mouth from mine, though his hand still lingers at my jaw and his thumb traces my swollen lower lip.

"Does that help?" he asks. "What do you think of me now?"

"Lila!" my grandfather calls my name from the direction of the dock, and the beeping of a boat horn follows. "Lila!"

"I have to go," I tell Thayer, leaving him answer-less as I jog toward the dock.

A man in jeans and a dingy t-shirt is unloading boxes, and my grandfather is placing them in a crate attached to a four-wheeler. The boxes keep coming and coming, and I'm guessing this will take several trips. It takes a lot of food to feed almost a dozen grown adults three full-course meals a day.

I get to the dock and pray my lips aren't red and the awestruck expression has left my face, and my prayers are answered when my grandpa hands me a box of groceries and turns to talk to the delivery man.

When the first load is packed, Grandpa drives it back to The Bertram, leaving me on the dock to wait for him. Alone. With my noisy thoughts and lips still burning from that kiss that ended way too soon and left me wanting more.

It was easier when I could deny the way I felt toward Thayer, when I could deny the blossoming crush and ignore the butterflies and chase those thoughts away like pesky gnats.

But there's no denying I'm attracted to him, to his kindness and his stormy blue eyes and the way he says all the right things at all the right moments.

And then he had to go and kiss me, the bastard.

I take a seat on the edge of the dock, crossing my legs beneath me and watching the ripples on the water.

Screw it.

I like him.

I like him a lot.

CHAPTER 9

THAYER

IT'S HALF past eleven when I check my watch. I'm not sure why I didn't give up hope hours ago. It's not like she's going to magically emerge from the darkness that surrounds us and join our stupid little bonfire.

My head is dizzy and despite the fact that I've had an ungodly equivalent of vodka shots, I swear I can still taste her—spicy like cinnamon gum and its signature burn followed by sweetness.

Fitting.

"Thayer, do you remember when we snuck out of our dorm after curfew last year?" Ashlan asks with slurred words as she sways by the fire, a near-empty bottle of Grey Goose in her hand. Out of all of us, she's hit it the hardest tonight, which isn't like her. "And do you remember when campus police chased us on their bikes and we hid behind those statues outside the library?"

"Yep ..."

She takes a swig before walking the bottle over to me.

"No thanks," I wave it off.

She collapses on her knees in front of me, motioning for me to scoot over on my sand-covered blanket.

"Fine," she says, crawling into my lap.

She didn't even give me time to move ...

"I'm so glad we picked the same school," she says, leaning against me. "It's almost like it was fate or something."

More like it was Ashlan being obsessed with me.

Ever since we turned sixteen, something changed in her. She got clingier. Called more. Texted more. Followed me around more. When we were heading into our senior years, she found out through her mother that my first pick was Yale and that I was thinking pre-law, and magically she went from wanting to be a kindergarten teacher to wanting to be a lawyer.

Every girlfriend I had, every female friend or person of the opposite sex who so much as looked at me in a certain way always had her to contend with. She would always criticize them under the guise of "trying to protect me from crazy bitches," but I always saw through it.

It's only gotten worse since we went to college.

She made sure her dorm was in the same building as mine,

and in addition to that, she made sure we had at least half of our classes together. I tried talking to my mom about it once, but she waved it off, saying I was reading into things too much and that I should be grateful to have a familiar face around.

I've made it clear to Ashlan on several occasions that I think of her as a sister, that I would never date her, but if anything, I think it only made her that much more determined to get what she wants—me.

I gave her a roadblock.

She saw a challenge and readily accepted it.

"Ashlan, get off me," I say, giving her a gentle nudge.

She slides off my lap and cozies up beside me, taking another swig from the bottle.

"Ash, maybe you should stop," Westley says. "You're going to feel like shit tomorrow."

"You're going to look like shit too," Whitley adds. "And then everyone will know we were drinking."

"It's nothing sunglasses and Advil can't fix," Ashlan says with a giggle before crawling onto her hands and knees like a damn animal.

"What the hell are you doing?" Whitley asks.

For the first time, it's not Westley making a fool of himself, and without any of us saying another word, I can almost feel the collective embarrassment for our friend.

Ashlan begins to say something, only to suddenly slap her hand across her mouth and scramble to get up. In her drunken haste, she trips, falling into the sand as she tries to get away.

"I think she's going to throw up," Whitley says, waving her hands and looking like she's going to be sick herself. "I can't. I can't deal with puke. One of you guys needs to take this one."

I get up and go to her, helping her up as she dry heaves, and with my arm around her, I lead her several yards away and hold her hair back as the liquid contents of her stomach splatter against the beach grass at her feet.

When she's done, she wipes her mouth on the back of her hand and turns toward me, though she won't look me in the eye.

"Got a little carried away tonight, I guess," she slurs, eyes half-open like she's about to pass out.

"Let's get you back to the house." I can't leave her like this. It wouldn't be right.

With my arm around her, I walk us past the bonfire and tell the twins I'm taking her to her room, and then we begin the half-mile stumbling trek back up the cliff.

She throws up twice more on the way.

"What would I do without you?" she asks, her arm hooked around my waist as we get closer to The Caldecott.

I take her in the back door and immediately dread the three flights of stairs it's going to take to get her to the guest room.

"You're my best friend, Thayer," she says.

"Shhh ..." I'd hate to wake my aunt and uncle.

By the grace of God, I manage to get her to her room a few minutes later, and I help her climb into bed. I flick on the light to her bathroom in case she needs to see in the middle of the night, and then I tell her goodnight.

"Love you," she calls out as I leave. She says it the way a friend would say it to another friend who just did them a solid, but I know better.

I say nothing in reply—I tiptoe down the hall, down the three flights of stairs, and head back to my house in the dark, stealing a passing glance at The Hilliard on the way.

Tonight would've been so much better had Lila shown up.

CHAPTER 10

Lila

I TOSS and turn for hours before deciding to face my insomnia head on. For whatever reason, sleep isn't coming easily to me tonight, so I tiptoe to the kitchen and make myself a cup of chamomile tea before heading to the front porch.

Rose Crossing was hit with a heat wave this week, so the cool evenings I've been growing accustomed to have now become stuffy and insufferable. Not even an open window helps.

Curled up in the white rocking chair, I sip my tea, knees against my chest, and take in my midnight surroundings.

Thayer invited me to another bonfire tonight, but that was before he kissed me, and we didn't have a chance to talk again after that. The last thing I want is to look like I'm becoming smitten with him, even if I am. I don't want to seem desperate or like I suddenly changed my mind all because of a kiss behind a shed (even if it was one of the best kisses of my entire life).

I was floating for a moment, lighter than air.

Yesterday didn't exist. Tomorrow wasn't so much as a thought in my head. It was just us, in that moment, and it was divine.

The sound of voices interrupt my quietude, and I peer ahead in the distance to see the outline of two figures stumbling toward the houses. The closer they get, the more I'm able to make them out, and within seconds I realize it's Thayer and Ashlan.

I can't hear what they're saying over the crash of the ocean waves that surround the island, but I don't need to.

His arm is around her shoulders.

Her arm is around his waist.

They're glued at the hip.

And they're heading to The Caldecott.

My stomach sinks, and I know I shouldn't watch, but I can't help myself. I'm frozen in my rocking chair, my tea growing colder by the second, and I watch as they go in through the back door.

A minute or so later, the light to her room flicks on, though the curtains are drawn. A minute after that, the light goes out.

Everything stings: my eyes, my chest, my ego.

I go back inside. I can't watch any longer.

I'm such an idiot.

CHAPTER 11

THAYER

IT'S mid-morning when I wake on Tuesday. My tongue feels like sandpaper and my head is pounding. The daylight pouring in from my open windows damn near burns my eyes, but I fight through it and make my way to the bathroom to shower.

I'm sure my absence at the breakfast table this morning will raise some questions and earn me a Spanish Inquisition from my parents, but I'll just say I stayed up late and wanted to get some extra sleep. With Ashlan's arrival, they won't think twice about it. They'll think we chatted all night, catching up like old friends who didn't just see each other less than two weeks ago at college.

I run the shower and toss my clothes in the hamper before grabbing my phone off the nightstand. We might not have cell service out here, but at least I can still listen to music. I shut the door, tap my playlist, and The Killer's Spaceman begins to play before I step under the hot shower spray.

When I'm finished, I step out and secure a towel around my waist, my headache beginning to subside. My mind begins to wander to Lila.

I kissed her yesterday behind the shed, after she said she didn't know how she felt about me. What she was really saying was that she liked me and she didn't know how she felt about that.

I don't know what came over me, but the next thing I knew, my mouth was on hers and my hands were in her hair and when it was over, she was looking at me in a whole new light.

We're playing with fire, I know. But I can't help myself.

She's an enigma.

A puzzle I want to solve.

A code I need to crack.

I've never met anyone like her. She doesn't throw herself at me. She makes me work like hell for an ounce of her attention. She's smart-mouthed and sassy, independent and stronger than most people would be given her current life situation. And then there's her beauty, which is nothing more than a bonus.

I've seen a thousand beautiful girls before and there's certainly no shortage of them at school, but Lila has what all of the other girls don't—a personality.

I brush my teeth and step out of the steamy bathroom, my

phone now blasting Modest Mouse's Missed the Boat. I'm two steps into my room when I stop in my tracks.

Lila's in my room, making my bed.

Her back is to me and there are earbuds in her ears.

I watch as she fluffs my pillows and tucks the corners of my quilt under the mattress, and when she finally realizes I'm standing in the doorway of the en suite, she gasps and yanks her earbuds out.

"You scared me." Her hand rests on her chest for a second before she shuts off her music. "I didn't know you were in here."

"You didn't hear my music?" I point behind me.

She lifts the cord of her earbuds.

"I'm almost finished," she says, turning away and grabbing a feather duster from her cleaning caddy. "Let me know when you're done in the bathroom so I can get out of your hair."

I linger for a second, my hand hooked on the back of my neck.

I want to talk about the kiss yesterday ... and the question she didn't have a chance to answer.

"Lila ... about yesterday," I say.

She whips around to look at me, brows lifted. "You don't have to say anything. I know it was a mistake. I'm perfectly capable of acting like it didn't happen."

"No. That's not what I'm saying."

"Well, that's what *I'm* saying."

She dusts my nightstand and lampshade before moving to the writing desk in the corner that once belonged to my grandmother.

"I'm confused," I say. "You kissed me back. I thought ..."

"You thought I liked it?" she asks.

"Yeah."

"I mean, you're not a bad kisser if that's what you're getting at. So congrats on that."

God, she's a smartass.

"I'm not fishing for compliments, Lila." I massage the back of my neck, watching her work her way around the rest of my room. "You didn't answer my question yesterday."

Her adorable little nose crinkles. "You're still hung up on that?"

"Yeah. I am." I fold my arms across my bare chest.

"That's the problem these days. Everyone is so obsessed with what other people think of them," she says, shaking her feather duster. "It's really restrictive, you know? You end up living your life for other people and not for yourself, and that's no way to live."

She turns to dust a bookshelf.

"That's not what I'm talking about and you know it," I say. "But if you'd like, I'd be happy to tell you what I think of you."

She says nothing as she continues to clean.

"You're fascinating and baffling—but in the best kind of way. I think about you way more than I should." I make my way to the dresser in the corner, grabbing a few things from drawers. "And I'd love to get to know you better. That's what I think of you."

She stands frozen, unmoving, her back still to me.

And then I return to the bathroom to get dressed. When I come out a few minutes later, she's gone.

CHAPTER 12

Lila

I SKIPPED CLEANING his bathroom today.

I had to get out of there.

If Thayer standing there dripping wet, a towel around his hips, highlighting his rippled abs and chiseled Adonis belt weren't enough, he then had to give me some mini speech on how special I am and how he wants to get to know me.

I'm sorry, but after what I saw last night, I'm not buying it.

But he's good.

I'll give him that.

He knows all the right words and has all the right moves and if I were a little more naïve, I'd fall for it in two seconds flat.

But I wasn't born yesterday. And there happened to be an abundance of assholes just like him at my old high school in

Santa Monica—guys used to getting everything they want because they were attractive, their parents had money, and they happened to be versed in the art of charming the opposite sex with a few lines.

I make my way to the master bedroom at the end of the hall and shut the door behind me. The room is floor-to-ceiling white wainscoting accented with dozens of windows covered in gauzy curtain panels that dance in the breeze. A king-sized bed with a seagrass headboard and a white, pick-stitched coverlet anchors the room. An antique walnut dresser covered in dozens of family photos is the only thing that personalizes this room and keeps it from looking like something straight off of Airbnb's website.

I finish making the bed before heading to dust the dresser, which requires moving each and every one of the family photos so I can clean beneath them.

Stopping for a moment, I study a few of them. Not surprisingly, most of them are Thayer through the years.

Thayer in a Little League uniform holding a bat.

Thayer in blue striped swim trunks on a sandy beach.

Thayer posing with Mickey Mouse in front of Cinderella's Castle at Disney World.

A braces-wearing Thayer posing with his parents, all of them dressed in Red Sox garb.

Thayer in a tuxedo, standing next to a stunning redhead in a lavender-sequined prom dress.

Thayer in a yellow cap and gown, holding his high school diploma.

A wedding photo of his parents rests in the middle of all of that. His mother, Tippi, reminds me of a modern-day Grace Kelly. Shoulder-length blonde hair that curls under. Fine features. Petite stature. His father, Mitchum, reminds me of a 1940s movie star, though I'm not sure which one. He's definitely the kind of man who ages well from what I can tell from these pictures over the years. There's something strong about him, something worldly, and yet there's a youthfulness, a light in his eyes—much like his son's.

I stop gawking and get back to work.

We can't help the family we're born into and I don't resent him for having a picture-perfect childhood. Good for him. But it only goes to illustrate how truly opposite we really are.

My mother was a saint in a lot of ways, though she still had her imperfections. We all do. She was overprotective at times. Stubborn and unrelenting when it came to certain things. She cried at weddings and laughed at funerals (when appropriate, of course). She dated here and there but once things started getting serious, she'd always find a reason to break it off. I knew her better than anyone, and yet there were times when I questioned if I even knew her at all.

She loved with everything she had, but she kept her own heart guarded, padlocked really. It's like she felt she was undeserving ... and now I'll never have a chance to ask her why.

I finish Tippi and Mitchum's bedroom before heading to their en suite and starting with the giant white tub in the middle of the room, the one beneath an oversized capiz shell chandelier straight out of a Serena and Lily catalog.

When I'm done with the bathroom, I make my way down to the main level. I'm hardly finished with The Ainsworth. I still have the living room, dining room, family room, study, kitchen, hallway, and half bath to do.

That's seven more opportunities to cross paths with Thayer.

If I'm lucky, he's already gone.

CHAPTER 13

THAYER

I COME out of the shed Tuesday afternoon, fishing rod in hand. I promised the twins and Ashlan I'd meet them at the cove for an afternoon of fishing—an old pastime of ours. Junie promised she'd cook whatever we caught today and told me to make sure we came back with enough for everyone, so we're going to be here a while.

To my left, damp sheets are being hung from the clotheslines and the faint scent of clean cotton fills the air as they flap in the wind.

For whatever reason, I stop to watch.

Two hands.

A clothespin.

A wet sheet.

A moment later, Lila steps out from behind it, bending low to grab another sheet from the wicker basket on the ground.

"Want some help?" I ask.

Her eyes flick to mine. If she's surprised to see me, she doesn't show it.

I don't wait for her to answer, I simply grab a sheet from the basket and a couple of clothespins and get to work.

"I don't know why you're doing this," she says, though she won't look at me.

"I do my own laundry at school," I say. "And believe it or not, I do a lot of laundry at home. We don't have ... help ... or anything. I mean, we have a cleaning lady that comes once a week, but other than that it's just the three of us."

I feel her gaze for a second, as if she's taking it all in or trying to decide if she believes me or not.

My grandfather is the one with all the money. He's the one with a private island and full-time employees. He bought my parents a comfortable house in Bridgeport, Connecticut as a wedding gift but as far as anything else goes, my father has always been the breadwinner, supporting us on his IT Security Consultant salary. He does well for himself, but we're certainly not rolling in the dough. I don't drive a BMW, and the only reason I go to Yale is because it's my grandfather's alma mater and he promised to pay if I went.

There's one sheet left in the basket and we both reach for it at the same time, our hands brushing. She lets me have it.

"Thank you," she says.

"Sorry if I made you uncomfortable earlier," I say when I'm finished. "And sorry if I'm coming on too strong."

"*If?*" she laughs.

"Okay, sorry *that* I'm coming on too strong," I say. "I just ... when I get excited about something, sometimes I get too excited, you know? It consumes me. And I can be a little intense for some people. I've been like that my whole life, and I realize now that you barely know me and maybe it freaks you out." I pause, studying her for a reaction that never comes. She wears her poker face and she wears it well. "If you want me to back off, I will. I just wanted you to know how I felt earlier, that's all. Because on the off chance you feel the same way but you're afraid to say it ... I—"

"Thayer! There you are." Ashlan appears out of nowhere, brushing one of the sheets aside. Half of it falls off the clothespin and she doesn't bother fixing it. "We've been looking for you. Westley has the bait ready and Whitley's got the golf cart so we can just ride to the cove."

Lila reaches to fix the fallen sheet, sighing as she bends.

I grab my pole from the ground and look at Lila one more time before we go.

"See you around," I say. Ashlan glances between the two of us. "Why don't you run ahead. I'll catch up."

"I can wait," Ashlan says, shrugging and grinning like she's oblivious to what's going on when I know damn well she isn't.

"No, seriously. Go on. I'm good. I'll take one of the four-wheelers and meet you guys."

Ashlan's dark brows meet in the middle and she does a slight pout, which makes me cringe because there's nothing adorable about a grown adult woman pouting like a spoiled child.

"Fine. Whatever." Ashlan leaves in a huff and I watch as Lila stacks and gathers the laundry baskets and hauls them under her arm back toward the house.

"Lila," I say. "Wait."

She stops. "You shouldn't keep her waiting."

Is that what this is about? Does she think I have a thing for Ashlan?

I almost think about inviting her along (even though I know she'll say no) and then I remember the promise I made a few moments ago about not coming on too strong.

"Can we finish this conversation another time?" she asks.

My chest inflates, warm and hopeful. This is a good sign. Unexpected too, which is ironically not surprising.

"I'll be in the abandoned cottage later," she says. "After dinner. We can talk there."

"The Lila Cottage," I say with a half-smile that she doesn't return.

She continues on her way back to the main house, and I head to the machine shed to grab one of the four-wheelers, counting down the hours until I see her again, until I can finally figure out what the hell is going through that pretty little mystifying head of hers.

CHAPTER 14

Lila

I PACE the living room of the abandoned cottage shortly after supper clean-up. Grandma fried up the haddock that the cousins caught earlier today so my hair smells like grease and fried fish, but there's nothing I can do about that until I wash it out tonight.

Besides, it's not like I need to impress him.

And who knows if he'll even show up.

I was pretty cold to him earlier. I wouldn't blame him if he decided I'm too much effort and not worth the work.

I unsnap the hair tie from my wrist and pile my hair into a messy bun at the top of my head before taking a seat on one of the dusty sofas and paging through an old issue of People magazine from January 1993. Jerry Seinfeld, Julia Roberts, and a few others are on the cover alongside the headline, "World's Richest Actors," and I find it ironically fitting.

My mom's crazy friend always said there was no such thing as coincidences.

The jury's still out on that for me.

Sometimes I think life is just a jumble of random events and there's no real path for anyone. Things just ... happen. And that's all there is to it.

The front door swings open when I'm halfway finished reading the Letters to the Editor page of my magazine. I fold it and toss it on the coffee table before resting my elbows on my knees and glancing up at the tall drink of water as he closes the door behind him.

There's a light in his eyes, a flicker of hope that doesn't belong.

When I told him we could talk at the cottage, what I didn't tell him was that I had every intention of calling him out on his playboy ways, confronting him about all the things he's said and then telling him I saw him and Ashlan together last night, arms around each other as he walked her home. I plan to tell him I'm not stupid and I refuse to fall for that, and then I plan to tell him to back off because he doesn't have a chance in hell.

Thayer takes a seat in the rocking chair beside the couch, and I clear my throat.

This was so much easier in my head.

Now that he's here, all I can think about is how gorgeous he looks and how nice he was earlier and I'm suddenly finding the words are stuck in my throat and my palms are clamming up.

Summoning all the strength I have, I clasp my hands together and sit up straight.

"So, just going to put it all out there," I say.

He nods, leaning forward a little. I have his full attention.

"You say a lot of nice things, Thayer. And you're hot as hell. And you're a good kisser. And you claim you like me, which is flattering as hell because you're ... you," I say. "But I know when something's too good to be true and—"

He laughs.

Which only infuriates me because I'm trying to have a serious conversation here.

"Too good to be true?" he asks. "Lila, I've meant every word I've said."

"See. That's exactly what I'm talking about." I point at him. "You always say the right thing at the right moment."

"And that means I'm not being genuine?" He scratches at his right temple, still fighting a smirk. He thinks I'm being cute. "I'm sorry, but your logic doesn't add up for me."

"I know your type. That's how you operate."

"My type? Now that's just cruel. I've yet to make a single assumption about you or pigeonhole you into some cheesy Californian stereotype." He stands. "Unlike you, I actually prefer to get to know people before I judge them."

I stand, though we're still not eye-to-eye thanks to the fact that he's easily a good seven or eight inches taller than me.

I try to say something in my defense, until I realize he's absolutely right.

I've judged and stereotyped him and aside from what I already know about him, there's still so much I don't know.

But it doesn't change what I saw last night.

"If you like me so much, why did you hook up with Ashlan last night?" I hate the way I sound. *Hate it.* But it all just came out like word vomit, sour and hot on my tongue, and there's no taking it back now.

"What the hell are you talking about?" His brows lift and his upper lip is almost snarling.

"Last night." I fold my arms across my chest. "I saw the two of you walking back from the bonfire. Your arms were around her and she was all over you. And then you took her to her room."

"And so then you just assumed we hooked up?"

"I mean ... it looked like you two were getting pretty cozy on the walk there." I shrug. "And you were alone."

"She was drunk out of her freaking mind. I walked her back because she'd just puked her guts out all over the beach. And I had to put my arm around her because she kept falling," he says.

I search his eyes, trying to decide if I believe him or if this is just another case of Thayer Ainsworth knowing exactly what to say.

"I've known Ashlan my entire life," he says.

"Yeah. She made that pretty clear to me yesterday."

"She's like a sister to me. Nothing more." He's breathing heavier now, like I've got him all worked up. If he were lying, I'd imagine he'd be calmer.

"Clearly she feels differently about you."

He rolls his eyes. "Yeah, I know. And believe me, I've made myself clear to her about a dozen different times over the last few years."

I knew girls like Ashlan back home. They'd become obsessed with a guy, creep his MySpace and Facebook, show up where he was, infiltrate his group of friends, flirt like hell and scare off other girls who so much as looked at the guy, and then when none of that worked, they got desperate.

It's like the more they couldn't have him, the more they wanted him.

I suppose it's not Thayer's fault ...

... if this is all true, anyway.

"I swear to you, Lila, I got her back to her room and left," he says, hand over his heart. "But can we get back on track here? We were talking about *us*."

Us.

There is no "us."

"Just tell me how you feel. If you're not interested, if you don't feel the same about me, I'll leave you alone," he says.

Drawing in a long breath, I take a seat, sinking into the stiff cushions of the dusty sofa with the scratchy fabric.

"It doesn't matter how I feel," I say before looking up into his dreamy, ocean-hued gaze. I never realized how dark his lashes were before, how they frame his almond-shaped eyes. "I promised my grandparents I'd keep things strictly professional while I'm here," I huff.

Thayer takes a seat in his chair, elbows on his knees and hands forming a peak that he breathes into.

"My grandfather gave me the same orders," he says. "Not to get involved with you ... for liability reasons. At least that's what he said."

"That's the difference between us, Thayer ... I have everything to lose if I defy my grandparents. If you defy your grandfather, you still have everything."

His dark brows furrow. "That's not true at all."

Yeah. Right.

"My grandfather holds the purse strings that keep this entire family under his thumb. He's got more money than he knows what to do with and he's always used it to get people to bend to his will—most of the time without them even knowing it," he says. "The houses he bought for his daughters as wedding gifts? He chose them. Which meant he chose the locations. He wanted them to be in Bridgeport, where he lived at the time. And my college tuition? He wanted me to go to his alma mater and promised to pay for my entire education if I did. Even bought me a Land Rover for my high school graduation because God forbid I didn't look every bit the part when I showed up that fall. You know what I drove before that? A used Nissan. Paid for it myself with money I earned working weekends at the golf course. And I loved the hell out of that car."

I let this sink in, trying to wrap my head around it and replacing my old assumptions with new facts.

"So while it looks like I have it all," he continues. "It's only because I walk a straight line with Granddad. One misstep and I lose it all. And honestly? Somedays I think I'd be okay with that."

I roll my eyes. "If you're trying to get me to feel sorry for you …"

"Please. I don't need your sympathy. I'm trying to illustrate a point to you."

"What? That you like me so much you're willing to throw away your entire future?" I chuff. "If that's the case, then I'm sorry, but you're not nearly as bright as I thought you were. No offense …"

"You don't have to be cruel to push me away. If you don't like me, just say it, Lila." His expression is blank but his eyes are searching.

I begin to speak and then I stop myself. Taking a deep breath, I try again. "You're too nice, and your persistence is just as flattering as it is infuriating. I hate how charming you are and how the things you say get stuck in my head like a catchy song. You're almost too good looking, which I know isn't your fault. You can't help that you're genetically doomed to look like a Greek statue the rest of your life. Everybody loves you. Everybody. Your grandfather adores you. Westley idolizes you. You're the center of your parents' world. And your mother is one of the sweetest people I've ever met. You're intelligent and kind and helpful. Everything about you and your entire world is perfect, Thayer.

Maddeningly perfect. And as much as I try not to ... I can't help but like you too."

His shoulders fall, as if he's relieved. And his subtle show of happiness makes my stomach flip and sends a tingle all the way to my fingertips.

"But." I raise a flattened palm. "Just because we feel a certain way doesn't mean we should act on it."

The flash in his eyes that was there a moment ago dims. "We're both adults. Maybe they won't be thrilled about this at first, but if we can prove to them that nothing bad's going to happen, that we're capable of handling this like adults should things go south ..."

"I've been here a week," I say. "And your grandfather didn't have to give me a job, but he did. If I didn't have this? I'd have nothing. Nowhere to go. I have zero dollars to my name. My mom barely had enough life insurance to cover the cost of her funeral. If I'm fired? I'll literally be homeless. And if my grandparents are fired because of me?" My stomach knots. "I couldn't live with myself knowing I was responsible for that."

"Granddad loves Ed and Junie. He would never fire them. Believe me. And I would never let you be homeless. We'd figure something out."

"And you? What if he cuts you off? Is a little summer fling even worth that risk?" I ask. "We're talking about your future here."

"He won't cut me off," Thayer says. "It means too much to him that I'm going to Yale. It's literally like a dream come true for him. He's been talking about this since I was four years old."

Thayer sounds so confident, so assured about all of this. Like he doesn't have a worry in the world. People who've lived comfortable lives with very little trauma and drama and loss tend to have that sort of world view.

He takes the seat beside me, and I inhale the faded scent of the ocean from his clothes. It's a strange scent. Not necessarily pleasant, but very much distinct. One I'll remember and associate with him for the rest of my life, just like I associate the smell of lilacs with my mother since she was always cutting them off trees in the spring and filling vases around our condo with them.

"They're only around for so long, Lila," she'd say. *"We have to enjoy them while we can."*

"I don't know if this is worth the risk," I tell him.

"Of course you don't know," he says. "Even I don't know. Yet. But I want to know, don't you? Because what if in a weird sort of way we were always meant to be together. What if we're meant to have this epic love story that would make it all worth it? If we let other people and the fear of the unknown keep us apart, we'll never know."

"And what if it isn't worth it? What if we fight and by the end of the summer we hate each other more than we ever thought it was possible to hate another human being?" I ask. "And let's say I lose my job and my grandparents lose theirs and you lose your college education and we've destroyed lives and futures, and for what?"

"Are you always this pessimistic?" he asks.

"Are you always this optimistic?"

"Yes," I say.

"Yes," he says.

"You realize we have nothing in common." I bite my thumbnail before folding my hands in my lap. "Like ... zero."

"No, I didn't realize that because between you not giving me the time of day and hiding from me, you're impossible to get to know."

"Then how do you know you even like me?" I mentally pat myself on the back, like I've just found a clue when I wasn't even looking, a hole in his story.

"I'm attracted to you, and I find you and all your confusing and mysterious and contradictory ways fascinating. Those reasons alone are enough for me to *like* the idea of getting to know you more," he says. "I get the feeling that underneath this invisible coat of armor you wear, there's a really amazing person, and I'd be remiss if I didn't try to get to know her."

No one's ever accused me of wearing an invisible coat of armor. It's funny. I could've said the same about my mother. Guess the apple doesn't fall far from the tree.

"How about this," he begins to say. "We test the waters. We sneak around, like Romeo and Juliet. We tell no one. We play it cool when we're around the rest of the family. And at the end of the summer, if what we have is real—"

"—that's another thing. You're going back to school in the fall. I don't think I could afford the rent on a closet in New Haven and the long-distance thing is the worst, so ..."

"Lila, will you just stop?" His voice is almost raised. Almost. He's much too kind of a person to yell at me. "Stop thinking of all the reasons it's going to explode in our faces and start thinking about all of the ways it could be the best thing to ever happen to us."

They say optimism is like a muscle. You have to exercise it to make it stronger. You have to practice it to make it second nature. They also say happiness is a choice, and it hits me now that perhaps I've been inadvertently choosing unhappiness for years without even realizing it.

Growing up, we had good years and lean years. Some years we needed help affording groceries. I back-to-school shopped at thrift shops more times than I can count. Used the same backpack through most of elementary school and into middle school until it fell apart at the seams. It wasn't until I was a sophomore in high school that Mom finally got a decent job with good benefits and a steady paycheck and life got a little more predictable.

My point is, I've spent the vast majority of my life waiting for the other shoe to drop.

It dropped when just weeks ago, I was getting ready for school and realized Mom still hadn't left for work yet, which was unusual. When I went to her room, I found her still sleeping in her bed.

Only she wasn't sleeping.

She was ice cold.

Turns out she'd had an aneurysm, died in her sleep.

If there's anything I've learned in my life, it's that it's not a matter of *if* the other shoe is going to drop ... but *when*.

"So what do you say?" he asks.

There's an earnestness in his voice that's hard to resist, and my brain is firing on all cylinders and in all different directions.

Do I listen to my gut? My heart? My head?

If my mom were still here, she'd know. She always gave the best advice. It was always equal parts rational and heartfelt. The irony isn't lost on me that if she were still around, I wouldn't be here, faced with this dilemma.

A random memory comes to mind from a few years back. I was having a rough time at school for whatever fifteen-year-old reason at the time and Mom called us both in sick. We took the day and drove to the ocean. She said sometimes life gets hard and it's okay to bend the rules a little if you need a break.

Well, life is hard as hell now.

And I could use a break.

Maybe I would have that with Thayer. If we kept everything on the down low, kept this strictly between us ... maybe this could work.

"No expectations," I say. "And full honesty. Brutal honesty if needed."

"Okay. Easy enough."

"We tell no one," I say. "We treat this like a secret our lives depend on."

"Got it."

"If this implodes ... there's to be no drama, no fighting, no going back and forth. We both walk away like it never happened."

"And if it doesn't implode?"

I don't have a response, at least not one that immediately comes to mind because my pessimistic monkey brain is convinced this won't work out, that we'll go our separate ways at the end of the summer and never see each other again and years from now, we'll be nothing more than foggy memories of a meaningless summer fling from our younger days.

"We'll deal with it when the time comes," I say. It's the best answer I can give him at this time.

A dozen other questions flood my mind ... like what do we do if we get caught? But I don't bring it up because we won't get caught.

And we won't because we can't.

My skin tingles and my lips go numb and for some bizarre reason, the thought of looking Thayer in the eye right now makes me anxious. It's like our entire dynamic has shifted and now the floodgates have been lifted and yet here we are, hesitating.

Or at least, I'm hesitating.

He's probably trying to demonstrate that he's still a perfect gentleman.

"So what do we do now?" I finally ask after I manage to steady my breathing.

Slow and steady, his hand reaches for mine, and I ignore my dizzying nerves in order to look his way.

His full lips inch up in the corner. "I think we kiss. But first ..."

Thayer guides me into his lap, running his palms down my outer thighs as my heart hammers harder than it ever has.

Our gazes catch, lingering for what feels like forever.

I secretly love that he isn't rushing this, isn't treating me like shark chum. That makes me think he wants to enjoy this, wants to take his time and prove me wrong.

Conversely it also makes me want him that much more ...

"When's your birthday?" he asks.

"What?"

"I'm trying to get to know you." He winks. "When is it?"

"November 8th," I say, adding, "Scorpio. In case you couldn't tell."

"Explains a lot ..."

"Yours?"

"April 3rd," he says.

"What's your favorite kind of ice cream?"

"Not a big fan of ice cream."

"You're lucky that's not a deal breaker for me. I'm a huge mint chip fanatic. Used to eat it by the gallons every summer. My parents practically had to put me in rehab for it once because I was so addicted."

"Not surprising," I say, "Seems like when you like something you really ... go for it."

He laughs. "I definitely do that."

A strand of hair falls over his forehead, and without thinking, I brush it away. It's strange to go from avoiding him to sitting in his lap playing fifty questions, but in an even stranger way, I'm actually having a good time.

I'm not thinking about anything outside that cottage door.

I'm simply here, in this moment, with him.

Like nothing else matters.

"Where did you grow up?" he asks.

"All over Orange County," I say, "But mostly Santa Monica. You?"

"Bridgeport," he says. "Born and raised."

"What's your biggest fear?" I ask.

His brows rise, like my question catches him off guard.

"I want to know the things about you that matter," I say. "So tell me: what are you most afraid of?"

He releases a breath through flared nostrils, glancing away. "That's a good question. I ... I don't know. I guess I've never really thought about it too much."

Of course he hasn't. He's Mr. Ray of Freaking Optimistic Sunshine.

"Can I answer you later?" he asks. "I could give you some

bullshit answer, but that wouldn't be fair to you, and I feel like I really need to think this one over."

"Fine," I say. "I'll allow it."

"Next question," he says.

"Okay."

"Can I kiss you now?"

CHAPTER 15

THAYER

"CAN I KISS YOU NOW?" I ask as my hands rest at the sides of her hips.

Lila lifts a hand to my cheek, leaving it there for a second as she looks into my eyes. Makes me think her exterior hardness is just a thing she does to protect the softness inside of her.

"Yeah," she says, biting her lower lip for half a second. "You can kiss me."

With my hands on the small of her back, I pull her closer against me, as if her being in my lap isn't nearly close enough, and a moment later we meet in the middle, my lips claiming hers, her lips surrendering to mine.

She rocks against me before resting her arms over my shoulders. Everything about her is pillow soft, her skin, the tendrils of hair that frame her face, her mouth, her movements. She's every bit as delicate on the outside as she pretends not to be on the inside.

I'm not sure how long we've been making out when we stop and come up for air. My guess is at least an hour, though time seems to act funny when I'm with her so it could be half that or it could be twice that.

My lips ache and if I touched them, I'm sure they'd be swollen.

"You okay?" I ask, fighting a grin. I can't help but smile when I look at her now because I know ... one day she's going to be mine and this is that sweet beginning that everyone always talks about.

I had a couple of girlfriends in high school and I've dated some in college, but I've never had anything real and I've never been in love.

When I look at Lila, I can't help but feel like this thing we have, whatever it is, is going to be special.

She climbs off my lap, taking a seat beside me.

"What are you thinking?" I ask.

Lila doesn't answer at first and for a moment I think she might be having second thoughts.

"I'm thinking that we should probably keep going," the little minx says as she pulls me over top of her.

She's pinned beneath me on the sofa, her thighs straddling my hips and me resting on my forearms above her. My cock begins to swell and throb the harder we kiss, but if I'm sent home with a case of blue balls, it'll have been worth it.

"I could do this all night," I whisper before gently taking her full bottom lip between my teeth and then kissing her swollen mouth over again.

My hardness pulses, throbbing harder than before.

"You have no idea how turned on I am right now," I say.

"Pretty sure I do ..." Her hand glides between our bodies, stopping at the waistband of my shorts. With an impressively deft move, she undoes the button and fly and takes my cock in her hand.

Lila kisses me, pumping the length, and while all of this feels incredible, all I can think about is feeling her, making her feel twice as good as she makes me feel.

Still hovering over her, I press kisses into her collarbone, working my way lower, and when I get to her stomach, I lift the hem of her shirt and kiss my way down. Her belly caves at my touch and her chest rises and falls faster and faster. When I get to the top of her shorts, I slide my fingers behind the waistband and tug them down her sides before tossing them across the room.

I go for her lace panties next, pulling them down her long legs before settling in between her thighs. With soft, gentle licks I taste her sweetness, and I take it as a compliment when her body writhes in response.

Running one hand up her stomach, I slide it beneath her shirt and bra.

The softest sighs escape her lips every few seconds, and she reaches down to grab a handful of my hair before her hips rock and her body undulates before she settles into a loose, limber, and breathless version of herself.

"Holy shit." She covers her face with both hands, breathing through her fingers. "That was ..."

She sits up slightly, resting on her forearms, and she looks at me with wild eyes that flash even in the dark.

I didn't plan for any of this to happen. I mean, I'd hoped things would move in the right direction, but I had no idea that things would be moving full throttle this soon.

Not that I'm complaining.

Lila rises from the chair, nothing but a t-shirt covering her spent body, and then she lowers herself between my knees. "Your turn ..."

CHAPTER 16

Lila

SHITTTTT.

My legs feel like Jell-O as I sneak back to The Hilliard Cottage. According to my watch, it's just past ten. My grandparents usually go to bed around nine, but since I wasn't home at nine, I'm one-hundred percent certain they're waiting up for me.

When I invited Thayer to meet in the cottage earlier, I had no intentions of messing around. I was going to tell him to stop pursuing me.

Nothing more, nothing less.

My mom's crazy friend always said, "Only fools make plans."

I never understood what that meant until tonight.

I take a deep breath before heading into the house. From the porch, I can see the light is on in the living room. And the TV is flickering.

"Lila. Oh my goodness." Grandma rises from her recliner and Grandpa mutes the TV. "Where have you been? Any longer and we were going to organize a search party."

I hope she's joking, but I don't think she is.

"Just went for a walk on the shore," I say, praying she doesn't check my shoes for sand. "The stars are so pretty out here at night. You can see each and every one of them. I'm not used to that back home ..."

Grandma studies me for a moment before sighing. She's too tired to argue or lecture. She just wants to go to bed. I see it in her eyes.

"Next time tell someone where you're going, okay?" she asks. "Or at least leave a note."

"I promise," I say before slipping my shoes off. "I'm sorry I kept you up."

My grandfather walks up and puts his arm around me. "You're all we've got, kiddo. It's our job to worry about you. Heck, we worry about you when you're in the next room. No more running off, okay?"

"Okay." Guilt sinks into my bones when I think about what I was doing just mere minutes ago. I hate that I made them worry, but this just means I need to be more careful next time. "Goodnight."

I trek down the hall to my room, closing the door behind me, and I peel out of my clothes and change into some clean pajamas before washing up.

In the bathroom, I trace my finger along my neck and collarbone, almost wishing I could feel his kisses again, though I'm sure I'll be reliving that entire experience as soon as my head hits the pillow tonight. It's already beginning to play in my head like a movie, and I can't wait to do it all over again.

Still, there's a nagging voice in the back of my mind telling me this is all too good to be true.

I guess only time will tell.

CHAPTER 17

THAYER

"YOU'RE LEAVING EARLY," Westley says Friday night. The flames from the bonfire between us light his face in shades of amber, and Whitley licks roasted, melted marshmallows off her fingers. "What's the deal?"

"It's been a long week. Going to get to bed early tonight," I lie. Earlier today, Lila pulled me aside and told me to meet her in the cottage around eleven tonight, and I wouldn't miss it for the world.

Apparently her grandparents were waiting up for her Tuesday night so she wanted to lay low for a few days, and I agreed that it was probably a wise decision.

"Ashlan wear you out?" Whitley asks with a laugh. "God, she's so out of control around you. It's sad, really."

"Nah. It's all good. See you guys in the morning," I grab my flip-flops out of the sand and slip them on before making the journey back toward civilization, only halfway there, I double check to make sure I'm not being followed, and then I take a detour to the cottage.

When I get inside, she's waiting for me on the sofa, her legs kicked up and an old magazine on her lap.

Her eyes light, though I can tell she's fighting like hell to act cool.

"Hey," she says, drawing her legs to the floor.

I take the seat beside her and we lock eyes for a moment. This past Tuesday night has played in my mind a hundred times since then and I've been waiting all week to have another chance to be alone with her.

My hair and skin reek of bonfire, and when I pull her into my lap, I inhale the sweet scent of her peaches and cream lotion.

"I want to take you on a date," I say. "A real date."

Lila gives me a half-chuckle. "Good luck. I feel like we're stuck on this island. And if the two of us left together ... at the same time ... like that wouldn't be obvious."

"No, no. I've been thinking about this all week," I say. "So the grocery boat comes Monday and there's always something we need from town. Supplies or something we can't get at Beekman Grocer's. Ask your grandma if you can go into town to grab whatever it is we need. Meanwhile, I'll organize an trip to town with the twins, and we'll play dumb when we realize we're all hitching a ride on the same boat back to the mainland. And when we get there ... we can ditch the twins and go off and do our own thing."

"Clever ..." she traces her finger up my chest. "But what if we can't ditch the twins? Westley's practically your shadow and Whitley goes wherever Westley does. Also, how would we get back?"

"Let me worry about the twins. And we'll charter a ride back. There are tons of guys around here who'll do it for a good price."

Her mouth bunches at one side as she thinks this over. I'm sure she's thinking of a million ways it could go wrong, but for once I need her to trust me. I've thought this through the last several days.

"I just want a day with you," I say, brushing a tendril of pale blonde hair out of her face. "A day of not sneaking around. A day where I can hold your hand and not think twice about it."

"As long as you're sure—"

"I'm positive." Hooking my hand around the back of her neck, I guide her mouth to mine, tasting her sweet lips. She grinds against me as we start to make out and my cock responds in record time.

I want her so badly.

I want every damn inch of her, every way possible.

Lila tugs at the hem of my shirt, pulling it over my shoulders, and I make a move for the waistband of her jeans.

I make a mental note to add condoms to the shopping list for Monday.

CHAPTER 18

Lila

I CAN'T BELIEVE we pulled this off.

Thayer takes my hand as we stroll down Hanover Boulevard, Rose Crossing's version of Main Street USA. The shops are quaint if not a bit touristy, but still fun to peruse.

Lorelai ended up tagging along on the trip, claiming she had some shopping to do in town. Thayer was nervous at first, but it all worked out because the twins ended up going with her after she promised Whitley a new purse from the Gucci pop up store in town and Westley a new watch.

"Oh, that looks like a cute place." I point up ahead, at a wooden sign with Pearlhouse Attic and Antiques painted onto it.

Thayer nods, as if to tell me to lead the way, and I drag him by the hand into a little antique shop filled to the brim with all kinds of curiosities—dolls and china and hats and cameras and furniture and tea cups and jewelry.

I stop by the jewelry display when an opal ring catches my eye.

My mom always loved anything opal, partly because it was her birthstone and partly because she thought it was one of the prettiest gems of all. Subtle and classy, she called it, each one with its own unique luster.

I take the pearly opal ring from the display and slide it over my right ring finger, stopping to admire the piece once it's in place.

The stone is oval and the metal is some kind of faded white gold with filigree details on the band. It's simple and under-stated, yet timeless. My mother would've loved this.

When I flip the ring over, I read the little tiny price sticker on the bottom of the band and almost have a heart attack.

This thing is seven hundred dollars ...

I decide to put the ring back before anyone notices—only there's a small problem.

It's stuck.

I glance around the shop as a cool sweat rushes through me, praying no one's watching me in my silent state of panic.

After a minute of trying in vain, my finger throbs, the skin around the ring turning an extremely obvious sign of pink.

"Hey," Thayer's hand lands on the small of my back a moment later. "What'd you find?"

Before I have a chance to respond, the middle-aged sales associate approaches the jewelry counter, her eyes immediately going to my hand.

"You like this, Lila?" Thayer asks.

"That's a beautiful piece," the saleslady says. "It once belonged to a Hedy Lamar, hence the asking price. We acquired that one last year at her great nephew's estate sale. We have the certification if you'd like to see it."

Thayer takes my hand in his, examining the ring, and another customer waltzes through the door. He must know the sales associate because her face lights like the Fourth of July and she waves before heading his way.

"Thayer," I whisper. "I can't get it off."

"Let me try."

I yank my hand away. My finger is already on fire from all the tugging and pulling. I wouldn't be surprised if I dislocated the damn thing.

"I've been trying," I say. "For, like, five minutes. It's stuck."

He's quiet for a second. "Do you like it?"

"What's that matter?"

"Just answer me. Do you like it?"

"Yes. It's beautiful. But that's not the point. I need to get this off. I can't afford this." I flip it over and show him the price sticker on the bottom.

"Do you want it?" he asks.

"Thayer ..." I lose my train of thought when I realize what

he's about to do. "You can't."

The sales associate returns just then, and Thayer doesn't give me another chance to protest before informing her that he's buying the ring.

"Can I box it up for—" she begins to ask.

"No," we both say at the same time.

"She'll wear it out," he says as he hands over a blue AmEx from his wallet.

I lean in, keeping my voice low as I tell him, "You don't have to do this."

He waves me off. "It's gorgeous and you like it and it suits you. You should have it."

The woman returns with a receipt for him to sign along with certification deeming that the ring once belonged to Hedy Lamar.

"Thank you," I say as I rise on my toes and kiss him. "So much."

I'll have to get the ring re-sized eventually, but for now I'll wear it home and hope some butter or lotion does the trick.

"We should probably stop at the hardware store before we forget," I tell him as we stroll down the sidewalk, hand in hand. He's been checking in with Westley here and there, making sure we're in separate parts of town so we won't be caught by the three of them. "Grandma said we needed oil for the mower. Silver polish. And some garden fertilizer."

Thayer checks his watch. "We still have a couple hours before we have to be back at the dock. There's a killer ice cream shop up ahead on the corner. I know you said you don't love ice cream, but you've never had their ice cream. I swear one spoon of their mint chip and you'll be a total convert."

"All right, fine," I say, my tone teasing. He leans down to kiss my forehead as we pass another couple on the sidewalk, and I relish in how normal and ordinary all of this feels. Being off the island with Thayer is liberating, and I wish this day could go on forever. I'm not ready for it to end.

Five minutes later we're sharing a double scoop of Meyerson Farms' famous mint chip ice cream, a local best-seller according to the description on the case.

"What do you think?" he asks, reaching across the table to wipe the corner of my mouth.

"Not bad."

"Not bad?" Thayer scoffs. "Not bad? Come on. You can do better than that."

Honestly it tastes like any other kind of ice cream to me, but the way it puts a smile on his face and gets him all excited like a kid at Christmas makes it special in its own right.

"What kind of law do you want to practice?" I ask. I know it's random, but I'm realizing that I haven't asked him that yet and I'm curious.

"Constitutional law," he says. "My dream would be to take on the kind of cases that would have a profound impact on society for the better."

"You're lucky you know exactly what you want to do," I say. "I still don't have a clue."

Just another way we're polar opposites ...

"You're eighteen. You've got plenty of time to decide." He licks the back of his spoon. "You'll know when you know."

"When did you know?"

"Tenth grade careers class," he says. "We had a guest speaker who was an attorney specializing in constitutional law and talked about some landmark cases he'd taken on. Opened up this whole other world for me, and I knew that's what I wanted to do. I want to leave this world better than I found it, you know?"

Why does he have to be so damn perfect?

I rest my chin on my hands, watching him finish the rest of his mint chip ice cream, admiring the way he takes his time and enjoys every bite like he's completely in this moment, which reminds me to stay in this moment as well ... instead of letting my mind fixate on all the ways we're still so opposite of each other.

So far, Thayer's shown that he's a pretty incredible person, inside, out, and every way in between, and I don't want to ruin this.

My entire life, I watched my mom chase guys away. Plenty of good ones, guys who were sweet and kind and crazy about her. She always found a reason to push them away as soon as shit got real.

I don't want to be like that.

I don't want to repeat her mistakes.

I want to enjoy this, I want to experience this with every fiber of my soul ... come what may.

CHAPTER 19

THAYER

"BROUGHT YOU SOMETHING," I say to Lila Tuesday night at the cottage.

She's been here two weeks now, but we've got a long, hot summer ahead and she's bound to get bored when we're not together ...

I place a stack of books on the coffee table in front of her. All of them are hardback first edition classics I took from my grandfather's study. He won't miss them. The man doesn't read anymore. He says he has to use a magnifying glass and it ruins the experience for him.

"Where'd you get these?" she asks, examining the leather-bound spines. "Are these first editions?"

"Yeah. I didn't know what you were into, so I grabbed a few different things."

"Sylvia Plath ... Charles Dickens ..." she rattles off the author names as she sorts through them. "Thank you. So much. This is amazing. How did you know I was into reading?"

"Lucky guess ..." I say, taking the spot next to her. My palms ache, antsy to touch her as soon as humanly possible.

"We used to have this hammock," she says. "Mom set it up on the balcony of our condo. I'd go out there and read for hours ... until the sun went down and I was forced to go inside or get eaten alive by bugs."

Lila runs her hand over the cover of The Scarlet Letter.

"This is one of my favorites," she says. "Did you know Nathaniel Hawthorne wrote this for his wife when she was dying? He wanted to make sure she was entertained when she was confined to her bed. Isn't that the sweetest? He never left her side. He just wrote and wrote and wrote and kept the story going." She offers a wistful smile. "That's intense, right? A little over the top? I feel like that's something you would do."

She elbows me.

"Is that a bad thing?" I ask.

"Not at all." Lila sets the book down before crawling into my lap.

"Wait," I say between kisses. "I brought something else."

She climbs off of me and I reach for the canvas bag at my feet, pulling out a stack of playing cards, a small chess set, a lighter and some candles, and finally two leftover slices of

Junie's salted caramel cheesecake that I stole from the kitchen after dinner.

"Thought we could make this into a date kind of a thing," I say before rising and leading her to the kitchen.

I place the desserts on the table, followed by two plastic forks I brought along, and then I light one of the candles and set it between us.

"You're too much," she says as she digs into her piece.

We sit side by side in silence, the candle dancing between us as we finish our treat. When she's done, she pushes her plate away and sighs a satisfied sigh.

"That was amazing," she says. "*This* ... is amazing. You are amazing. I wish we never had to leave here. It's like nothing bad happens in this house. Ever."

She rests her pretty face on the top of her hand and stares at the empty wall in front of us, lost in thought.

"You really like this place, don't you?" I ask.

"Love it."

"Then someday, when this is all mine, I'll give it to you," I say.

Lila turns to me, half laughing and half looking at me like I'm insane. "You can't just give someone a house."

"Why can't I?"

"Is it even yours to give?"

"It will be. For whatever reason, Granddad's leaving me the

island in his will," I say. "If you want this house? Consider it yours."

"Thayer ..."

Getting up from the table, I search through a few drawers until I find one filled with miscellaneous junk. I locate a black Sharpie and remove the cap, hoping it's not too dried out to work, and then I proceed to scribble on the wall beside the table.

For Lila, forever.
Signed,
Thayer Ainsworth
May 25, 2009

"THERE," I say.

"You're insane!" Lila claps her hand over her mouth. "I can't believe you just did that."

"It's yours now," I say, pulling her against me as she stares at the writing on the wall. "Or it will be someday."

CHAPTER 20

Lila

I DUCK into the cottage the next night, fully intending to spend some time alone with one of the beautiful books he brought for me last week, but the second I step inside, something catches my eye.

A flash of red just beyond the back door.

With my heart in my teeth, I immediately scan the room for a place to hide—assuming that someone's lurking just beyond the back door. But when I manage to calm myself down a minute later, I summon the courage to peek out one of the kitchen windows toward the little brick patio off the back of the cottage.

"Oh my god." I suck in a breath.

It's a hammock.

A week ago, I casually mentioned how I used to lie in our

hammock and read on the balcony ... and now a hammock magically appears.

I have no idea where he got it or how he pulled this off, but it's truly one of the sweetest things anyone's ever done for me.

Tears fill my eyes, clouding my vision as I head outside to check it out. A folded piece of paper is taped to the red canvas cloth, and I open it to find a note scribbled in blue pen and small, meticulous handwriting.

L-
A housewarming gift. Now your cottage is complete.
-T

CHAPTER 21

THAYER

WE'VE BEEN SAILING the better part of the day, Westley, Granddad, and I, with no end in sight when out of
nowhere, Granddad mutes his radio and clears his throat.

"Boys. Come closer. I want to tell you a story," he says.

Westley and I exchange looks before making our way to the
back of the ketch.

"When I was about your age, there was this young woman
by the name of Emeline. She worked at the bakery down
the road. Her parents owned it. My mother always loved
their bread. Anyway, one day, my mother had a cold and
decided she'd send me to the bakery to get that week's bread
order." He adjusts his aviators, peering straight ahead.
"Anyway, long story short, that's the day I met Emeline."
He chuckles. "Legs up to her neck. Dimples. Dark hair.

Always wore this red lipstick that made her look like Snow White, always smiling. Pretty thing. For an entire summer, she was the object of my affection. I was obsessed. Nothing mattered but her."

Westley and I exchange looks once again and he shrugs. We're both lost as to where he's going with this story, but seeing as how we're stuck here, we have no choice but to humor him with our attention.

"Anyway, that fall, I was going off to Yale and my father made me break up with her," he says. "Hardest thing I ever did. Broke her little heart to pieces too." Granddad pauses. "It's been almost fifty years, and I still think about her some-times. But a few months later I met your grandmother. And she was twice the woman Emeline was, and I never looked back. Your grandmother was it for me. And I can't imagine what my life would've been like had I married the girl from the bakery down the street."

"Good story, Granddad," Westley says. Kiss ass. "I never knew about this Emeline."

"Yeah, me neither," I say. "You've never talked about her before. What brought this on?"

My heart races, though I try my best to play it cool. Lila and I have been extremely careful each and every time we've met up at the cottage. We do everything by candlelight. We sneak out after the rest of the island is asleep. We erase any and all signs that anyone was ever there.

Granddad shrugs, his hands gripping the steering wheel. "Just felt like something the two of you needed to hear."

His answer does nothing to quell my suspicions. Granddad is playing coy. I'm well aware of the fact that he's smarter than he acts, and "manipulative" is his middle name—a fact I always keep in my back pocket.

CHAPTER 22

Lila

"HEY, we can't meet up tonight," I tell Thayer after dinner Thursday night. "Grandma got up in the middle of the night last night to check on me and noticed I was gone. I told her I was outside on the porch and she bought it because apparently she didn't think to look outside ... but I think we should lay low for a while."

His lips rub together and his brows furrow. "Yeah, Granddad made this weird comment a couple days ago on the boat."

I gasp. "You think he knows something?"

"God, I hope not."

Sometimes I love sneaking around and having our own little secret—other times I hate it because at any time, it could be swept out from under us.

"I have to go," I tell him when I hear my grandma calling for me from the kitchen.

He hooks his hands around my waist and pulls me against him, stealing a kiss that only makes the thought of not seeing him tonight that much more painful.

And then I walk away, trying my damnedest to wipe the ridiculous grin from my face before anyone sees it.

CHAPTER 23

THAYER

LILA SITS cross-legged on a checkered picnic blanket, tying a ring of dandelions into a crown that she places on her head.

"How's do I look?" she asks.

"Like a dandelion queen," I say.

She lies on her back, staring up at the puffy white clouds that hover above us in the perfect blue sky. It's a miracle we managed to pull this off. I packed us a lunch, she brought the blanket, and we took alternate routes to the alcove where we met up at the grassy section just outside the beach.

I lie beside her, resting on my elbow and leaning in to taste her mouth. The sweetness of the strawberries she just ate lingers and the warmth of the sun bakes our skin.

Everything about this moment is perfect.

Over the last couple of weeks, she's really opened up. She's not as pessimistic, not as closed off. She answers every question I ask, no matter how intrusive, and she tells me things she's never told anyone else before. Sometimes they're painful memories, other times they're nostalgic stories of her childhood that make her eyes water. She even opened up about her mother's death, and I let her cry in my arms.

I knew Lila was multi-faceted. I knew she had layers and depth that would take time to peel back, but everything's happening so quickly, so naturally. Nothing in my life has ever felt so right.

The sunlight kisses her with its warmth.

And I kiss her again.

I'd live in this moment with Lila forever if I could.

CHAPTER 24

Lila

"OH, LILA. THERE YOU ARE." Grandma shoves an empty punch bowl in my arms. "Get started on this, will you? The ingredients are on the counter along with the ratios. When you're done with that, you can help your grandfather set up the tents by the dock."

The way everyone is acting, you'd think the president is coming to visit, but nope. It's just Bertram's annual Fourth of July Extravaganza.

I head to the counter and find a handwritten recipe on an index card, and then I begin dumping two-liters of soda and frozen sherbet and fruit cocktail and seltzer water into a giant punch bowl.

From what I've been told, neighbors from all the surrounding islands boat in for this party, and Bertram hires a professional to put on a fireworks show from the edge of the dock. Supposedly it's the best one in the area, beating out all the local shows put on by mainland townships, and not only that, but it's invitation only.

"We're expecting at least fifty people," Grandma says, flitting around the kitchen. "And they're going to start arriving in about two hours." She digs around in a utensil drawer. "It's a lot of work, but Mr. Bertram throws the best party around. You'll see."

More like his staff throws the party and he takes all the credit …

When the punch is done, I head outside to help Granddad set up the tents, only to find Thayer and Westley also helping. I have to fight like hell to keep the smile from claiming my face when I see Thayer, and my insides are going insane … all butterflies and tingles.

Things with him are getting better by the day, if that's even possible. For six weeks now, we've managed to sneak around and not a single person has caught onto us.

We've had a few scares and a couple of close calls, but nothing major. It helps that everyone's so caught up in their own little world out here. No one's on edge. No one's watching for anything out of the ordinary. Every day is a vacation for them and they go about their time without a care in the world. I've yet to see Tippi or Lorelai without a glass of pinot or rose in their hands and Ari and Mitchum are connected at the hip, always fishing or enjoying an afternoon sail with Mr. Bertram. By the end of each day, everyone's so sun-worn and exhausted, they crash early, and with the island being so dark at night and the sound of the ocean drowning out excess noise, sneaking around is ridiculously easy.

"Can I help?" I ask, sliding my hands in my back pockets.

Thayer avoids looking at me, though I can tell he's fighting a smile just like me. He's better at this than I am, at acting cool and casual and not showing all his cards—which is funny because you think it'd be the other way around.

"I think we're about done, kiddo," my granddad says. "Thank you though."

Westley and Thayer finish up the last tent and on their way back to the main house, Thayer slips a folded piece of paper in my hand.

Meet me at the cottage at 9 tonight.

IS HE INSANE?

He's gone before I have a chance to ask him.

There are going to be tons of people here tonight. What if someone sees us? What if he gets stuck in a conversation and can't get away?

I cross my fingers and hope it works out. And I'm sure it will. Seems like when it comes to Thayer, everything always works out.

————

I SIT on the sofa in the cottage living room, waiting for Thayer. It's a quarter past nine and I've decided to give him twenty more minutes before heading out. If he got caught up in conversation or can't come for whatever reason, it is what it is. I really want to watch the fireworks with him tonight, but ultimately that's beyond my control.

I wait a few more minutes before pacing by the window, stopping every few seconds to peek out from behind one of the curtains.

In the distance, I see the first firework light the sky, spraying electric reds, whites, and blues into the pitch-dark sky.

There's no point in sticking around now. By the time he gets here, the show will be over.

Heading out, I shut the door behind me and make my way down the shadowy path back to the main house. I'm not sure what I'm supposed to do ... if employees are allowed to mingle and enjoy the party or if we're supposed to stay hidden and out of sight until it's time to clean up, but I'm sure I'll figure it out once I get there and find my grand-parents.

I'm halfway back when I spot the outline of a man several yards ahead, and the closer we get to one another, the more I realize it's Thayer.

"Hey," he says as his walk turns into a light jog. "Sorry. I got stuck talking to someone."

More fireworks fill the sky, their colors shading Thayer's face before they fade to nothing.

"The show's going to be over soon," I say.

"No, no. We still have time. Come on." He takes my hand and before I know it, we're sprinting up the hill past the cottage until we reach the top of some cliff.

The show is still going, the booms and pops echoing from the dock as the night sky lights with every color in the rainbow.

Thayer slips his hand around the small of my back, pulling me against him. It's colder up here, windier, but he keeps me warm.

From way up here, you can see everything. The Bertram, The Ainsworth, The Caldecott. The Hilliard Cottage. The dock. The machine shed. The Lila Cottage ...

All of it looks so small, so inconsequential.

The fireworks begin to explode faster and faster, several at a time, electric brilliance like nothing I've ever seen before.

"The grand finale," Thayer says as he kisses my forehead.

When it's over, everything becomes dark again, nothing but smoke and the distinct scent of sulfur lingering in the air.

"What'd you think?" he asks.

"Pretty amazing from all the way up here," I say. "Thank you for bringing me here."

"Lila." Thayer places his hands on my hips, turning me to face him. Under the light of stars, I can tell his expression is stoic, and for a half second, I'm positive he's about to drop something major on me. "I know we haven't known each other that long, but there's something I think you should know."

I suck in a breath, keeping my inner panic to a minimum.

"I'm falling in love with you," he says.

I release my held breath, letting his gaze hold mine and letting his words play in my head a couple more times.

"I love you," he says, his lips dancing into a hesitant grin. "I've been wanting to say it to you for a while. Wasn't sure how you'd take it."

"I love you too," I blurt out before rising on my toes and kissing him harder than I've ever kissed him before. I've never been in love before, but I'm pretty sure this is what love feels like. That can't sleep, can't eat, can't function until you see him again feeling that consumes your every waking moment. The kisses that make you feel like you're dancing on air and the constant fullness in your chest, like it's two seconds from exploding from sheer excitement that you can't possibly contain.

"I've never loved anyone before," Thayer says, sweeping a strand of windblown hair off my face as he peers down at me. "Never said that to anyone."

"Me neither."

"I love you so much," he says. "Feels so good to finally say that."

I press my cheek against his chest, breathing him in as he wraps his arms around me.

This moment is everything.

His love means the world to me.

But at the same time, I can't ignore the slight ache in my

center when I think about the fact that he leaves to go back to college in six weeks.

It's going by way too fast.

I just want time to slow down or stop altogether.

I miss him when I sleep and he's just a house away—how's it going to feel when he's in a completely different state?

Looking into his eyes, I promise myself not to fixate on that so I can enjoy what time we have left together this summer.

He kisses me, and it quiets my mind the way it always does.

"We should probably go back before they notice we're missing," I say a moment later.

Thayer takes my hand in his and helps me down the rocky cliffside. When we reach the cottage, he tells me to go ahead without him so no one spots us walking back alone together.

When I get back to the main house, I spot guests heading to their boats in droves, leaving behind them a giant mess that my exhausted grandparents and I will be cleaning up until midnight tonight I'm sure.

Without saying a word, I grab a trash bag from a nearby table and get to work. From the corner of my eye, I spot Thayer making his way down the path and heading in the direction of The Ainsworth, and then I watch the man I love disappear inside.

Part of me wonders what would happen if we came forward to our families. If they saw us in love, saw how much we cared for each other, they'd have to see that it couldn't possibly be a bad thing, right?

The other part of me doesn't want to so much as test the waters in case it backfires in our faces.

I have to take Thayer any way I can get him, and for now, all we have are stolen moments.

It won't always be this way though.

I'm sure of it.

CHAPTER 25

THAYER

MY GRANDFATHER BLOWS out the candles on his cake
as the rest of my family sings and claps.

Seventy-five years and he's still going strong.

My mother grabs the cake knife and Aunt Lorelai grabs the
plate and Whitley sticks her finger in the frosting to steal a
lick and claim her corner piece.

It's the first week of August, which means I'll be leaving in
two weeks to go back to school. A year ago this time, I was
excited, now all I can think about is the fact that two weeks
from now, Lila and I will be separated.

To go from seeing her several times a day and sneaking
moments with her and spending hours in the cottage in the
middle of the night ... to nothing ... is a transition I've spent
all summer trying not to think about, but now that it's

almost here, we're going to have to figure out where we go from here.

She hasn't brought it up either, which makes me think we're in the same boat, swimming in the same denial-and-avoidance-filled waters.

Westley takes a seat beside me at the end of a long table on the back patio. The rest of our family is gathered around the birthday cake, dishing out slices topped with vanilla ice cream.

"Hey," Westley says.

"Hey."

"So ... I ... uh ... I saw you and Lila the other night."

I shoot him a look, like I'm confused and I have no idea what he's talking about.

"You guys were coming down the path by the old nurse's cottage," he says, keeping his voice low and leaning in. "It was late. Maybe midnight or so. I know it was you two."

Shaking my head, I'm fully prepared to deny, deny, deny, but he continues.

"Dude, you're playing with fire here," Westley says. "You know how Granddad feels about this. He's warned us both a thousand freaking times to stay away from her. He'll spaz if he finds out."

Sucking in a long breath, I adjust my posture and grind my teeth.

"How long have you been sneaking around with her?" he asks, like it's any of his business.

"What were you doing out at midnight the other night?"

He shrugs. "Couldn't sleep. Went for a walk."

"You can't say a word." I lock eyes with him.

My whole life, Westley's been like a brother to me. And a shadow. I'm pretty sure he'd kiss the ground I walk on if I asked him to.

He places his hand over his chest. "I promise."

"I'm serious."

"So am I," he says.

"Take this to the grave," I tell him.

"Dude. I get it."

The two of us glance down to the end of the table and his mom waves at us, asking if we want vanilla or chocolate cake.

"You realize what's at stake here, right?" Westley asks. "If Granddad catches you, he'll cut you off. Trust me. I speak from experience."

A year ago when Westley announced he wouldn't be going to Yale (because he couldn't get on their lacrosse team) and would instead be attending a private, hole-in-the-wall college in Eastern Pennsylvania, Granddad wasted no time de-funding his college account. To this day, he still refuses to acknowledge the name of Westley's college—or that Westley even goes to college.

"I don't think you realize how much control he has over every single person in our family," Westley says.

"No, I'm well aware."

"Then why are you putting your entire future on the line for some girl."

I shoot him a look. "She's not *some girl*."

He lifts his hands in protest. "All right. Fine. Just be careful."

"Trust me," I say. "We're being careful."

"What are you going to do when you go back to school in a couple weeks?"

I shrug. "We haven't talked about that yet."

"Oh. So it's nothing serious. You guys are just messing around?"

"I wouldn't say that."

"So it *is* serious?" He shakes his head. "Thayer ... you realize if he's not cool with it now, he's not going to be cool with it ever. And you still have a lot of school left ..."

"I'm not worried," I say. Things always have a way of working out.

"Yeah, well, maybe you should be."

CHAPTER 26

Lila

"YOU'RE SURE ABOUT THIS?" Thayer holds a foil packet between two fingers. Apparently he bought condoms back in May when we went to the mainland and he's been carrying one around with him ever since. He claims when I confessed to him that I was still a virgin and I'd only ever fooled around with guys before, he wanted to take it slow and make sure this is what I really wanted before he went for it.

"Yes, now come on." I trace my fingers down his bare thigh. and he rips the foil between his teeth and proceeds to slip it over his fully engorged cock.

The two of us are completely naked for the first time, which is risky because on the off-chance someone busts in here, we'd be screwed—literally, no time to tug on pants, zip zippers, or mess with shirts. But he leaves in less than two weeks and I want my first time to be special. All of him and all of me. Nothing quick, nothing rushed.

He positions himself between my thighs, which I now realize are shaking, and drags the tip of his sheathed cock along my seam before slowly guiding it in.

It's the strangest sensation at first—slightly painful before a satisfying burst of pleasure once he's all the way in.

"You doing okay?" he asks as he looks into my eyes.

I bite my lip before nodding. "Yeah. Keep going."

Thayer fills me again and again, taking his time, his hips moving in perfect rhythm, not too fast, not too slow, and my body unfurls beneath him, relaxing and sinking into the mattress below.

I've never felt this close to anyone, and my only regret now is that we didn't do this sooner.

"I love you, Lila," he whispers into my ear.

"I love you too."

I run my hands along his sides, his muscles rippling beneath my palms with each thrust, and my hips buck in response.

With his head buried against my shoulder, he kisses my neck before working his way down to my breasts, taking each nipple between his soft lips before getting back into his rhythm.

I could so do this forever with him.

When the ache between my thighs intensifies a few minutes later, I know I'm getting closer and there's no turning back, and when I ride the wave that follows, I swear I see stars.

He thrusts harder, faster ...

And when we're both finished, he collapses beside me, breathless, his hand interlaced with mine.

I curl up against him, resting my cheek against his chest and hooking my arm over his stomach. He kisses the top of my head, and we lay there, still and basking in the moment.

"I want to go to Italy," I say.

"That's random." He sniffs a laugh through his nose.

"I know. I don't know why, but I just decided that," I say. "We should go there someday."

He traces his fingers down my arm, leaving a trail of tiny goosebumps. "Maybe we should talk about next month before we talk about someday..."

The delirious smile I've been wearing leaves my lips and I know it's time to have the conversation we've both been putting of all summer.

"Yeah." I sit up. "So ... where do we start? Who goes first?"

"Why don't you tell me what you think and we'll go from there?"

"What I think about what? Staying together? Splitting up?"

He winces. I don't know if that's good or bad, if he's wincing because I mentioned "splitting up" or wincing because he thinks I want to stay together and that's not the same thing he wants.

"I'll be right back," he says, getting up. He disappears down the hall, cleaning up I assume, and when he returns, he lies down and pulls me up against him. His heart drums against my ear. He's just as anxious about this talk as I am.

This conversation isn't going to be easy, but we have to have it, so I stuff my nerves deep down, take a second to gather my thoughts, and let him have it.

"I love you, Thayer," I say. "Like ... beyond obsessed and addicted and insanely wild about you. I can't see myself feeling this way about anyone else. Ever. You have my heart. And I think you know that. When you leave, you're going to be spending the next two semesters on a campus filled with thousands of beautiful women, and odds are some of them are going to cross paths with you and when they do, they'll realize what a catch you are. And I'll be here. On this island. With your grandfather and my grandparents, missing you, thinking of you, and wondering every single day if you still feel the same way."

He's quiet, but I realize he's holding my hand.

"I've thought about the long-distance relationship thing," I say. "But there's no cell service out here. No internet. We can't send each other letters for obvious reasons. If I called you from my grandparents' phone, they're going to see it on their phone bill and figure it out. I've got no way to leave the island and come visit you for days at a time without that being a huge red flag. This whole thing is a logistical nightmare." I take a deep breath. "But all of that said ... I'm not ready to let you go."

"Then don't." He sits up and pulls me into his lap, our naked bodies touching at every curve and bend, fitting together like two perfect puzzle pieces. "Lila, you have my word that when I go back to school, I'll be one-hundred percent focused on my studies. My heart will belong to you and only you. And I know you're going to worry. That's in your nature. That's who you are and I've known that from the day I met you. But you'll just have to trust me."

"So when will I see you again? Will you come back here for winter break?"

His shoulders fall. "Maine winters are brutal. A lot of times there's no travel to and from the mainland. Granddad usually comes to Bridgeport for the holidays and your grandparents stick around to take care of the grounds. Coming back here while the rest of my family is in Connecticut isn't going to be an option."

"So I won't see you again until ... next May?"

"Right." He softens his voice, but it only amplifies the disappointment in his tone. "It's not going to be easy, but with a little trust and a little faith, I know we can do it. I mean, I kind of think we make a pretty amazing team, don't you? Look what we pulled off this summer."

"Yeah ..."

"So what do you say?" he asks. "Are you in this with me?"

I lose myself in his calming ocean eyes for a moment before kissing the lips I'm going to spend the next nine months missing like hell.

"Yes," I say. "I'm in this with you."

CHAPTER 27

9 MONTHS LATER...

THAYER

"*WHERE ... ARE ... THEY?*" My lungs burn after sprinting from The Lila Cottage to my grandfather's house where I stormed into his study, a man on a mission.

"Thayer." He rises from his leather chair, a cordial smile on his face as he dog-ears his Architectural Digest magazine and rests it on a coffee table. "What a pleasant surprise. Wasn't expecting you until tomorrow. Come on in. Have a seat."

He waves me over, but I remain planted. I won't rest, I won't make myself at home until I know why the Hilliards are nowhere to be found.

The boat dropped me off at the dock a half hour ago, and as I made my way to the main house, I couldn't help but notice from a distance that The Hilliard Cottage looked ... off. And then I realized there were no flowers. Junie always plants flowers at the end of April, and it's the middle of May. Also there were weeds growing out of the old flower beds. Ed never would've allowed that to happen. Curious—and concerned—I made my way to their cottage, only to find the front door unlocked and the place looking different from the last time I was there.

I made my way from room to room, and it only took me a minute to realize all the family photos that Ed and Junie had were gone. In their place were the faces of smiling and posing strangers. I went to the main bedroom next, only to find the closet half-filled with women's clothes, not so much as a hint of anything a man would wear. When I went to Lila's old room next, I found it stripped to the bones. Not a picture. Not a book. Not a single article of clothing on the dresser.

The Hilliards were gone.

I left their cottage and sprinted to the abandoned cottage. I know Lila—she wouldn't have left without an explanation. I was positive I'd find a note somewhere in the house, and I tore the place up looking for it only to come up empty handed—except for the notes I'd written and hidden for her before I left.

She didn't find a single one, never had a chance to read them.

Granddad rises from his chair, the corners of his lips turning down. "I'm not sure why that's any of your business." And then he chuckles. "Or why you're so visibly upset." Walking toward me, he places a hand on my shoulder. "Let's head to the kitchen. I'll have Bernice prepare a snack for you. I'm sure you're hungry after your travels."

"Bernice?"

He ushers me out of his study. "The new help."

"Where are the Hilliards?" I ask as we walk.

He chuffs through his nose, taking his time answering. "They retired, Thayer. That's what people do when they reach a certain age."

I exhale, the tension in my shoulders dissipating in small increments. Retirement makes sense. They were in their early sixties last I knew, and they'd been caring for the family's island off the coast of Maine since before I was born. Junie did the cooking and the cleaning and Ed tended the garden, maintained the landscaping, combed the private beaches, and kept up the boats and three main houses all twelve months of the year.

"They moved to the mainland then?" I ask.

"I haven't the slightest. I sent them on their way last fall and haven't heard from them since. For all I know they're living their golden years in sunny Florida, or perhaps they made their way to Arizona. I believe Junie has a sister there. Either way, they're having themselves a time, I'm sure of it."

His nonchalance is nothing short of concerning.

Ed and Junie were like family. They'd been around for decades. I can't imagine they wouldn't stay in touch—or that my know-it-all grandfather wouldn't have so much as a clue as to where they went. That coupled with the fact that Lila didn't so much as leave a goodbye letter tells me that he's not giving me all the facts.

I follow him to the kitchen where a middle-aged woman with gray-brown hair stands at the sink, washing dishes by hand. She's shorter and thinner than Junie, her hair straight and cut blunt at her shoulders. There's a permanent scowl etched on her face. She doesn't light the room like Junie did.

"Bernice, this is my eldest grandson, Thayer," Grandfather says.

The woman glances over her shoulder, offering a blink-and-you'll-miss-it half-smile and a nod, her yellow-gloved hands still deep in the dirty dishwater.

"Very nice to meet you," she says, her back toward us. "I've heard so much about you. Your grandfather tells me you're pre-law at Yale?"

"Yes, ma'am," I say.

"Just finished his second year." Grandfather beams from ear to ear. It thrills him to no end that I've chosen to follow in his collegiate footsteps. "Anyway, he's made quite the jaunt today and my boy is starving. Would you mind preparing him a sandwich?"

"It's fine. I'm not hungry," I say.

"Don't be ridiculous." He puffs his chest and follows with a pompous chuff. "You just drove several hours and then you ferried in."

He's right.

I drove four straight hours from New Haven, not stopping once, because all I could think about was getting here—to Lila. And then I waited two hours for a ferry that took three hours to get me here because of all the other island stops we made.

Mile after mile, the thought of seeing Lila kept me going. The sheer excitement and anticipation of being together again was all the distraction I needed.

I daydreamed about sneaking up behind her and wrapping my arms around her waist.

I pictured her sweet smile and her sparkling amber-green eyes.

I felt her hands on my face and her hair between my fingers as I stole her away and claimed her pink lips with a kiss behind the boathouse.

"How can I find them?" I ask my grandfather.

His thick brows knit. "Who, Thayer? I'm afraid you're going to have to be a bit more specific."

He's playing dumb. I know better than to buy into his act.

"The Hilliards," I say, without naming Lila specifically.

"And what reason on God's green earth would you have to contact them?" my grandfather asks. "They're *retired*. I'm sure we're the last people they want to hear from."

"They were a big part of my childhood. I considered them family," I say. "It'd just be nice to be able to keep in touch is all. Would've been nice to know the last time I saw them was going to be ... the last time."

Granddad hooks a hand on my shoulder and gives it a squeeze.

"You're too sentimental, boy. Just like your mother. Speaking of which, she'll be here in two days. The rest of the crew should be here by the weekend. Say, I was going to get the ol' ketch out and go for a sail this afternoon. You'll join me." In true Howard Bertram fashion, he isn't asking.

"If you don't mind, I think I'm going to pass. Not in a sailing mood today."

His cheery disposition fades and he studies me for a moment. "This isn't about the Hilliards, is it? If you'd like to write them a letter, I'd be happy to have my attorney work on locating them and sending it on."

I consider his offer. "And how long do you think that would take?"

He squints. "Is this an urgent matter? I was under the assumption you were simply wanting to keep in touch."

Yes, it's urgent.

The woman I love—the only woman I've ever loved and will ever love—is out there somewhere and I haven't the slightest idea as to where she is, how to contact her ...

... or why she would've left without saying goodbye.

Lila had my address at school—before I left, I gave it to her for emergency purposes as well as my number and email address. She could've written me a letter. The Hilliards didn't own a personal computer of any kind, but there was a lab at the public library in Rose Crossing—she could've easily looked me up and emailed me.

I believe that the Hilliards retired, but I don't believe that Lila would have left here without so much as leaving a letter in the cottage.

Something isn't adding up here.

"Thayer." My grandfather clears his throat. "I'm speaking to you. Are you all right?"

I realize now that I'm sitting at the base of the grand staircase in my grandfather's foyer. I don't remember walking here. I don't remember sitting down and placing my hands in my hair, tugging until my scalp throbs.

Coming to, I pull in a deep breath and force myself to stand. "I'm fine. Think I just need to lie down for a bit."

His mouth flattens. He's disappointed I won't be sailing with him this afternoon, but he's not going to push it. The summer is young, I'm sure he's thinking.

"All right. I'll have Bernice get you the key to Ainsworth," he says. "We weren't expecting you home this early, but everything should be in order. If it isn't, let me know. This is her first time opening the island for the summer."

Opening the island ...

He opened the island the way other people open their pools for the summer: with checklists and procedures and quiet fanfare. "Opening the island" was always his expression for this time of year, when our entire extended family would abandon their modern lives, their work and school in favor of sun, sand, and sailing off the coast of a New England island hideaway. It was always Ed and Junie who would prepare for our arrivals. All the linens would be freshly washed, beds made. Junie used to fold our towels into little animal shapes, like we were at some resort, and Ed would shine up the boats and hose off the dock. Junie would place freshly picked and trimmed flowers in vases in every living room, kitchen, bathroom, and bedroom—that alone must have taken her hours if not days considering each home had at least five bedrooms and six baths. But she always loved to go the extra mile to make our annual homecoming a splendid affair.

My grandfather disappears into the kitchen, returning with a set of keys to my family's designated house just a few hundred yards down the drive.

"Dinner will be at six," he says, dropping the key ring in my hand. "Get some rest, but don't be late. We have much catching up to do."

As soon as he's gone, I realize I'm squeezing the set so hard, the metal teeth are leaving indentations in my palm. Relaxing, I show myself out and head down the path to Ainsworth, gaze locked on the cedar shake siding that covers the backside. Last summer, I stole a kiss from Lila next to the white peony bushes on the north side of the house.

The bushes are lackluster now, appearing as if they hardly intend to bloom this year.

Once I get to the house, I unlock a side door and head in. My lungs fill with stuffy, slightly damp air. Apparently Bernice didn't air out the house the way Junie always did in anticipation of our arrival, but I know she's new so I won't fault her for it.

Passing down the hall, I make my way to the living room before cutting through the foyer to get to the kitchen. There's no bowl of fresh fruit waiting on the counter. Not a single vase filled with picked hydrangeas or lilacs as per tradition.

A moment later, I climb the stairs to the second floor and find my room at the end of the hall.

No folded swan towels.

No welcome note in Junie's whimsical handwriting.

No secret welcome note from Lila tucked into my pillowcase.

I head to the windows first, sliding up the sashes and letting some much needed fresh air fill the space.

Collapsing on the bed next, I slide my hands under my neck and stare at the lifeless ceiling fan above. Everything … and I mean everything … has taken on an empty quality.

The island.

The house.

Me.

It's like a substantial part of me is missing—and that part of me is her.

Squeezing my eyes shut, I try to rest despite knowing damn well my head isn't going to stop spinning long enough to make that possible. But I need to calm down so I can come up with a game plan.

There's no internet access on the island—my grandfather

contacted the local phone company once, and they were told there was not enough infrastructure to support running cable or DSL lines to Rose Crossing at the time, and then they said that running those lines to the island would've been humanly impossible. The only options he was given were satellite or dial up. My grandfather made the executive decision to forgo both—deciding that the island was better off with as minimal technology as possible because family time was too priceless to sacrifice for *"computers and video games and the like."*

I grab my cell from my pocket and check the service. It's always been spotty out here, even at the highest point, which happens to be the attic of my grandparents' house, so I don't hold my breath.

One bar.

One bar is enough to make phone calls if you're okay with the sound cutting in and out, but it makes any internet capabilities virtually useless.

I try to refresh my email inbox as a test ... my point proven in under two minutes when the app times out before it has a chance to load.

I'll have to try and sneak away to town in the next day and use the computers at the library.

I'm sure a quick online search will tell me exactly where she is ...

Placing my phone aside, I close my eyes once more and listen to the crash of the ocean outside my windows.

It doesn't sound the same without her here.

And it sure as hell doesn't feel the same.

I close my eyes and try to get some rest.

I'll look for Lila forever if I have to.

I'll start first thing tomorrow, and I won't stop until I find her.

PART TWO [PRESENT)

May 2019

CHAPTER 28

Lila

"JUNEBUG!" My grandfather's eyes light when I walk into his room at the Willow Creek Care Center the Thursday before Mother's Day.

Exhaling, I take the seat beside him and softly shake my head. "No, Grandpa. It's me: Lila. Grandma Junie isn't here."

I decide not to explain to him, for the dozenth time, that Grandma passed away last year. It's been a hell of a day and I don't think I can bear to watch him reduced to tears like the first time all over again.

"Lila?" His wrinkled face is washed in confusion. It always depends on the day, but sometimes he remembers he has a granddaughter. Other times he doesn't. Every once in a while, he mistakes me for my late mother, but that hasn't happened in weeks. "Oh. Yes. Lila."

He places his hand on mine, but his moment of clarity is gone in a flash.

His Alzheimer's is progressing and the meds aren't helping as much as they did in the beginning. Sometimes he gets combative with the staff. Lately he's refusing to eat, as evidenced by the way his clothes hang from his once strapping and broad-shouldered physique.

The TV in the corner plays some black-and-white Western on mute and his eyes focus on the screen for a bit.

"Are you hungry?" I ask. One of his nurses stopped me on the way in, asking if I could coax him to eat. He skipped breakfast this morning and only ate a few bites of his lunch, and he can't take his meds on an empty stomach. "Grandpa?"

He reaches for the remote control beside him, staring at the buttons in silence, as if he can't quite recall which one he needs to push—or perhaps he's forgotten why he grabbed it in the first place.

"Grandpa, you need to have some dinner," I say. "Grandpa ..."

He ignores me, and I rise from my chair, heading out to the hall to find a nurse. I ask her to have his dinner delivered to the room. I'll stay here as long as it takes to get him to eat. His mind might be wasting away, but I refuse to let him die of physical starvation.

I return to his room—a private double suite at the end of the hall, one with every amenity Willow Creek has to offer and not one but two picture windows with a view of a small courtyard with a koi pond, flower garden, and a walking path.

Sometimes I catch him staring out the window with this wistful look in his eyes, smiling. Waving. And when I follow his gaze there's nothing, no one.

I imagine he thinks he's seeing Grandma.

Or maybe he does see her ... in his own special way.

I can only imagine the reunion those two are going to have on the other side. And my mother, too. I'm sure he can't wait to see his daughter for the first time in almost ten years.

One of these days I'm going to have to let him go.

And probably sooner than later.

"Knock, knock," a voice calls from the doorway. An orderly in pink scrubs brings a food tray in and places it in his kitchenette.

"Thank you," I say, hopping up and situating his meal at his little table for two by the window. "Grandpa, come eat. It's your favorite. Beef and noodles. And orange Jell-O."

None of those things were his favorites, but I don't think he remembers, nor does he care at this point.

To my surprise, he pushes himself up and uses his walker to push his way across the room to the table, having a seat in the chair I've pulled out for him. He eyes the plastic tray filled with hospital-grade food and smacks his lips a couple of times before reaching for a spoon.

I take the spot across from him, hand resting beneath my

chin, and watch him the way I always do, wishing I could have asked him more questions when I had the chance, wondering what goes on in that once-brilliant mind of his during his bouts of mental lucidity that always tend to happen when I'm not here.

"You're not eating," he says. "Tell that waitress to come back here and take your order."

"Already had dinner," I lie.

"Get yourself a slice of pie then," he says. "I'm buying."

"No, thank you, Grandpa."

"At least get one to take back to Junie," he says. "She loves rhubarb, you know."

Sighing, I say, "I know."

He reaches for his glass of cranberry juice with a shaky hand before finishing the rest of his dinner. When I spot his nurse peeking in the doorway, I give her a nod, and she returns a few minutes later with his evening meds.

"That one there reminds me of Eloise Bertram," he says under his breath as the nurse stands by the door and makes a note on his chart.

I peer across the table.

He hasn't mentioned Eloise Bertram in ages ... not since her husband forced my grandparents into retirement and gave us a three-hour notice to pack our things and leave.

"You remember the Bertrams?" I ask.

He chuffs. "Of course I do. You don't work for a family for thirty-six years and forget them, do you?"

The nurse places a white paper cup filled with an assortment of colorful pills between us, followed by a plastic glass of water. I push them toward him.

"What do you remember about the Bertrams?" I follow up with another question.

He takes his meds without so much as a fight, and his nurse and I exchange looks.

"Grandpa, what do you remember about them?" I ask again.

He places the cup on the table, eyes narrowing. "Who?"

"The Bertrams," I say.

Grabbing his fork, he clears his throat. "Never heard of 'em."

Deflated, I bury my head in my hands and let it go. I'm not sure what I was trying to accomplish anyway. Maybe a piece of me wanted one last validation that that part of our life happened.

It feels like forever ago.

And sometimes it feels like it was all a dream.

After what happened the summer of '09, Howard made his demands and my grandparents had no choice but to accept them. The moment we left the island, the two of them quickly swept our former lives under the rug, refusing to so much as utter the name "Bertram" in any context.

This August will mark ten years since we left Rose Crossing

Island, and while we've never set foot on that soil in all the time that's passed, there's still a piece of me there.

And his name is Thayer Ainsworth.

CHAPTER 29

THAYER

I STAND in the doorway of my Granddad's Rose Crossing kitchen the Saturday before Mother's Day, watching the pockets of conversations taking place as the rest of the family settles. My father talking shop with my uncle. My mother and her sister passing a newspaper between them. Whitley chatting her dad's ear off about her upcoming nuptials while her dead-eyed fiancé scrolls his Instagram.

Once again, Westley's nowhere to be seen.

Ever since the summer of '09, he's been a completely different person. More withdrawn, less engaging. Sometimes he visits the island. Most of the time he doesn't.

"Oh my goodness! Thayer's here, everyone." My mother throws her arms in the air as she abandons the kitchen table chit-chat the moment she sees me.

I had no intentions of returning to Rose Crossing this year, and if it weren't for my cousin, Whitley, getting married next weekend, I'd likely be holed up in my Manhattan office wearing my workaholic badge of shame like an Olympic gold medal.

But ever the loyal family man, here I am.

"So good to see you, lovey," my mom clasps her hands on my cheeks and kisses my forehead like I'm not a full-grown man. "We're so glad you're here. The last few years ... haven't been the same without you."

I glance away, unsure of what to say.

I stopped summering in Rose Crossing with the family years ago. The first couple of summers after the Hilliards left filled me with dread and anxiety. Dread because I wasn't looking forward to spending another June, July, and August without knowing where the hell Lila was. And anxiety because despite all of my best efforts and intentions, I still couldn't find her, and being trapped on some private island with limited cell and network connectivity only amplified that helpless feeling.

No matter how many years have passed, I've never quite been able to accept the fact that one summer she was here and the next she was ... gone. It was like the sea swallowed up all those promises of forever without any kind of warning, leaving nothing but a gray island and a gaping void in my heart I'd never be able to fill with anyone else so long as I lived.

My life trudged forward, but only on paper.

After my senior year, I landed a paid summer internship in the city and shared a place with a handful of guys I knew from school. That fall I started law school and before I'd even graduated, I was looking at five job offers. Took the best one and never looked back. Every May after that, like clockwork, I always managed to come up with plausible work-related excuses as to why I wouldn't be able to make it out that summer.

"Anyway," my mother says, placing her hand on mine for a brief instant. "I was just telling Aunt Lorelai about your latest case," she says, wearing a humble smile to hide the brag she's about to drop in her sister's lap.

My phone buzzes in my pocket—which is shocking because very rarely do I ever get a signal out here. Then again, cell towers are more powerful now than they used to be and my phone's a 4G.

Checking the caller ID, I'm taken aback when I see it's the private investigator I've been working with the last couple of years. He only calls when he's got a lead and his last couple of leads were dead ends, so I try not to get my hopes up.

"Excuse me. I have to take this." I make a beeline for my grandfather's study and close the door behind me.

Unbeknownst to my family, I've spent tens of thousands of dollars on private investigators over the years, some of the best of the best, and every search has stopped at the same dead end—as of August 2009, Ed, Junie, and Lila Hilliard seemingly vanished off the face of the earth.

No paper trail. No proof of life. Not a bread crumb of any kind.

My biggest fear is that something unspeakable happened to them and that's why I can't find them.

"What do you have for me?" I ask when I answer. When it comes to these matters, I don't have time for formalities.

I hold my breath and refuse to get my hopes up.

They've been dashed far too many times.

"Well, I came across something interesting," Roland says on the other line. "So I've got my new software set to scan obituaries and the like, and it alerts me if any names match the ones on my list. One of the features it comes with searches for partial matches and we got a hit on a Jane Hill in Summerton, Oregon. At first glance, Jane Hill seems like it'd be a pretty a common name. Nothing unique or remarkable or strange. But I took a look at the obit and saw something else. It mentioned she had a granddaughter named Delilah and a husband named Ted. So then I thought … what are the odds that Ted, Jane, and Delilah Hill are actually Ed, June, and Lila Hilliard?"

My heart's racing so fast I forget to breathe, and I take a seat in Granddad's leather wingback. Dragging my hand through my hair, I say, "Go on."

"So I wasn't able to find anything social media-wise on this Delilah Hill, but I did find a mention in a newspaper article where it said she made the dean's list at some community college. No pictures or anything. Honestly, this could be a coincidence. A strange coincidence, but if it isn't, it sure as hell explains why you haven't been able to find them all these years."

"Where did you say they live?"

"Summerton, Oregon. Looks like it's about sixty miles from the coast. Nice little town from what I can gather."

"Was there a picture with the obituary for Jane Hill?"

"No, I'm afraid not."

"Thanks, Rol. Going to head out there. I'll keep you posted."

I end the call and run a search for airline tickets from Portland, Maine to Portland, Oregon.

I'm going to take the next flight out. If this is her, if this is my Lila, it's not something that can wait.

As absurd as it seems, the three of them living under aliases is the only thing that would make sense. It would mean all those fruitless searches for her were simply due to the fact that she was living under another name—which actually begs an entire new set of questions that I plan to address once I finally find her.

The pages take forever to load, timing out a handful of times before finally filling out, and I manage to find one seat on a red-eye that leaves tonight.

"Thayer, you doing all right?"

I glance up and find my grandfather standing in the doorway, his hands in the pockets of his khakis and his lips shaped into a concerned frown.

Shoving my phone into my pocket, I rise. "Something came up at work. I'm going to have to take off for a couple of days."

He frowns. "It's Mother's Day weekend."

I wince. "Yeah. I know."

"And Whitley's wedding is next week. We've got a full itinerary, family coming in from all over the country. Whatever this is, I'm sure it can wait. Or maybe one of your associates can handle it for you?"

I head toward the doorway, but I get the sense that he's blocking me in.

"I would strongly advise you not to leave," he says. It's funny, now that he can't hold my tuition over my head, his threats have a little less weight.

"Excuse me," I say, glancing over his shoulder then back to him.

His chest rises for a moment. Even at eighty-five, it's amazing that he still has his wits about him, still has his broad shoulders and barrel chest, even if he moves a little slower these days.

"Mom, I'm so sorry. I've got a work emergency," I say to my mother when I pass through the kitchen. "I'll make it up to you."

"Is everything all right, lovey?" she asks as I give her a peck on the cheek.

"Yeah, no need to worry," I say before making my rounds and giving everyone a quick goodbye. "I'll be back in a couple days. Three max."

I grab my suitcase by the door and head to the boat dock, dialing a local guy I know to see if he can come get me as soon as possible.

I offer him three hundred dollars cash to get me off this God-forsaken island.

He tells me he's on his way.

Forever is a promise.

Love is a promise.

Someday, too, is a promise.

I'm a man of my word and no amount of time or distance, no amount of unanswered questions will ever change that. She's the only woman I've ever wanted.

I won't rest until she's in my arms again.

CHAPTER 30

Lila

"HE'S REFUSING TO EAT AGAIN." A nurse from Grandpa's assisted living facility is on the line. "And this morning he attacked one of our dietary aides. She had a pitcher of coffee and was making her rounds at breakfast and he grabbed her arm. Wouldn't let go. That could've ended very badly."

"I'm so sorry," I say, burying my face in my hands. "He's on a wait list at the Alzheimer facility in Northrup. They say it could be a few more months still."

"Do you have time to come in today? He always seems to calm down after he sees you."

I glance at the mile-long to do list I scribbled onto a piece of yellow legal paper. I'd planned on running a million errands today, getting caught up on laundry and the like, and I was going to visit him after dinner, but family comes first. Always.

"Give me a half hour," I say.

I take a quick shower, throw my hair into a wet ponytail, and change into leggings and a t-shirt before hightailing it across town to the Willow Creek Care Center.

I'm stopped at a red light at 5th and Vine when I happen to look over at the car beside me—a red sedan of some kind. For whatever reason, the driver reminds me of Thayer. Same mussy brown hair, same strapping shoulders. But he's wearing sunglasses and I can only see him from the side, so maybe it's wishful thinking.

I laugh at my delusion.

Thayer would *never* be in Summerton.

And who knows ... it's been almost a decade since he last saw me.

I'm probably nothing but a faded memory by now.

CHAPTER 31

THAYER

I STOP at a little coffee shop on the square in downtown Summerton. I'm running on adrenaline and a total of four or five intermittent hours of sleep, but I refuse to slow down.

My flight arrived early this morning, but I had to wait until the rental kiosk opened at five thirty so I could grab a car.

I order a coffee. Black. And take a seat at the bar next to a sweet-looking elderly couple drinking hot tea and sharing a cranberry scone.

"And here you are," the barista, a woman who looks to be in her late twenties, slides the coffee cup and saucer in my direction.

According to Google, Summerton's population is around twenty thousand. The odds of this woman knowing "Delilah Hill" are slim to none, but I'd be remiss if I didn't ask.

"Excuse me," I say before she gets too far away.

"Yes?" She comes back, dark brows arched. Everything about her is harsh. Penciled brows. Pencil-lined lips. Pointed features. She looks nothing like the kind of person I'd picture hanging out with Lila, but you never know.

"Do you know anyone by the name of Delilah Hill? She lives around here."

The woman looks me up and down, skeptical almost. "You're not some crazy stalker ex-boyfriend, are you?"

"No," I laugh, though I realize in a way there's very little difference between me and a crazy stalker ex-boyfriend at this point in time.

"Delilah Hill, you said?" she asks.

"Yes."

"Never heard of her. Sorry." The woman struts to the cash register to help another customer.

I'd be disappointed if I weren't already accustomed to having my hopes dashed.

"I couldn't help but overhear that you're looking for Delilah Hill," the woman-half of the elderly couple beside me swivel in their bar stools, facing me.

"Yes," I say. "I am. Do you know her?"

The woman places her hand over my arm and smiles. "We sure do. We were friends with her grandparents for years. We got to know Delilah and MJ quite well."

"MJ?"

"Her daughter," the woman says. "Adorable little thing."

The idea of Lila having moved on, met someone new, and started a family with them is a shock to my system, and for a second everything around me fades out as the woman continues talking. Over the years, I'd always known anything was possible, but hearing someone confirm one of my worst fears? She might as well be ripping my heart out sans anesthesia because I'm feeling it all right now.

I remind myself that I don't yet know if it's even Lila, and until I have the facts, I have no business assuming the worst.

"Do you know where I can find her?" I ask. Earlier this morning when I was waiting for the rental car kiosk to open, I performed a dozen searches trying to find an address for "Delilah Hill in Summerton, OR," only to come up empty-handed every time. For all I know, she doesn't even live here. The obituary Roland found was from last December. People move all the time.

"I'm sorry ... how do you know her again?" the woman asks.

"We're old friends," I say. "We lost touch. I'd like to see her again. She was a very special part of my life many years ago."

The woman and her husband exchange wistful grins before she turns back to me. "Isn't that the sweetest thing you've ever heard, George?"

"It is," her husband says, picking bits of scone from his white mustache.

"Does she still live around here?" I ask.

The woman takes a deep breath. "Well. Let me think. Last

time I saw her was back in December at Jane's memorial service. And I know Ted's over at the Willow Creek Center. You know, I don't know where Delilah lives these days, but I can tell you they used to live over in the yellow house on Bayberry Lane."

Yellow house.

Bayberry Lane.

Willow Creek.

This is good. This is a start. I can work with this.

I ask the barista for a to-go cup and thank the elderly couple for their help, and then I head to Bayberry Lane.

CHAPTER 32

Lila

I SPENT the better part of the morning at Willow Creek with Grandpa. By the time I left, he seemed to be in better spirits, though he was still calling me "Junie." The important thing is, I got him to eat three-fourths of his breakfast, so it was well worth the trip.

I hover over the kitchen island as I take a bite of my turkey sandwich lunch, and then I circle a Help Wanted ad in the paper for a part-time assistant at a local insurance agency with one of my daughter's Mr. Sketch scented markers that smells like cherries.

A couple years after MJ was born, I finished my dental hygiene program at the local community college and landed a good job at Kellerman Family Dentistry here in town, but as it turned out, Dr. Chad Kellerman was a sexist asshole who had no sympathy for the fact that I was a single mom and sometimes motherhood and working a 9 to 5 schedule got in the way of each other.

I worked for him for five years before Grandma got sick, and between running her to doctor's appointments and taking Grandpa to his part-time job and running MJ to kindergarten and soccer and dance, I was spread paper thin and had no choice but to quit my job.

We were fortunate in that the money Bertram sent more than covered expenses, but now that Grandpa's at Willow Creek and Grandma's stipend is no longer coming, we're going through our monthly budget faster than ever. Plus, I want to set a good example for MJ. I don't want her to think all I do is relax all day between running her all over town. She doesn't see everything I do during the day or all the hours I spend with Grandpa at the care center. She needs to see me work, just as I grew up watching my mother's insane work ethic.

Eventually I hope to land another full-time dental hygienist job, but with Grandpa and everything going on, I'm going to have to take something part-time.

I take another bite of my sandwich and turn the page, circling another job for a part-time receptionist at a bank.

There's a knock at the door just as I'm finishing the last of my turkey on rye, and I wipe my hands on a napkin before heading that way. Sometimes Ms. Beauchamp gets deliveries that need signatures, and she's designated me as an approved third party. Anytime there's a knock on the door this time of day, it's almost always FedEx.

I swing the door open, prepared to greet Mark the FedEx driver.

Only it's not Mark the FedEx driver.

It's Thayer Ainsworth.

CHAPTER 33

THAYER

I FOUND HER.

I found Lila.

"Oh my god." She gasps when she sees me, and then she takes a step back, though I can still see her perfectly through the screen door that separates us. "What are you doing here?"

"Lila," I say, breathless and frozen with shock. "It's you. I can't believe it's actually you..."

She steadies her hand on the interior knob, eyes shifting.

"You can't be here." She glances over my shoulder, peering up then down the street. She's closer now, and though we're still separated by a thin gray screen, I can tell she's just as stunning now as she was a decade ago.

She definitely looks more like a twenty-eight-year-old than an eighteen-year-old, but in the best of ways. Like she grew into her features. She still has a crown of pale blonde hair and her deep-set eyes are still the same shade of amber-green framed with long lashes.

"You should go," she says.

This isn't exactly the long-awaited reunion I'd conjured up in my mind, but I didn't come all this way just to turn around and leave.

"Can we talk first?" I ask.

"No," she says. "We can't. You have to go. Please."

"Lila. I don't understand. You just left …" my voice trails. "I flew three thousand miles to find you, and I'm not leaving without an explanation."

If she had any idea how much this mystery has haunted and plagued my life for the last decade, she might relent. But she doesn't know. And now I'm beginning to think she doesn't care.

And maybe she never did.

Maybe I had her all wrong all those years ago.

Maybe I projected something onto her that was never there, convinced myself she was someone she wasn't.

The woman I thought she was would've never left like that. And the woman I thought she was wouldn't turn me away from her door ten years later.

Her gaze flicks all around me, not lingering in any one place for too long. I don't know if she's nervous or scared, but I hate seeing her like this.

"Come in," she says as she gets the door. "And hurry."

CHAPTER 34

Lila

THAYER'S STANDING in my small foyer, looking at me like it's the first time all over again. This isn't ideal—having him here, inside my house—but I know how persistent he is, and I think he would've stayed on my doorstep all day until he got what he wanted, so I had to bring him in.

"You really can't be here," I tell him. "Does anyone know you're here?"

"One person."

My stomach free falls.

If Bertram were to find out, we would be completely cut off, we'd be forced to leave the only home MJ has ever known, and I don't want to even think about how I'd pay the exorbitant fees at the assisted living center.

"Who?" I ask.

"The private investigator I hired to find you."

I glance away, smirking. Of course he did that.

"Ten years," he says. "For ten years, I've looked for you. Wondered about you. Missed you. Worried about you. Finding you was the only thing that mattered."

"Come on, Thayer," I say. "You can't expect me to believe you never moved on and that you've literally spent ten years looking for me."

He says nothing.

"That sounds sweet and all, but you've always been gifted in the art of telling people exactly what they want to hear," I say. "I find it extremely hard to believe that someone like yourself would waste the best years of your life looking for someone like me."

My coldness is intentional.

I hate speaking to him this way.

I'd love nothing more than to tell him everything, to introduce him to his daughter, and to make up for all the years we've lost ... but that isn't an option for me. Not at this point in time.

"I don't understand," he says. "You're acting like you're angry with me, but you're the one who left."

He has a point.

And I don't have a good response for him right now.

My cell phone rings from the kitchen.

"Wait here," I tell him before leaving to answer it. The

caller ID reads SUMMERTON ELEMENTARY. "Hello?"

"Delilah Hill?" a woman asks.

"This is she."

"This is Jacqueline," she says. "I'm the school nurse at Summerton Elementary. I've got MJ here, and she's complaining of a headache and she says her ears hurt. I took her temp and it's 101.3 right now, so unfortunately we do require that you pick her up within the hour. Sooner if possible."

"Of course. I'll be right there." I end the call and return to the foyer where Thayer stands waiting for me.

He's dressed in navy slacks and a white button down cuffed at his elbows, and I can't help but notice the sleeve of tattoos that covers his left arm—completely unexpected.

As if he wasn't already a Greek Adonis at nineteen, he had to grow up and become an even hotter version at twenty-nine, all filled-out and equal parts edgy and clean cut.

"I have to pick up my daughter from school," I say, swallowing the lump that forms in my throat when I realize I'd do anything to kiss him this very moment.

"Will you be around later?" he asks.

I shouldn't see him again.

This is risky. Entirely too dangerous. But I'm not ready to watch him go yet.

"Let me get my daughter to bed tonight and you can stop by for a little bit. Maybe eight or so," I say. "But after tonight, you have to leave Summerton. And you can't come back."

I grab my purse and keys from a nearby console table and usher us out the door, locking up behind me.

He makes his way to a shiny red car, confirming that it indeed was him that I saw earlier today on my way to Willow Creek, and I make my way to MJ's school.

I can't believe I invited him back.

————

MY WHOLE LIFE has been full of surprises. The fact that Thayer Ainsworth is sitting on my sofa while our nine-year-old daughter is asleep upstairs is easily top five.

I always knew we'd reconnect someday, somehow, in some way, I just never knew how so I never bothered wasting my time dreaming up scenarios that were always going to be better in my head anyway.

"Look. I know you have questions, and I'm sure you want closure," I say.

"Closure?" Thayer scoffs. "Lila, I want answers and explanations. I want to know that you're okay, that you're safe and healthy and happy."

"All right. Well, I'm safe and I'm healthy."

"But are you happy?"

"I have MJ." It's the truth. She's my happiness. She's my little piece of him. My memento from one of the greatest summers I've ever had the joy of knowing. For three months, I loved and I was loved and every time I look at our daughter, I'm reminded of that.

"What happened after I left?" he asks. "Something happened."

"I can't answer that."

He pinches the bridge of his nose, and when he sits hunched over with his elbows on his knees, his muscles strain against the white fabric of his dress shirt. I imagine him in the courtroom, fighting the good fight and using his charm and intelligence to win cases left and right.

A few times over the years, I read about some of his work in articles. I'd be in a wistful, nostalgic mood after a few too many glasses of wine and I'd find myself lying in bed Googling the hell out of this man, almost hoping to find something that would make me miss him less ... like an engagement announcement. Something to show me he'd found love again and moved on. If he was happy and successful, that's all that mattered.

"When I came home that May, Granddad told me Ed and Junie had retired," he says.

I force myself to remain stoic.

If I so much as hint to him that his grandfather was responsible for any of this, he'll confront him, we'll lose *everything*, and this will have all been for nothing.

"Is that true?" he asks.

"In a way, yes," I say, neglecting to mention they were forced into retiring.

"What does that even mean?" There's a hint of justifiable frustration in his voice.

"Mom?" MJ's angel-soft voice interrupts our conversation, and I find her standing at the bottom of the stairs. "Who's here?"

Rushing to her, I slip my arm around her shoulders and turn her away from him.

"Go back to bed, sweetie. I'll be there to tuck you in again in a few minutes, okay?"

She trudges up the stairs in her panda pajamas and I return to the living room. "I'm sorry. This was a bad idea. You should go."

He draws in a long breath before rising, and he doesn't take his eyes off me for one second. "Obviously you're not going to tell me anything. And I can't force you to. But whatever happened, Lila ... whatever you think you did that's so horrible you had to run away and hide for ten years ... "

"Thayer, you *have* to go. Please." I place my hand on his back and guide him to the door. "I'm so sorry you came all this way for nothing. Really I am. But I hope you can find some peace now. You checked on me. I'm okay. I'm fine. Life moved on and you should too."

His hand lifts to his face and he rakes his palm along his chiseled jawline as he draws in a hard breath.

"We were spectacular together," he says. "Weren't we? You remember it the same way I do, right? Please tell me that summer meant something to you and I didn't come all this way because I'm some heartsick idiot who romanticized some teenage summer..."

He speaks with a confidence that makes me think he isn't so much as looking for validation as he is wanting to remind me that what we had was meaningful—as if I need the reminder.

"It was one of the best summers of my life," I say.

I'll give him that, but only because he came all this way and quite frankly I have nothing more to give him.

"It's not too late," he says.

Clearly he has mistaken me for someone else—for the girl I used to be, the one he fell in love with over a single endless summer forever ago.

But I'm not her.

And I haven't been since I left Rose Crossing.

But my God, what I wouldn't give to be her again ... so that *we* could be *us* if only for a moment.

He steps outside, but before he leaves, he turns back to me. "Just so you know, I kept my promise. For nine months I focused on school and I didn't so much as think about another girl. I waited for you. And when I came back, you were gone. Not even a letter. You destroyed me. And you ruined me for anyone else. But I see now that you moved on, so ... good for you. I hope whatever your reasons are, they were worth it."

With that he climbs into his car, and I close the door and fight the burn of tears that sting my eyes so I can go upstairs and tuck our daughter into bed.

CHAPTER 35

THAYER

I SIT in my idling rental car in Lila's driveway, my hands white-knuckling the steering wheel as I think about the picture I saw on my way out. Sitting on a table by the front door was a school photo of a little girl, only she wasn't little. She was more like eight or nine if I had to guess.

"No fucking way." I sit back into my seat and run the numbers in my head one more time, trying to piece everything together.

If her daughter is nine, that means she got pregnant ten years ago. I know she wasn't pregnant when I left for college, and we were always diligent about using condoms, though there was one time we thought one of them might have torn but we weren't sure …

I left in the middle of August.

Westley left in the middle of September.

He wouldn't have …

She wouldn't have …

I think back to Thanksgiving that year, when he was acting standoffish. I brushed it off until it happened the next year and the next. Something changed after that summer and we went from being as close as brothers to perfect strangers over the last ten years.

But I still have his number in my phone.

I grab my cell and call the bastard. I don't care how late it is in Connecticut.

"Hello?" Westley answers.

"Did you know Lila had a kid?" I ask, hoping to catch him off guard. It's an old interview technique I learned in law school. Westley's never been good at lying on the spot.

"Did you find her?" He ignores my question.

"Answer me. Did you know Lila had a kid?"

"No." He almost answers too quickly.

"I take it you found her?" he asks. "Where was she? I always wondered what happened to her. She was there one summer then the next summer she was gone."

He's rambling now, a red flag.

He knows more than he's letting on.

"Don't lie to me, West," I say. "You know something."

He's quiet, and I hold my breath as I wait for him to answer.

"Tell me," I say through gritted teeth. "This is your chance. Tell me what you did."

For a second, I wonder if he assaulted her, knocked her up, and Granddad paid her to go away for "liability reasons."

If he hurt her, he's a dead man.

I don't care if we're family.

"I think we should talk," Westley says. "In person."

"Why, so you can look me in the eye and tell me you fucked my girlfriend and got her pregnant?"

"Thayer ... I'm sorry. It's beyond complicated and I can't tell you anything. Not right now. Just ... don't tell anybody you found Lila, okay?"

"Did you hurt her?" I ask.

"What? God. No. I would never."

"Fuck," I say, punching the steering wheel. "You knew where she was all these years and you didn't say a goddamned thing? You saw how much this destroyed me, you saw me put my entire life on hold and you sat back and ... you're pathetic, Westley. You know that? And now you're dead to me."

He's silent on the other end, and all I keep picturing are the two of them together. I'm not sure which one I feel most betrayed by at this point.

"We'll talk when you come back," he says.

"No need. I've got nothing more to say to you." I end the call and throw my phone into the passenger seat.

I've got a flight to catch tomorrow, but before I go, I want to have one last word with Lila, and then she'll never hear from me again.

CHAPTER 36

Lila

THERE'S a persistent tap coming from downstairs, like someone rapping on the screen door.

I glance down to see MJ's out cold again, and then I tiptoe out of her room, making my way back downstairs. Flicking on the porch light, I find Thayer standing there.

He still hasn't left, not that this surprises me.

"We have to talk," he says when I open the door. "*Now.*"

There's a wild flash in his stormy eyes, and he's breathing so hard his nostrils are flared. But I'm not scared—I'm curious.

"I just talked to Westley."

Oh, God.

"Come in," I say, though I don't take him to the living room. I make him stand here in the foyer.

"How could you, Lila?" he asks. "How could you lie to me? How could you keep me in the dark? You made a promise and then you betrayed me."

I hug my sides, listening to the cocktail of pain and anger in his tone, unable to look him in the eye any longer.

I can't believe Westley told him what happened—as far as I knew, his grandfather forced him into signing an NDA as well, threatening to cut him out of his will if he breathed a word to anyone about any of this.

"For ten goddamned years, I didn't love another woman. I didn't go on a single fucking date. I was obsessed with finding you, with making sure you were okay and finally knowing what happened. But all this time it turns out I've been chasing after an illusion. You never loved me. You wouldn't have done this if you did."

"You're wrong," I say. "I did what I did *because* I love you."

"Justify it any way you want ... at the end of the day, that's not love. Lying is not love. Betrayal is not love."

I can't say his anger isn't warranted, but I won't stand here and take the misguided anger another minute longer.

"You need to go," I say. "Before my daughter wakes up again."

"Answer one last question for me," he says. "And then I'll never bother you again ... why?"

"Why did I do it?"

"Yes. Why did you do it?"

"I didn't have a choice," I say. "Plain and simple. I didn't have a choice."

"So someone forced you."

"In a way, yes."

"Who?" he asks.

"I can't tell you. Not yet."

His hand runs through his thick dark hair, and he grabs a fistful. "I don't understand."

"Someday you will."

"Do you remember that time when you asked me what my greatest fear was? And I told you I didn't have an answer for you. Well, I figured it out about halfway through my sophomore year," he says. "My biggest fear was losing you. But it turns out, I'd lost you long before I realized that."

He shows himself out.

I hate that he had to find out from Westley.

I can only imagine his version of events.

There are two sides to every story. I can only hope someday I'll get the chance to tell him mine.

CHAPTER 37

THAYER

I STOP at the coffee shop on the square before hitting the road. My flight leaves in two hours and as soon as I get back to the island, we'll be in full wedding prep mode for Whitley's big day next weekend. I'm not exactly looking forward to breathing the same air as Westley for a whole fucking week, but I'm left with no choice.

"Coffee. Black." I toss a five-dollar bill on the counter and tell the kid behind the cash register to keep the rest before moving down the line.

A little girl with dark pigtails and a unicorn backpack is in line ahead of me. She turns to glance up at me. She smiles, and I can't help but notice her eyes are the exact same shade of amber-green as Lila's.

"Hi," the girl says.

For a second, I think she's with the woman ahead of her, but that woman grabs two coffees off the counter and leaves alone. The girl's in here by herself.

"Hi."

"Were you at my house last night?" she asks. "You look like the guy that was talking to my mom."

"Are you MJ?" I ask.

Her face lights. "Yep. It's short for Mary June. I was named after my grandma and great-grandma 'cause I was born on Mother's Day."

She tugs at a gold chain around her neck, and I realize there's something attached to it, like a pendant or something. Upon closer inspection, I realize it's not a pendant at all—it's an opal ring.

The very one I bought Lila from that antique shop in Rose Crossing the summer of '09.

"That's a very nice necklace you have," I say.

She toys with the chain. "Thank you. My mom gave this to me. She says my daddy gave it to her before I was born."

PART THREE [PAST]

September 2009

CHAPTER 38

Lila

"LILA, HEY."

I'm sitting at the edge of the dock when Westley finds me. Turning away, I dry my tears on the back of my hand.

"You okay?" he asks, sitting beside me.

Thayer left almost a month ago and Whitley left shortly thereafter, but Westley's semester doesn't start until the middle of September, so he isn't leaving until this weekend.

"You miss him, don't you?" he asks.

My heart flips. There's no way he knows ...

Thayer would've told me if he told Westley.

"I know about you and Thayer," he says, voice low even though we're the only two around. "It's okay. Your secret's safe with me."

I say nothing. There's nothing to say. Or at least there's nothing I can say to Westley right now.

"If you want to write him a letter or something, I can take it back with me and mail it from campus." I can feel Westley watching me. "I mean, is there anything I can do here? I have this thing where I can't handle girls crying."

He's sweet to try and comfort me, but I realize now that I went the whole summer without saying more than a handful of sentences to him. He kept his distance. I kept mine. We're practically strangers, but I know he thinks the world of Thayer and if Thayer did entrust him with our secret, then maybe I can trust him with mine ...

"Can I tell you something?" I ask.

"Of course. What's up?"

I slide my hand into the pocket of my hoodie, my fingers wrapped around the positive pregnancy test I took an hour ago.

A few days ago I realized I was late.

Two weeks.

My whole life my period has come every four weeks like clockwork, no matter what. My grandma happened to be sending me to the mainland for supplies the next day, so I grabbed a test from a local pharmacy while I was there.

I didn't have the courage to take it until today.

I kept thinking that maybe if I waited just another day and another day ... my period would come.

But it never did.

And now I'm pregnant with the baby of a man I was explicitly told to stay away from.

My grandparents are going to kill me.

Mr. Bertram is going to kill Thayer.

Pulling the test from my pocket, I hold it in my palm.

"What's tha—" he begins to ask. "Oh. Shit. Um ..."

"Yeah." I shove it back into my pocket.

"Oh, shit," he says again. "Shit, shit, shit."

"What am I going to do?" I ask.

I have no money aside from what I've saved over the summer, which is hardly enough to get me on my feet. I was hoping to have at least another year of earnings in the bank before figuring out the whole school-work-independent woman chapter of my life. If I can't support myself now, how am I going to support a baby too?

"If Granddad finds out about this ... " Westley's words taper into nothing.

"What do you think he's going to do?" I ask. "Worst-case scenario. I want to be prepared."

He blows a hard breath between his lips. "Honestly?"

"Yeah."

"Well, first he'll probably fire you," he says. "And then he'll probably stop paying Thayer's tuition."

Shit.

"But this is his great-grandchild. Why would he do that?"
I ask.

"You have to know my grandfather to understand him," he
says. "And half the time we don't even understand him. He
makes the rules, we're expected to follow them. If we don't,
there are consequences. Trust me. I was the first to learn
that the hard way. I didn't take his threats seriously."

"You really think he'll cut Thayer off?"

"In a heartbeat. Without question."

"What do I do? Obviously I spent the entire summer on the
island. When my belly starts to grow, they're going to know
it was him."

"No, they won't," Westley says before turning to me. "They
might think it's me."

I bury my face in my palms.

Unplanned pregnancies happen every day, but I never
knew something so small could have such a ripple effect and
complicate so many lives.

"I have an idea," he says. "What if we tell them it's mine?
I've already been cut off. I've got nothing to lose. He'll be
pissed at me and probably say a bunch of shit that's going to
hurt and he'll still probably fire you, but at least Thayer will
be in the clear. We don't have to tell Granddad the truth
until Thayer's done with school ... you know, if Granddad's
still around then."

"You would do that?" I ask. "You would take the fall
for him?"

"He'd do it for me," he says. And he's probably right. "It makes sense. I've got nothing to lose. He's got everything to lose."

"And what will you tell your parents? They'll think they've got a grandchild on the way."

He sucks in a deep breath, pinching the bridge of his nose. "Yeah. I guess we'll have to figure that out too."

We linger in silence for a few moments. I imagine he's mulling over the ramifications of what he's about to do.

"Are you sure about this?" I ask again.

He's quiet, contemplative, and he peers across the rolling waves just beyond the cove.

"Yeah," he says. "I'm sure."

"When do we tell them?" I ask. "Do we wait until I'm showing or do we just do it now and get it over with?"

I'm on the taller side ... maybe I'll be able to hide this a little longer so I can put a few more paychecks away?

"We're going to have to do it now, Lila," he says. "I leave this weekend and I won't be back until next summer."

He's right.

"We'll do it tonight," Westley says. "After dinner, after everyone leaves, we'll pull him aside and do it then."

My body fills with little earthquakes and my stomach churns, though it could be morning sickness for all I know.

"Don't stress," he says, taking my hand. "Think of me as your surrogate Thayer."

I laugh at his absurd comment.

And then I cry at his generosity.

CHAPTER 39

THAYER

"HEY, HEY!"

I hit save on my paper and spin in my desk seat to find one of my friends standing in the doorway of my dorm room.

"Are you kidding me right now? It's Friday night," Noah says. "Don't make me unplug that thing."

"I dare you," I say, teasing though not really. He struts across my dorm room giving me a half-handshake, half-high five and then takes a seat on the edge of my bed. A few more pages and the paper's done, but he has a point. It's Friday night and it's been a hell of a week.

"Bunch of us are going to Carter's place for drinks. You in?"

I rest my hands behind my head, leaning back in my chair. "Yeah. Sure. Why not."

I've been back in New Haven for a month now and this

marks the first time I've actually gone out of my way to socialize. Ashlan's begged me to hang out a few times, but so far I've been able to excuse my way out of those.

I grab my jacket, phone, wallet, and keys and follow Noah to the hall, locking up behind me.

Friday night on campus is alive and buzzing, everyone's laughing, their good moods spreading like wildfire. A group of girls that I recognize from my philosophy class pass me going the opposite way and the blonde in the middle smiles and waves.

A year ago, something like that would've made my night. Now? It only makes me miss Lila.

CHAPTER 40

Lila

"DO EITHER of you have any idea what you've done?" Howard's eyes are wild and spittle leaves his lips when he talks. "Do you know what this means? No, you don't. How could you?" He's pacing back and forth in his study as Westley and I sit in the leather guest chairs, holding hands for show. "I told you, Westley!"

He points a crooked finger at his grandson.

"I told you to stay away from her!" He's yelling now, his face cherry-red.

"This is going to destroy everything I've worked so hard to build for us," he says. "Our family name. Our legacy. And the two of you have ruined it." He rests his palm over his wrinkled forehead. "You can't keep this baby. No one can know about this. *No one.*"

The thought of handing Thayer's baby off to a perfect

stranger to raise is one that never crossed my mind. The baby is mine. Ours. No matter how hard it's going to be, I'm not giving it up.

"You know, I had my suspicions over the summer," Howard said. "Went for a walk one morning and noticed the front door to the cottage was open. Went inside and no one was there, but why else would it have been open? Someone had to have been in there. I knew it was one of you boys, I just couldn't figure out who ..." he's rambling, mostly talking to himself I think. "And you." He points at me, his eyes even wilder than before. "I never should've given you a job here. You're just like your harlot of a mother."

"*Granddad.*" Westley stands up.

"Sit. Down. Westley," he bites back before straightening his shoulders and resting his hands on his hips. He's facing us square on, his gaze traveling between us. "There's something the two of you need to know now that you've brought this plague upon our family."

Westley squeezes my hand.

"The two of you are half-siblings," Bertram says.

Westley and I exchange looks, and for a second I think I misheard Howard.

"H... how?" Westley asks.

My stomach churns and my entire body is clenched as I wait for his answer.

"Lila's father is your father," Howard says. "While your mother was pregnant with you and your sister, your father was sneaking around with Mary on the side."

I hate the sound of my mother's name in Bertram's voice. It doesn't belong there. He's a vile human being and she was a saint.

"So my father is Ari?" I ask.

Howard clucks his tongue. "Unfortunately, yes."

Westley and I release our hands from one another's grasp. He's my half-brother. We can't pretend to be lovers anymore.

"I banished your mother from ever setting foot on this island again once I found out," he says. "And I forgave Ed and Junie. Told them their positions here were safe as long as they agreed never to let Mary or the baby anywhere near Ari and Lorelai. My daughter was in love. She was starting her family, her life. I refused to have all of that ruined over some meaningless copulation."

Oh my god.

It makes sense now ...

The reason my mother refused to set foot in Maine.

The reason she kept herself so closely guarded.

Howard banished her.

And Ari broke her heart.

My mind goes to Ari next. The number of times the two of us interacted over the summer I could probably count on one hand. He was always standoffish and avoidant, and I assumed that was just his personality.

Now I know better.

He was avoiding me, the bastard.

Howard begins to pace again, raking his hand against his bristly jaw and muttering to himself.

"I'm going to handle this," he says. "You'll tell no one, you understand?"

"Yes," we both say.

"I'll come to you when I have this sorted out," he adds.

I decide right here and now that I hate this man, and I've never hated anyone in my life. Who is he to think he has any say in what I do with my child? "Now leave."

Westley and I waste no time exiting Bertram's study and when we get outside, we're out of breath and talking over each other.

"Holy shit," I say.

"Yeah, I can honestly say I've never seen him that angry before," Westley says. "And the fact that he needs time to think about this means he definitely wants to punish us for this."

"Also, um ... we're half-siblings," I add.

"God, Yeah. That too." Westley runs his hands through his auburn waves. I guess I've never studied him long enough to realize that we do share some resemblances. Same square jaw, same hairline, same gold-green eyes, though his are a shade lighter than mine. And Whitley ... she's blonde like me but other than that, she's the spitting image of Lorelai. "This is a lot to take in."

"I know, right?"

We stand in front of The Bertram for a few more minutes, the last half hour playing on a reel in my head.

"I should probably head back," I say.

"Right." He rests his hands on his hips, studying me. I wonder if he's searching for resemblances too. "Try to get some sleep, okay?"

I give him a hug—one I feel wholly entitled to now that I know he's my half-brother.

"We'll talk more tomorrow," he says as he heads to The Caldecott.

I make my way back to my grandparents' cottage, numb with shock. By the time I get there, I have no recollection of the short walk. When I go in, I find both of my grandparents passed out in their recliners as a cable news show plays on their TV.

Sneaking to my room unseen, I collapse on my bed, my head dizzy with all these thoughts and revelations.

I so badly wish I could talk to Thayer.

He always knows exactly what to say to put my mind at ease.

CHAPTER 41

THAYER

"HEY, you going home for break at all?" My roommate asks the Friday before a three-day weekend.

"Yeah. Going to Bridgeport for the week. You?"

Jonah shrugs. "Staying put. My parents booked a freaking Caribbean cruise this week. Can you believe that? I'm like ... what am I supposed to do? They knew we had no school this Monday."

I pack my bag for the weekend and glance around the room to make sure I've got everything. I need to hit the road in the next forty minutes if I want to avoid rush hour.

"Taking off," I tell Jonah, giving him a two-finger wave as I sling my duffel bag over my shoulder.

"Have a good one, man." He waves back, his eyes still glued to his MacBook screen.

I pass a mailbox on my way to the student parking lot and for a second, I wonder how hard it would be to get a letter to Lila. Junie always gets the mail this time of year. If there's no return address, maybe she'll think it's an old friend from California wanting to say hi?

There's also the grocery boat. If it's the same guy, I'm sure he'd do me a favor and hand deliver a note to Lila. I'd just need to call him. And mail the letter to him ...

I decide to work out the logistics on my drive home, and I take solace in knowing I left a dozen haphazardly hidden notes all over her cottage for her to find. Even if I'm not there on the island, I want her to still have a piece of me with her at all times.

CHAPTER 42

Lila

I'M LYING on my bed the next morning, earbuds in my ear as I make my way through a first edition copy of *The Bell Jar*, when Grandma bursts into my room. Her eyes are red, filled with tears, and her lower lip trembles.

The last time I saw her undone like this was at Mom's funeral.

"Get up," she says, motioning with her hands like I'm not moving quickly enough.

I know what this is about, but I don't dare say a word.

"Come on now," she says, waving me toward her.

I follow her down the hall, and I stop in my tracks when I get to the living room and find Howard standing in the middle. It's so weird seeing him in this house. He sticks out among all of my grandmother's pastel throw pillows and milk glass knick-knacks. He brings a heaviness that normally isn't here.

"Lila, have a seat," Howard says. "Actually, I'd like the three of you to take a seat on the couch as this conversation pertains to your entire family."

"Lila, what have you done?" My grandmother's lower lip trembles and her voice is a thin whisper.

My grandfather won't look at me.

The three of us take the sofa. I'm sandwiched between them. Grandma wrings her hands in her lap and Grandpa rests his hands on his knees, though when I look closer, I can tell one of them is shaking.

"Ed. Junie," Howard says as he stands before us. "I'm not sure if you're aware, but our Lila here is with child."

Grandma gasps.

Grandpa's shaking hand turns into a clenched fist.

"And the person who did this," Howard pauses for dramatic effect. I'm almost positive he's enjoying the hell out of this, dragging it out just so he can watch us squirm. "Is none other than her half-brother, Westley."

My grandmother claps her hands over her mouth, her eyes filling with tears, and I realize now that she had to have known, and in a way, I imagine she blames herself for this.

I so badly wish I could tell her the truth.

I can't imagine how difficult it's been for her to bury a secret of this magnitude and for nearly two full decades.

"So now that we have this little ... situation," he says, booming voice filling the small cottage living room as he commands our attention. "I'm afraid I'm going to have to make some changes that are to take effect immediately."

He retrieves a manila envelope from the coffee table, pulling out small stacks of paperclipped paperwork and three shiny gold ballpoint pens.

"Because of the sensitive nature of this ... pregnancy and its details ... I'm afraid I have no choice but to relieve all three of you from your duties," Howard says, fingers coming to a peak beneath his bulbous nose.

"I'm sorry. I don't understand," my grandpa says. "We had no idea ..."

"Lila was your responsibility," he says. "You were to watch her. And keep her away from my grandsons. You failed. Just like you failed with Mary. I already gave you a chance with your granddaughter. I don't do second chances."

"I'm so sorry," I whisper as the three of us stare ahead at the paperwork sitting in front of us.

"Not now, Lila," Grandpa whispers back.

I realize now that their relationship with Mr. Bertram was never based on respect or admiration for him, but fear. He must have controlled them exactly the way he controls his own family.

"So here's how it's going to go," Bertram begins. "First, the three of you will pack up your personal belongings and leave by noon today. I'll have a boat waiting for you at the end of the dock. Second, I need each of you to sign a non-disclosure agreement that ensures you will never breathe a single word about this child or its existence to anyone in my family or extended family."

I open my mouth in an attempt to protest, but my grand-mother grips my forearm. I have to tell Thayer. As soon as I'm off this island, I'm going to find him. This is his child. He deserves to know.

"In exchange for your silence," Howard continues, "I'll ensure that the child is well-cared for for the next eighteen years. Lila, you'll receive a monthly stipend of five thousand dollars until the child goes to college. At that time, I'll have a trust in their name that should cover most if not all of their college expenses. In addition, I require that the three of you live under aliases. Shorten your last name to Hill. Alter your first names. Do what you need to do to become untraceable. Since that might complicate your ability to get loans or housing, you should know that I've already thought ahead. I'll buy a modest home for the four of you, and I've already made transportation arrangements. When you arrive on the mainland, there will be a man there. He's to give you keys to the car I'm giving you. As for where you settle, I'd prefer that it's as far away from here as possible, the Pacific Northwest perhaps? I'll let you decide. Last but not least, Ed and Junie, I know you weren't planning to retire for at least another four years, so I'll be providing a small stipend for you as well. I know it's difficult getting employment at our age and with neither of you having high school diplomas, it's going to be a bit of a challenge. I'll give you each three thousand dollars a month for the next twenty years. With your housing and transportation covered, the four of you should be more than comfortable."

While this offer seems mutually beneficial, this feels like

making a deal with the devil, and I have no intentions of signing.

"What's the catch?" I ask.

"There is no catch," Howard says. "The three of you keep quiet and make yourselves impossible to find ... and you'll be taken care of. If any of you so much as opens your mouth or contacts a single person in my family, the contract is null and void. You'll lose the house, the car, and the monthly allowances and you'll be completely on your own."

Grandpa reaches for the pen.

Grandma follows suit.

The hot sting of tears fill my eyes. If I sign this, I'll never be able to tell Thayer about the pregnancy—I'll never be able to contact him in any way, shape, or form for the next two decades.

"This isn't right," I say as thick tears slide down my cheeks and land on the paperwork below.

"Neither is that *thing* growing in your belly right now," he says.

"You mean your first great-grandchild?" I ask. I know family means the world to him and while it sickens me to know this baby has a drop of Bertram's blood, I'm also not afraid to give him a taste of his own medicine and use that fact against him.

"Why do you think I've so generously provided for its education?" he asks. "Given the strange and bizarre circumstances that I tried my damnedest to prevent, I think I'm being awfully generous here."

"Sign the paperwork, Lila," Grandpa says under his breath.

"What happens if I don't?" I ask.

"Lila, you don't have a choice," Grandpa says, shoving the pen in my hand. "*We* don't have a choice."

I look into his pain-filled eyes and think about everything this is costing them. Their job security. Their home. Their livelihood.

Everything they've worked their entire lives for.

And then I think about Thayer and the great things he's going to do with that Yale law degree someday. If I don't sign the paper and if I tell Thayer, my grandparents will be homeless and Thayer will have to drop out of school.

It's lose-lose.

I try to look at this the way Thayer would. He was always good at finding the upside to every troublesome situation. I can't be certain, of course, but I feel like he would make his decision based on what's in the best interest of the baby, the innocent life who didn't ask to be dragged into this.

Without saying another word, I sign the NDA and toss the pen when I'm done.

"Excellent," Howard says, gathering the paperwork into a pile. "And here are your copies. I'd like you to ensure that every line of this is memorized frontwards and back. If you have any questions, you can contact my attorney. His number is at the top of every page."

He speaks to us like we're morons.

"Don't forget," he adds, checking his watch. "The boat will

be at the dock at noon. That leaves you with three hours to pack your things."

Grandma looks at Grandpa, her eyes glassy. I'm sure she's wondering how she's going to pack a lifetime of personal belongings in a three-hour window.

Howard leaves without saying goodbye and without so much as thanking my grandparents for their decades of loyalty and service to his family.

"I have to tell you something," I say. I'm going to tell them about Thayer.

"Not now, Lila," my grandmother flits around the room, gathering small glass knick-knacks and framed photos of my mother and I in younger years. "Pack your things. We don't have time to chat."

I rush down the hall, passing my grandparents' bedroom and watching as my grandfather stuffs clothes into an open suitcase on the bed.

The gravity of the situation sinks into me when I get to my room. Grabbing my suitcase from under the bed, I pack my things with tear-stained vision.

I didn't just sign an NDA today.

I signed away a future with the man I love.

CHAPTER 43

THAYER

"WHAT ARE YOU DOING ON SATURDAY?" Ashlan is sprawled on my bed, thumbing through the photos on her phone. This is what she does. Shows up unannounced. Makes herself at home. Tries to weasel her way into my social life.

"I'm doing some intramural lacrosse thing with some guys from my philosophy class," I say. At least this time it's the truth.

"You suck." She rolls to her stomach, eyes still glued to her iPhone. "Don't you ever hate being so busy all the time?"

"No, I love it." If I keep busy, it distracts me from missing Lila and makes the days go by faster, which puts me that much closer to May.

"Are you going home for all of Christmas break?" she asks.

"That's, like, three months from now. Why are you asking?"

"Because I'd like to hang out with you at least once before the year is over. I feel like you never make time for me anymore." She sits up, her bottom lip pouting. "At least at home you don't have intramurals or clubs or study groups or whatever."

Damn it.

She has a point.

"I'm still mad at you about last summer," she says.

"Mad at me for what?"

She scoffs. "Thayer. I came all the way to the island to visit you for five days and you barely gave me the time of day. You were all hung up on that blonde girl. That maid."

That maid.

Nice.

"What was her name again?" Ashlan asks, messing with her phone.

"Lila," I say. God, it feels good to say her name again. It's been too long.

"Yeah, that's right," she says. "You totally had the hots for her."

"What are you talking about?"

"You were always checking her out when you thought no one was paying attention," she says.

"Yeah, well, she was pretty. And I'm a red-blooded American male. That's kind of what happens when you put those two things together." I know I sound like a chauvinistic asshole, but I have to downplay this. If Ashlan gets so much as a whiff or inkling that I feel a certain way about Lila, she'll tell her mom ... who will tell my mom ... who will innocently tell Granddad under the guise of thinking it's a cute story to share. "She's not my type though."

"Obviously," Ashlan laughs. "She was kind of weird."

"Definitely."

"Did you guys ever hook up?"

"God, no. I'm not that desperate."

"Okay, now answer this: who's hotter? Me or her?" she asks.

I have no choice but to tell her what she wants to hear. "You. Hands down. All the way."

"Aww, I love you so much," she says, singsong-y. "Do you love me?"

"Of course I love you," I say, but only to get her to shut up.

"Say hiiiiiii to everyone." She raises the phone and zooms in on me before tapping the screen.

"Did you just take a video?" I ask.

"Yeah." Her nose crinkles. "Why?"

"You need to tell people when you're filming them. Delete that."

"No, I will not delete that. It's adorable," she says.

I reach for the phone, and she tucks it behind her back and

lays on my bed. If I want it, I'm going to have to pin her down and wrangle it out of her hands, and I think she'd like that too much.

"Seriously, Ash, delete it," I say.

She sits up, her phone still clutched in her hand. "You're way too sensitive sometimes, you know that? Did you say something in the video that you don't want people to hear?"

"No," I lie.

"Okay, then you have nothing to worry about."

I'll watch her social media accounts the next few days to see if she posts it, and if she does, I'll file a copyright infringement so it's taken down immediately. Thank God Lila doesn't have a computer or internet access on the island, and as far as I know, she doesn't know Ashlan's last name, so even if she did have those capabilities, there's no way she'd see the video.

CHAPTER 44

Lila

We pull up to a roadside motel outside a little town called Summerton not far from the Oregon coast. Shortly after reaching the Rose Crossing mainland and getting the keys to the shiny economy-sized car Bertram gifted us, we hit the road driving west, stopping first in Pennsylvania for gas, where I bought a prepaid smart phone so we could use the internet for navigation.

We were halfway across Iowa when I found Summerton on a list of "most desirable places to live in the Pacific Northwest."

"Top-rated schools," I read off the list to them as we drove down I-80. "Twenty thousand people, low unemployment ... You want to see the pictures?"

With all the lush vegetation and evergreens, it almost looked like a West Coast version of Maine, but it was described as being progressive and laidback, which reminded me of California. I showed them both photos on my phone as we drove and an hour later, we'd settled on Summerton.

"We're supposed to call Bertram when we get here," I remind them. All those hours in the car meant I had plenty of time to read over the NDA as well as the little instruction sheet he had typed up for us.

We were halfway across Pennsylvania when I finally had the nerve to ask my grandparents about my mother and Ari Caldecott and ... me. It turns out she was working for Bertram the summer after Ari married Lorelai and as part of their wedding gift, Bertram gifted the newlyweds a housekeeper: a young, naïve Mary Hilliard.

She was sent to Connecticut to live with Ari and Lorelai, and shortly thereafter Lorelai fell pregnant with the twins and spent nearly four straight months on bedrest. It was during that time Ari became smitten with my mother, pursuing her relentlessly. My mother was pliable and impressionable and made the foolish decision to get involved with a married man. By the time she realized she was pregnant, she was almost three months along and Lorelai was due to give birth any day.

Shortly after the twins were born, Lorelai asked her father if he'd be willing to swap out a housekeeper for a nanny and he agreed without hesitation, but when my mother returned to the island it wasn't long before her pregnancy was glaringly obvious.

She was five months pregnant when Bertram cornered her and got her to tell him everything. He prefaced the conversation as though he was concerned and wanted to help her, only to flip his narrative as soon as she admitted the baby was Ari's.

He banished her after that and swore my grandparents to secrecy, holding their jobs over their heads and ruling from his throne of fear and manipulation.

My grandmother must have gone through half a box of tissues as she told me everything, and my grandfather never let go of her hand once.

She asked me if I could forgive them, but I assured her it wasn't necessary.

None of what happened was their fault.

I hand my phone to Grandpa and Grandma, and I head into the hotel lobby to see about getting a room for the night.

Tomorrow we're supposed to look for housing and when we find the one we like, we're supposed to send the listing to Bertram to handle the rest.

Grandpa meets us in the lobby a few minutes later, handing the phone back to me. Later when we're settled, I'm going to connect to the hotel's WiFi and see if I can find Thayer on social media.

I can't contact him, of course. But I don't see the harm in sneaking little glimpses of his life, making sure he's happy and doing well.

Placing my hand on my lower stomach, I try to look on the bright side—that at least I'll forever have a piece of him with me.

CHAPTER 45

THAYER

"HELLO, HELLO!" My mother calls as we head into the Caldecott home in Bridgeport for Thanksgiving dinner.

"We're in the kitchen," Aunt Lorelai calls over the sound of a football game blasting from the family room. "It's just about ready."

"I know, I know. We're late," Mom says as she sits a couple of store-bought pies on the counter. "Thayer, you can put the sweet potatoes next to the turkey. Thanks, lovey."

I glance into the family room, spotting the back of my grandfather's balding head as he snoozes in a recliner. Whitley is sprawled out on the loveseat, texting away on her phone.

I take a seat on the sofa next to Westley.

"Hey," I say.

He turns, jerks away when he realizes it's me. "Oh, hey. When did you get here?"

"Like two seconds ago."

"Cool." He turns back to the game.

"How's school?" I ask.

He shrugs, still watching the TV. "Fine."

It's not like him to be so cold, then again, everyone has off days.

"Everything okay?" I ask.

"Of course," he says, still turned away.

"You want to throw the football in the back yard later?" I ask. It's always been our tradition.

"Eh. We'll see," he says. A second later, his phone rings and he takes the call. "Hey, man, what's up?"

His tone is noticeably more upbeat than it was a second ago, and he walks away to take the call in the next room. I can't make out what he's saying, but by the inflection in his voice, I can tell he's engaged and happy to be talking to whoever's on the other line.

Well, shit.

I get up from the sofa and head to the kitchen. I wasn't going to take that personally, but now ...

"Thayer, you want to call everyone to the dining room?" Aunt Lorelai asks. "I think your uncle's in the garage with your dad."

I make my way around the house, telling everyone it's time to eat, and we all head to Aunt Lorelai's wallpapered dining room. Granddad takes the seat at the head of the table, in a throne-sized chair that's always reserved for him, and I take the spot to his right.

Uncle Ari says grace and my dad carves the turkey.

"Thayer," Granddad says as we wait for the food to go around. "How's the semester going so far?"

"Great," I say. "Acing all my classes. Finals are in a couple of weeks. Just trucking along."

"Wonderful, wonderful." He pats my shoulder, his eyes lit with pride.

"How's the island life?" I ask. I can't directly ask about the Hilliards, but I'm hopeful if we start taking about Rose Crossing, they might come up in conversation.

"Same old," he says as he takes a roll from a serving platter.

"Anything new?" I ask.

He answers me with a laugh, and I know that's all I'm going to get from him.

"Westley, pass me the green beans, will you?" Granddad says, pointing toward the middle of the table. "Let's keep everything moving."

After dinner, I help with clean up while Granddad, Uncle Ari, and Westley settle back into the family room. It's strangely quiet in there. Usually when the three of them are together you can't get a word in edgewise, they're usually debating politics or whatever the hot topic of the news is at the time ... but they're just sitting there, staring at the flickering TV screen like zombies.

"What's with them?" I ask my aunt, nodding toward the next room.

"What? What's wrong?" Of course she's oblivious.

"Not used to them being so quiet together."

"Ohhh." Aunt Lorelai laughs as she dries a china plate with a taupe checkered dish towel. "Yeah, good question. Ever since Westley came home for break he's been quiet, and when Dad got here, he didn't even get up to say hi. He went up to his room."

"Is he *depressed*?" my mom asks, whispering. "You know when people get antisocial or withdrawn, sometimes that can be a sign ..."

Aunt Lorelai sighs, watching her son from afar. "Yeah, maybe? I'm not sure. I tried to get Whitley to talk to him, but he wouldn't even open up to her. I'm hoping to have a moment alone with him when all the holiday craziness is over."

I think of Westley and the phone call earlier. Maybe he was upbeat because it was regarding a job or internship or someone he was trying to impress? Then again, he referred to the person on the other line as "man," and that's not exactly the kind of verbiage you use when trying to sound professional.

Something's going on with him.

Just wish I knew what.

CHAPTER 46

Lila

"DO you want to know what you're having?" the ultrasound tech asks as she runs the transducer across my lower stomach. This is only the second ultrasound I've had—the first one being back in October. They said everything looked normal and gave me a due date.

May 8th.

A year to the day I arrived at Rose Crossing Island.

"You can tell already?" I ask. I'm only seventeen weeks along and I'm hardly showing.

"I can," the woman says with a sweetness in her voice that makes her perfect for a job like this.

"Yeah. I want to know," I say. I've had enough surprises this year. I don't know if I can handle another one.

"All right," she says as she highlights a fuzzy black and white image on the screen. "You're having a girl!"

"A girl? Are you sure?" I ask.

The woman nods. "I'm ninety-nine percent sure. Our technology is pretty incredible, but every once in a while we get a little one that likes to trick us."

She hands me a warm, wet wash cloth, and I wipe the gel from my stomach before climbing down from the bed.

"I'll send the doctor in shortly," she says, printing off a few pictures and placing them in my chart before she leaves.

I take a seat in one of the guest chairs and wait in the dimly lit room, letting my eyes adjust.

I hate that Thayer is still in the dark.

I'd give anything to be able to tell him he's going to be a dad, that he's going to have a little girl. I bet he'd be so good with her, and I bet she'd have him wrapped around her finger in no time.

My OB, Dr. Caraway, makes a quick stop by the room to let me know that everything looks great and to answer any questions, of which I have none. And then she tells me to come back in four weeks for my next appointment.

I check out at the front and head out to the car I share with my grandparents. It isn't the most convenient arrangement, but so far it works out. The two of them were recently hired part-time at a retirement home in town, Grandma cooking in the kitchen and Grandpa doing general maintenance around the grounds. The pay isn't the greatest, but it keeps them busy and supplements the money Bertram sends every month.

So far we've saving almost everything we get.

Grandpa hates that Bertram owns the house we live in, he hates that it gives him that much more power over us. He hopes in a few years we'll have enough money to buy a house of our own with cash. Until then, we save, save, save.

Last week I signed up for classes at the local community college, which I'll pay for with cash, and when I was finished, they told me to head to the student library to get my laptop. Apparently as long as you're enrolled here, you get to use one of their laptops.

My appointment ended early, and I still have another hour before I have to pick up my grandparents from work, so I stop at a local café to grab a coffee and use their WiFi on my new-to-me laptop.

The internet on my prepaid phone is infuriatingly slow and the screen is temperamental. Every time I wanted to check up on Thayer, I ended up throwing in the towel because I could never get anything to load half the time, and when it did load, it was so tiny I was afraid of accidentally clicking on a "like" or a "follow" or something.

Five minutes later, I'm seated in a two-person booth in the front of The Mocha Bean on Summerton's downtown square, sipping a peppermint latte and connecting to their lightning-fast Wi-Fi.

As soon as I'm on, I log into my fake Facebook account and do a search for Thayer Ainsworth.

He shows up as the top—and only—result, and my

stomach flips when I click on his profile picture. I zoom in, making it fill my screen like I'm some kind of creepy stalker girl, but I don't care. It feels so good to *see* him again. The picture says it was uploaded two weeks ago, so I know it's current. The only thing different about him is his lack of a suntan, but he still looks as gorgeous as before.

I zoom out and scroll down his page, which is unfortunately under lock and key. I can't see a single status update. And his current profile picture is the only one made public.

I've hit a wall.

Clicking on his friends' list, I scroll through to see if I can find Ashlan. I know he mentioned they went to school together, and she seems like the kind of person who'd have their entire profile wide open for the entire world to see, so I'm hopeful I might be able to find Thayer in some pictures or tagged posts.

I just want to know what he's been up to.

And I want to see that he's having fun, enjoying his life, living it up.

I type the name "Ashlan" into the search bar above Thayer's friends' list and the only result that comes up is for an "Ashlan Potthoff." Clicking on her picture confirms I've got the right girl, and scrolling through her page proves my assumption correct—this thing is an open book.

I start with the most recent post—one of Ashlan taking a selfie and posting about her "Thanksgiving food baby," which is non-existent because her stomach is flat as a board. It's nothing more than an attention grab, and the comments section is filled with a half a dozen other girls telling her how wrong she is and how amazing she looks.

Yawn.

I keep going, scrolling faster and faster because none of these pictures contain anyone who looks remotely like Thayer. Ninety-nine percent of them are selfies or huge group pictures that turn blurry when you try to zoom in too much.

Not only that, but she posts at least four times a day.

It's almost time to go pick up my grandparents when I make it to September.

There's a video posted on September fifteenth. I fish my earbuds from my bag and stick them in the jack on the laptop before hitting play.

The sound of Ashlan's nasally voice precedes the camera coming into focus. It looks like she's filming Thayer, only he's at his computer so all I can see is the back of him.

"I'm still mad at you about last summer," Ashlan says.

"Mad at me for what?" Thayer asks.

"I came all the way to the island to visit you for five days and you barely gave me the time of day. You were all hung up on that blonde girl. That maid. What was her name again?"

"Lila."

"Yeah, that's right. You totally had the hots for her."

"What are you talking about?" he asks.

"*You were always checking her out when you thought no one was paying attention,*" she says.

"*Yeah, well, she was pretty. And I'm a red-blooded American male. That's kind of what happens when you put those two things together. She's not my type though.*"

"*Obviously. She was kind of weird.*"

"*Definitely,*" he says, his tone so convincing it stings.

"*Did you guys ever hook up?*"

"*God, no. I'm not that desperate.*"

"*Okay, now answer this: who's hotter? Me or her?*" Ashlan asks.

"*You. Hands down. All the way.*"

"*Aww, I love you so much,*" she says, singsong-y. "*Do you love me?*"

"*Of course I love you.*"

I slam the lid down, eyes welling with tears, and I pack up my things and dash to my car.

I knew it.

PART FOUR [PRESENT]

May 2019

CHAPTER 47

THAYER

I CORNER WESTLEY outside The Caldecott the moment I set foot on the island that night. I spent the entire plane ride home trying to piece everything together, trying to rectify what I thought I knew with this new information. If MJ was born in May, that means Lila would've been pregnant in August—when we were still together. And if Lila told MJ the ring was from her daddy ...

"Tell me everything," I say as I charge him. "Now."

Westley's hands lift in the air. "Thayer, come on. Don't make a scene."

"You're not going anywhere until you tell me everything."

Westley glances around. The island's been full of various vendors and contractors all week, setting up for his sister's wedding and ensuring everything's going to go off without a hitch.

"Lila's daughter," I say. "Is she yours or is she mine?"

Westley hooks his arm into mine and pulls me to the east side of his house, away from the hustle and bustle.

"Lila's daughter is yours," he says.

"I don't understand. Why wouldn't she have told me? Why keep it this secret and disappear?" I think about all the things I've missed. Milestones. Celebrations. The birth of my first child...

How could she?

"She found out she was pregnant in the middle of September," he says. "She confided in me and as we were trying to figure out what she should do, we realized that she was going to lose her job regardless ... but she didn't want you to lose your education. I didn't either. We figured I had less to lose than you, so I told her I'd take credit for her ... predicament." He draws in a breath, hands on his hips. "But our little plan backfired because it turns out, Lila's my half-sister."

"Wait. What?"

"My dad and Lila's mom," he explains.

Oh, thank God.

"So yeah, all those times Granddad was warning me to stay away from Lila? It was for that reason. And when he was warning you? It was because he couldn't stand her, what she represented," Westley says. "Anyway, it wasn't twenty-four hours and Granddad had the Hilliards shipped off. We all had to sign NDAs. And Thayer, I'm telling you ... you cannot repeat any of this to anyone. Lila will lose everything. I'll lose everything. I don't even think Granddad knows the kid is yours anyway. We didn't exactly have a chance to tell him. Everything happened so fast."

"Is this why you've been so distant to me?" I ask.

His lips press flat. "Yeah. All of it felt so wrong. I couldn't look you in the eye seeing you so torn up and knowing what I knew. It was easier to avoid you. I'm so sorry."

"So what now?" I ask. "Do you still have the NDA you signed?"

"Yeah. I'll let you look it over. But dude, please don't cause a scene. It's not worth it. Lila was provided for. The kid was provided for. Things could've been a lot worse."

I'm not so sure about that.

I should've been there for her. I should've been the one taking care of her, providing for them.

"Go get yourself a drink. Go for a walk. Cool off," Westley says. "And for the love of God, don't do anything stupid."

CHAPTER 48

Lila

"WE'RE ALMOST THERE, sweetie. Hurry up and finish that," I say to my daughter as she inhales the blueberry muffin she begged to have for breakfast this morning.

I pull into the frenetic chaos that is the school drop off zone and MJ unbuckles her seatbelt before grabbing her backpack.

"Oh, Mom," she says. "I forgot to tell you. I saw your friend at the coffee shop."

"Which friend?" I inch up half a car length and wait as six kids climb out of a sagging Dodge Caravan.

"The guy who was at our house last night," she says.

She only saw him for a few seconds. There's no way she could recognize him. It was probably someone who looked similar.

"How do you know it was him?" I pull up another car length. We're almost next.

"Duh, Mom. I asked him," she says.

"Ah. So the two of you had a conversation?" I glance up at her in the rearview.

MJ shrugs. "I don't know. He asked about my necklace."

She tugs at the opal ring hanging from a chain around her neck—the ring Thayer gave me ten years ago when we spent a day strolling around in Rose Crossing, hand in hand. The ring is still too small for me and it's too big for MJ, so she wears it like a pendant.

"Oh, yeah? What did you say?" My hands are wrapped tight around the steering wheel, palms sweating.

"I told him my daddy got it for my mommy before I was born," she says, scooting across the backseat and reaching for the handle.

"And what did he say?"

"He said he must have loved her very much to give her such a special ring. Why are you asking so any questions?"

"No reason," I say. "Time to go, babe. Have a great day, okay? I'll see you after school."

MJ climbs out and shuts the door before running toward the school entrance and disappearing into a crowd of multi-colored backpacks, and I drive home, thankful that she didn't notice the tears behind my sunglasses.

CHAPTER 49

THAYER

I LOOSEN my tie and unfasten the top two buttons of my dress shirt before shrugging out of my suit jacket. I'm hot. Burning. My skin is crawling as I pace my grandfather's study. I need to get out of this suit and off this fucking island as soon as possible.

Whitley's wedding was nothing short of beautiful. At least I think it was. It was like I was there, but I wasn't. I couldn't focus. Couldn't enjoy a damn thing. I probably looked miserable, though I tried my hardest to put on a good face. Despite the live band and open bar and good-spirited guests, I kept myself away from the merriment. It wasn't that I was trying to be an ass ... I just wanted to keep myself from doing something stupid at my cousin's wedding—like confronting Granddad ...

But the wedding's over.

The guests have left.

There's a hired crew outside taking down tents and chairs and the dance floor. The caterer is cleaning up and the band is packing up and Whitley and her husband are already halfway back to the mainland by now.

My parents, aunt, uncle, and Westley have all retired to their houses, and last I knew, Granddad was outside talking to a member of the clean-up crew.

He'll be coming inside any minute.

And I'll be waiting for him.

Westley mentioned he and Lila were forced to sign NDAs, but if he threatened them and coerced them to sign the documents, they could be legally challenged. A contract signed under duress isn't enforceable, and I can only imagine the fear of God he was putting into a frightened, eighteen-year-old Lila.

Westley also mentioned Granddad had been providing for Lila and MJ. I imagine that was part of the deal, him buying her silence with money, but they're not his problem anymore. They're mine. I'll be the one taking care of them from here on out. His power, his money ... it's no good here.

Not anymore.

Not now.

Not ever.

I toss my jacket over the back of his leather chair when I hear the front door open and close. His heavy footsteps follow, growing louder with each passing second. Any moment now, he'll see the light on in his study.

With my hands on my hips, I straighten my shoulders, hold my chin up, and wait.

"Thayer," Granddad says a few seconds later when he steps in. "What are you doing in here? I saw the light was on, but I had no idea—"

"Sit," I say. "I'd like to have a word with you."

I've never spoken to him like this before, and the incredulous look in his eyes paired with the open-mouthed smile on his mouth tells me he isn't sure whether to take me seriously.

"Mind telling me what this is about?" He doesn't sit. He stays planted in the doorway, blocking me in. I realize now he's always done this. It's a power move, a silent way to show who's in control.

"You lied to me, Granddad," I say.

He scoffs. "Thayer. I don't know what you're talking about or why you feel the need to have this conversation at this very moment, but it's been a long day. Hell, it's been a long week. And I'm exhausted. If you don't mind, I'm going to wash up for bed. We'll have this talk tomorrow. We can go on a sail, just you and me. How's that sound?"

"I'm afraid that won't be an option," I say. "I'm leaving tonight."

He checks the Rolex on his left wrist. "It's one in the morning. Where are you going to go?"

"We're having this conversation *now*." I ignore his question. It's none of his business that I plan to hitch a ride back to the mainland with the wedding crew, where my rental car is parked in a public lot a few blocks from the inlet. I planned to find a hotel, but I'll sleep in the damn car before I spend another night on this island with him. "You lied to me. You told me the Hilliards retired, that you didn't know where they were."

He squints. "The Hilliards? This is about the Hilliards? Thayer, that was a lifetime ago. Why are you bringing this up now?"

"Because you banished them, you made them change their names, and because of that, I've spent the last ten years killing myself trying to figure out what happened to them ... all the while not knowing that I had a daughter."

His brows rise before meeting in the middle, and he strokes his thick fingers along his bristled jaw. I remember Westley saying he didn't think Granddad knew Lila's baby was actually mine, that everything had happened so fast.

"I have a daughter," I say it again, louder and clearer in case he didn't hear me the first time. "And I've missed *everything*. Every birthday, every milestone. Every opportunity to be there for the two of them."

My jaw tightens.

His eyes wince and his face turns a shade darker. "I was protecting you."

"What do you mean, you were protecting *me*?" I ask. "Are you saying you knew the baby was mine from the start?"

Granddad snorts. "Of course I did. Do you think I'm a damn idiot? I saw the way you two looked at each other all summer. I saw you sneaking around. I saw the evidence in the old nurse's cottage."

"And you never said anything?" Not that it matters at this point, but his revelation stuns me.

"I warned you several times to stay away from her early on," he says. "When it became clear you were going against my direct orders, I kept my mouth shut. I knew she was nothing more than a summer fling ... until you had to create that ... *situation*."

"You had no right."

"I had *every* right. You were throwing away your entire future over a girl!" His yell sends an ache to my ears, and he's marching toward me with his finger ready to poke in my face. The number of times I've seen him lose his cool over the years, I can count on one hand. It's almost comical, really. Seeing this once all-powerful, controlling puppet master reduced to a powerless parody of his old self.

"That girl *was* my future!"

"You're a fool if you believe the two of you had any business being together. She's a harlot. Her mother was a harlot. They're trash, Thayer. *Trash*." He shakes his head at me, glaring. "You know, all I ever wanted was for you to have the best of everything. The best education. The best opportunities. The best—"

"—Lila was the best thing that ever happened to me," I say.

"You ungrateful prick," he spits at me. "I give you the world and it's not good enough, eh?"

I know what he's doing. He's deflecting and distracting, trying to turn this around and make *me* look like the asshole.

"Well, I'd hate to stand in the way of the rest of your life," he says, sneering. "So consider yourself relieved from any and all familial ties and obligations you might have to me. First thing in the morning, I'll get my attorney on the line and have a new will drafted up. I'll be damned if I give you a damn thing after the way you've spoken to me. You have some nerve, boy."

I smirk.

I don't need his money.

I don't need a damn thing from him.

And this might actually be the greatest thing he's ever given me: freedom.

"I would expect nothing less from you." I gather my jacket and fling it over my left arm as I head toward the hall.

"Don't walk away from me, Thayer." His voice booms from the study, but I keep walking away. "This conversation is far from over."

That's where he's wrong.

I have nothing more to say to the bastard. Not now, not ever.

"Fine," he yells. He must be a few yards behind me now because his voice is louder and closer than it was a second ago. "Then don't you dare set foot on this island again. You no longer have a place here."

I hear it in his voice—panic.

He's realizing that he's lost the last bit of control he ever held over me. And he's also realizing that the cat's out of the bag now. This secret, this secret that he's spent probably hundreds of thousands of dollars—if not millions—to hide ... has now cost him everything.

If that isn't justice, I don't know what is.

I slam the door behind me when I leave, and I make my way to the dock.

CHAPTER 50

Lila

"GO BRUSH YOUR TEETH," I tell MJ Sunday morning after breakfast. "We're going to visit Grandpa. And wear a sweatshirt today. It's going to be chilly."

MJ carries her cereal bowl to the sink, rinsing it out before skipping upstairs, and I pour myself my second coffee of the day.

Across the room, my phone buzzes, and I head over to grab it off the charger, only I stop when I'm met with a hauntingly familiar 207 area code. For a moment, I think it might be Thayer, but he lives in Manhattan. He wouldn't have a Maine area code and he never would've had one. It has to be Bertram.

Clearing my throat, I glance at the bottom of the stairs to make sure MJ isn't within earshot.

"Hello?" I keep my voice down.

"Lila," the voice booms from the other end.

My stomach sinks.

It's Bertram.

I decide to take the call outside, on the back patio. Given the information that's recently come to light, nothing good is going to come from this phone call.

I asked Thayer not to say anything.

No, I pleaded with him.

I said it again and again, probably sounding like a crazy person, but I needed him to understand the gravity of the situation without having to divulge all the details.

I pull the sliding glass door open and glide it shut behind me. It's a cold spring morning, but sunlight dapples across the patio and the breeze makes the new budding leaves on the trees dance.

In a matter of seconds, I know this perfectly beautiful day is going to be demolished.

Damn it, Westley.

The contract forbade Westley and I from communicating these past ten years or else I imagine we'd have been on the same page.

"It has come to my attention that you're in breach of your contract," Howard says. "I'm calling to inform you that effective immediately, I will no longer be upholding my end of the agreement. All forms of financial assistance will here on cease to exist and you have twenty-four hours to vacate your home."

"Twenty-four hours?" There's absolutely no way I'm going to be able to pack up a decade worth of our lives and find us a new place to stay in twenty-four hours. I don't even know if I could do that in a week. All the apartments around here require credit checks, and given the fact that I've never so much as had a credit card or car loan to show I'm capable of paying my bills on time, I can't imagine anyone's going to let me sign a lease. There might be a few places in town with sketchy landlords desperate to fill empty units, but I refuse to force my daughter to live in a place that literally lets anyone move in.

"Goodbye, Lila. I'll be sending someone to collect the keys and change the locks first thing in the morning." With that, Howard ends the call, not that it's surprising. There's never any arguing with him, and I know what the contract said.

I hug my sides and let my lungs fill with the cool breeze.

Suddenly this house feels like so much more than a house to me. Standing on the porch where I used to lounge with a book while my daughter ran around in the back yard, I can think of a hundred other memories just as ordinary and precious.

I wipe the tears that start to fall and compose myself in record time before heading back in.

"Mom, what's wrong?" MJ asks. She's standing in the middle of the kitchen. "Why were you outside with no coat on?"

"Change of plans, sweetie," I say. "We're not visiting Grandpa today."

"Why not?"

"I'll tell you later. I promise. I just have a few things I need to take care of. You want to play with Lucy today? I can call her mom and see if you can go over for a few hours?"

MJ hops up and down, her face lit and vacant of the concern that filled it a second earlier. "Yes, yes, yes!"

"All right. Go change into some play clothes," I say as I call my friend, Taylor.

I met her the year we first moved here. The two of us were the only single moms at the parenting seminars the local hospital held for pregnant women, so we ended up pairing up and then we promised to be each other's birth coaches, even though neither one of us had ever done it before.

She ended up having Lucy three weeks before I had MJ.

We were there for each other then, and we've been there for each other ever since.

"Tay," I say when she answers. "I need a huge favor ..."

"Of course, anything," she says.

I begin to talk, but my throat constricts. My voice is going to be shaky and she's going to ask me what's wrong, and I'm going to lose it and I don't want MJ to see me like this.

"Delilah?" she asks.

"Yes, sorry." I clear my throat and take a deep breath. "Can MJ come over today for a few hours?"

I keep my voice light and upbeat. I'll tell her everything later, when I've had a chance to sort through all of this.

"Oh, God. Yes. Send her over. Lucy's been begging for a playdate all week."

"Thanks, Tay. I'll drop her off in a few."

I load MJ into the car a few minutes later and run her across town to Taylor's house. I wait in the car as I watch her go inside, and I wave to Tay and Lucy from the driver's seat before backing out and heading home.

Halfway there, I stop at a home improvement store to pick up as many cardboard boxes as I can. We might have to stay in a hotel for a while, but I can put the important things in these and keep them in my car.

Last I checked, we had a decent amount in savings that should get us through these next few months. For several years the three of us had saved up quite the nest egg, but between Grandma's sickness and subsequent stint in a nursing home and Grandpa's Alzheimer's and the insane cost of keeping him at Willow Creek, we've blown through a depressing amount of it.

I pull into my driveway a few minutes later and start carrying the empty cardboard boxes to the house. Across the street our long-time neighbor, Ms. Beauchamp, is pruning her flowers.

"Hey, Miss Delilah!" she calls, waving with a garden-gloved hand.

"Hi, Ms. Beauchamp," I say, giving a nod because my arms are full.

She pushes herself up before waddling across her lush green yard and making her way across the street.

"How's Ed doing? I've been meaning to ask, but I haven't seen you around much. We must keep missing each other." Her bushy gray-blonde hair bounces in the breeze and there's a smudge of dirt on her oversized red sunglasses. There's something carefree and effervescent about her, and I've always loved that.

"He's hanging in there," I say. "Taking things one day at a time."

"Well, it's just so sad," she says. "I watched my own mother suffer from that horrible disease, and I know it isn't easy. Is MJ doing okay?"

I nod. "She is.

Kids are amazingly resilient, but I've always felt that MJ was a notch above average in that department. Sometimes I think she's stronger than me.

"Well, I won't keep you," she says, waving her garden shears. "Looks like you're about to embark on a little project or something ... are those moving boxes? You're not moving, are you?"

"We are," I say. "Unfortunately. Our landlord has asked that we leave by tomorrow."

"And you're just now packing? Oh, dear ..."

"Well, his request came as a surprise to us," I say before realizing she's going to assume we're being evicted. "He was an old family friend." I hate referring to Bertram as a friend, but in this case, it's just easier than explaining what he truly is: a monster. "He bought the house for us when we first moved here, but our families have had a recent falling out so he'd like us to be out as soon as possible."

"Well, that just seems cruel." She folds her arms and clucks her tongue. "With your grandfather in the nursing home and it just being the two of you ... how could someone be so heartless?"

"If you knew him, you'd understand." I glance at my front door. "I should probably start packing."

"Where will you go?" she asks. "Do you have anything lined up?"

I begin to speak, but my throat tightens. I can tell her we're staying in a hotel for the time being, but that doesn't change the fact that we're officially homeless, and the thought of saying that out loud sends a painful jolt to my stomach.

"You don't, do you?" she asks, yanking off her big sunglasses as she takes a step closer. Placing her hand on my arm, she shakes her head. "You're staying with me. And I won't take no for an answer. I've got two extra bedrooms and a spare bath. They're all yours until you can get on your feet."

"Are ... are you sure?" She's being entirely too kind and it pains me to take her up on this generous offer, but I think of my daughter, and how much easier this change will be if I keep her on her same familiar street with the same familiar faces.

"Oh, honey. Yes." She nods. "And you know ... I have a couple of nephews back from OSU for the summer. I'm sure they'd like to make a little cash. Want me to see if they can help with the move? Pretty sure one of them has a truck."

I'm too choked up to speak, so I drop the cardboard boxes and throw my arms around Ms. Beauchamp.

"Thank you," I finally manage as the scent of her perfume fills my lungs.

It smells of lilacs.

It smells like my mother.

If I believed in signs, I'd almost think ...

"All right, dear. You better start packing," she says. "I'm going to call the guys and tell them to get over here ASAP. Don't you worry, Delilah, we'll get this done."

The strangest sensation washes over me, a lightness or a weightlessness, and I realize now that I don't have to be Delilah Hill anymore.

For the first time in a decade, I'm free from Howard Bertram and all of his chains.

And that feeling? Priceless.

CHAPTER 51

I'M in my office Monday morning, but my mind is elsewhere.

Tapping my pen against my desk and staring into space, I lose myself in little vignettes that play like daydreams in my head. I try to picture what our life would've been like had I known from the beginning. She'd have left the island and I'd have left New Haven, but where would we have gone? And what would I have done for work? I imagine we'd have been broke as hell but stupid happy. And I imagine she'd have been stressed and nervous and worried and I'd have been making it my mission to remind her that the best is yet to come.

I try to imagine what Lila would've looked like pregnant.

How her soft belly would've felt under my palm.

I try to imagine the tears in her eyes when she heard the

heartbeat for the first time and the pain she must have felt going through all of this without me.

My reveries disappear for a moment and my focus shifts. I spent all of yesterday mourning what might have been and redirecting my anger from Granddad to Westley to Lila and back. Maybe it isn't fair to be upset with Westley and Lila, but I can't help but feel betrayed by them for keeping me in the dark. Contract be damned, I had a child out there and she was kept from me by the very three people who meant the most to me.

The shrill ring of my office phone jolts me back into the present moment, and I grab the call.

"Mr. Ainsworth, your mother is on line three," my assistant says.

Any time my mother calls me at work, it's usually to tell me she's in the city and wants to do lunch or to remind me of some upcoming family engagement she RSVP'd me to.

"Tell her I'll call her back," I say.

"She says it's urgent."

Sucking in a deep breath, I mull it over. My mother has never deemed anything "urgent" in her life. She's always been patient and unhurried and unburdened by even the most stressful of situations.

I think of my father, and I hope to God nothing happened.

"All right. I'll take it," I say, hanging up with her and pressing the blinking light. "Mom, what's going on?"

She doesn't answer right away.

And then I hear sobs, gasping, breathless sobs.

"Mom, talk to me. What happened? Is Dad okay?" I ask, heart going a million miles an hour. I rise from my chair, unable to sit and wait.

"Thayer," she says between sniffs. "I'm so sorry to tell you this ... but Granddad passed away."

I sit back down.

And I feel nothing.

"Thayer?" she asks. "Did you hear what I said?"

"Yes, Mom." I remind myself that Granddad may have been a deplorable person to me, but he was never anything but wonderful to his daughters. They knew him as their loving father. Their protector. Their everything.

"I'm so sorry." I'm sorry for her loss, but I'm not sorry that the asshole died.

"Beatrice found him in bed. They're thinking heart attack, but of course we won't know yet until ..." she stifles another sob.

"Is Dad there with you?" I ask.

"He's on his way home. He should be here any minute."

Good. I don't want her to be alone. I could leave now, but it'd be at least another three hours before I could make it to Bridgeport.

"You'll come home, right?" she asks. "Please tell me you're not going to work at a time like this. I know you love your job, but you loved Granddad even more. It's okay to mourn, lovey. You *need* to mourn."

"I'll see what I can do," I say. The thought of sacrificing perfectly good work days pretending to be upset over Granddad's passing makes me sick to my stomach.

"They're planning the funeral for Thursday," she says. "Visitation is Wednesday. It'll be here in Bridgeport."

"I'll be there," I say, but only to support my mother.

I end the call and grab my suit jacket off the back of my door, and then I make my way down the hall to talk to my partner, Jackson, about taking some time off for the foreseeable future. Fortunately we're heading into the summer, so we've got interns to pick up some of the slack and handle the more tedious parts of our job, but he agrees to cover my cases for as long as I need.

I let my assistant know what's going on, and I promise to check my email while I'm out in case there's anything urgent, but as soon as I'm out the door and hitting the pavement, I have one priority and one priority only.

CHAPTER 52

Lila

"GIRLS? I made goulash. Would you like some?" Ms. Beauchamp asks Tuesday evening.

MJ shoots me a look that Ms. Beauchamp can't see, but I ignore it.

"Sounds amazing. Smells amazing too ... we'll be down in a few. MJ's just finishing up her homework," I say.

"Mom." My daughter hates goulash with an unreasonable amount of passion.

"MJ, we're guests here, and being a good guest means eating what your host has prepared for you. We're only here for a little while. We're going to make the best of it and show her how grateful we are to be here. Understood?"

MJ closes her social studies textbook and places it on an old roll top desk in the corner of her temporary bedroom. We brought only the essentials over here since Ms. Beauchamp's house is already fully furnished, and I managed to find a medium-sized storage unit in town for fifty dollars a month. While I carried boxes upon boxes of clothing and keepsakes across the street to Ms. Beauchamp's pastel green split level, her nephews loaded up all our furniture in the back of a truck and hauled it to the storage center.

"Come on. Let's get some dinner," I say before leaning down, "if you eat at least half, maybe I'll take you out for ice cream later ..."

She smirks. It's an old trick I haven't used on her since she was much younger, but I'm hoping it still works just the same.

"Deal?" I ask.

"Deal."

The smell of pasta and peppers and garlic bread fill the air, and while Ms. Beauchamp tends to the oven, I begin to set the table. Passing by a window in the kitchen that overlooks the front yard, I steal a quick glance at our old house.

Just like Bertram promised, a man came yesterday morning, took my keys, and changed the locks.

Despite the origins of us living in the house, it was a bright, cheerful, happy place ninety-nine percent of the time.

I brought MJ home to that house.

She took her first steps there.

Said her first words.

Blew out her first birthday candle.

I force myself to stop reminiscing, and I tell myself it's just a house. I'm about to glance away when I spot a black SUV pulling into the driveway, so I stop and let my gaze linger. The man who came yesterday drove a small white car. No one else has any business being there right now that I know of.

A moment later, the driver side door opens and a man in pale jeans and a white v-neck tee steps out and makes his way to the front door. When he lifts his arm to knock, I spot the sleeve of tattoos.

It's Thayer.

CHAPTER 53

THAYER

LILA'S CAR isn't in the driveway and I'm sure she isn't home, but I knock anyway. I stand back a couple of steps and wait, but it's only then that I realize the curtains on the large window beside the front door are pulled open wide and the entire house is dark—not so much as a stove light on.

Cupping my hands around my eyes, I peer inside (like a creep, I know) and find myself looking at a house that's been completely emptied out. Nothing but carpet and walls.

I was just here less than a week ago.

How can they be gone?!

I take a seat on the front steps, resting my elbows on my knees and staring off.

I came all this way to make things right ... and she bolted?

Maybe she was afraid I was going to try to take MJ? Maybe she's worried I'm too much like my grandfather and she wants nothing to do with me? I wouldn't blame her for being traumatized at having to live in secret the last ten years, but my God, this is my child we're talking about here.

Pushing myself up, I trudge back to my rental. Westley calls just as I'm backing out of Lila's driveway, so I stick it in park and wait, hoping maybe he's calling because he knows something.

"Hey," he says after I answer. He doesn't ask me how I'm doing. He knows better. "You at work?"

"Nope. In Oregon. Looking for Lila. She left. Again."

He says nothing at first, and then he sighs. He knows how fucked this whole thing is and he knows better than to offer some pithy words of comfort. "So, they wanted me to call you and let you know that the reading of the will is this Saturday at the Hageman Law in Bridgeport. Eight o'clock. They want everyone there."

"I'll be there Thursday for the service, but I can't promise I'll stick around after that."

"Really?"

"Granddad told me Saturday night he was writing me out of the will," I say.

"What? What'd you do? Tell me you didn't ..."

"Of course I did."

"Seriously?" His tone is cutting. "I bet he wrote us both out because I wasn't supposed to tell you. And you knew that. Thanks a lot, asshole."

"Do you really want to go there with me? Right now? As I look for the mother of the child that you hid from me for almost ten fucking years so you could keep your inheritance?"

Westley begins to say something, but I end the call.

I don't have time for his shit.

I shift into reverse and begin to back out, only I slam on the brakes when I catch a glimpse of Lila in my rearview. She's coming from across the street, run-walking toward my SUV. Rolling down my window, I begin to ask where she was, but she cuts me off.

"Can we go somewhere and talk?" she asks.

CHAPTER 54

Lila

WE'RE SEATED in a corner booth in a sparsely filled café on the north side of Summerton. Thayer's hands are folded on the table in front of him, and I can't stop shredding the paper napkin in my hands into hundreds of tiny pieces.

We order two coffees.

We've got a lot to talk about.

When I saw Thayer at my old house a little while ago, I asked Ms. Beauchamp if she wouldn't mind watching MJ for a little bit so I could catch up with an old friend, and she happily obliged. In my frenzied state, I stepped into a pair of flip-flops, grabbed my purse and phone, and ran out the door just in time to catch him backing out.

"So what brings you back?" I ask.

"I came back because I wanted to apologize," he says. "Last

week, when I talked to Westley ... he didn't give me the full story. And I assumed ..."

"You assumed what?"

"I assumed you and Westley slept together after I left for college and that he got you pregnant and that's why you left," he says. "When I saw the picture of your daughter on my way out of your house, I guessed her age to be about eight or nine, and I started piecing everything together. And when I called Westley to ask him if he had anything to do with this, he just kept saying it was complicated and he needed to talk to me in person. And in my mind, I figured that if he didn't do it and he's innocent, all he had to say was 'no,' but he was so vague and kept circumventing my questions so the only logical explanation was that the two of you ..."

I reach across the table and place my hand over his. "Oh my god. No. I'm so sorry you thought that."

"The next day, I saw MJ at the coffee shop on my way out of town," he says. "She was wearing that opal ring I gave you, the one from the antique shop? She had that on a chain like a necklace. I asked her about it and she said her dad gave it to her mom before she was born."

Thayer takes my hand in both of his.

"I had a flight to catch and Whitley's wedding to go to, so I left," he says. "But as soon as I got to the island, I found Westley and demanded the truth." Thayer's blue eyes are intense as they hold mine. "And he told me everything, Lila."

"Everything?"

"*Everything.*"

"So you know about the NDA?" I ask.

He nods. "I know that you were coerced into signing it. I know that you were young and scared and you probably felt like you had no choice. He knew you had no legal representation, he knew you were naïve, and he took advantage of that."

I drag in a breath that cools me from head to toe. "You have no idea how terrified I was."

"Any reputable judge would throw that contract out the window because you signed it under duress," he says. "But that's neither here nor there. I want to move forward, Lila. I don't want to focus on everything we missed. It's upsetting, and I don't want to be upset when I'm around you. And MJ."

Our waitress brings our coffees and he releases my hand.

"I hate that you went through that alone," Thayer says, his strong, steady hands wrapped around the white ceramic mug.

"I had my grandparents." I stir a splash of creamer into mine before reaching for a sugar packet. "And my friend, Taylor."

"I wish I could've been there to welcome her into the world," he says. "Last thing I said to the old bastard was that I'd never forgive him for taking that away from us."

I almost choke on my sip of coffee. "I bet that went over well."

Thayer shrugs. "I mean, he wasn't thrilled to hear that. Nor was he thrilled to hear all the other things I said to him after that. Crazy thing is, he dropped dead the next night. Heart attack in his sleep, they think."

The way he's so nonchalant about this is strange. I know he's angry, but I also know his grandfather was his everything growing up. They had a bond like nothing else.

"Isn't that so typical of him?" Thayer asks. "It's almost like he died of a broken heart just to spite me. He was always manipulative like that."

"He called me Sunday morning," I say. "Told me I had twenty-four hours to move out of the house."

"Ah. That was the morning after I had words with him," he says. "I'm sure the moment he hung up with you, he speed-dialed his attorney to have me written out of the will. That was his last threat to me, like the promise of money was worth more to me than you."

His words catch me off guard.

I know he's spent all these years looking for me, but I had no idea his feelings were still so strong that he'd be willing to risk his inheritance, his future, and guaranteed financial security. I sip my coffee, convincing myself that I'm reading into it too much. People say a lot of things when their emotions run high.

"So where do we go from here?" he asks after an extended pause.

"I guess we should have you meet MJ— properly and as her father," I say. "We can transition you into her life and then we can talk about some kind of visitation—"

His head tilts and he half-laughs. "Lila. That much I

assumed. I'm talking about us. You and me. Where do *we* go from here?"

So many times over the years I imagined what it'd be like to reunite with him. I'd always imagined I was in a better place than this. That I was financially independent and successful and the kind of grown woman he'd be proud to have on his arm.

I'm lucky if I wash my hair more than twice a week, and I'm pretty sure most of my lipsticks are expired. I can't remember the last time I wore a dress, and I've been using up my current bottle of perfume going on three years now.

Every time I Googled him during our time apart, I'd be met with dozens of photos of him—mostly work-related. He was always in a tailored suit, polished and clean cut, standing tall and proud like the successful man he clearly grew up to be.

He's Manhattan in every sense of the word: metropolitan, worldly, dapper and debonair.

And I'm Summerton: safe, a little boring, and otherwise unremarkable.

"I don't know." I bury my face in a sip of coffee, buying time to think about how I'm going to answer him.

"Lila." He chuffs. "What don't you know? I've waited years to find you so we could be together again."

"You act like it's so simple. Like we just pick up where we left off."

"It can be as simple or as complicated as we make it."

"Look." I place my mug down and fold my hands. "I love

you. I always have and I always will. I miss what we had so bad it hurts sometimes. And I love the idea of us being together again. But it'll never be the way it was. You grew up. I grew up. We've built completely different lifestyles that couldn't clash more."

Not to mention, I'm homeless and jobless. While I know Thayer would never judge me for that, a woman needs to have a little dignity and confidence before she goes barreling headfirst into a relationship she wants to work out more than anything in the world.

He's all gung-ho about this now, but what if months pass and he's tired of flying across the country? Tired of spending his weekends in Summerton, where people drive around the square for fun on Friday nights and hang out in the parking lot of the Target after it closes.

Summerton has been a wonderful place to raise MJ, but Summerton isn't his style, his vibe, or his speed, and no amount of exciting relationship newness will change that.

"I'm not her anymore, Thayer," I say. "I'm not the girl you fell in love with. I'm what happened to that girl after life kicked her when she was down. I stood back up, but I'm not the same."

"You know what I see when I look at you?" His full lips rub together. "I see a strong woman who has held herself together with a string and a paperclip, survived insurmountable loss, spread herself thin as the glue of her family, and raised a beautiful, thriving child on top of it all. If that doesn't make you the most beautiful thing I've ever seen, I don't know what does."

"You and your words," I say with a bittersweet smile.

The waitress stops by with a check, and when she leaves, he places a ten on the table. My gaze is fixed to his tattoos, and I wish I could ask him about them, but the question would seem out of place.

Some other time.

"So what do you say?" he asks, and I think of his trademark persistence.

"You should probably take me home. I'd like to get back in time to tuck MJ in. It's her third night in a new place, and I—"

"—you don't have to explain," he says. "I'll take you back."

We slide out of our seats and he follows me outside.

The ride back is uncomfortably quiet, but it doesn't seem appropriate to make small talk.

"We're staying across the street." I point to Ms. Beauchamp's split level when we reach Bayberry Lane.

Thayer pulls into her driveway. "We should probably exchange numbers."

"Right." I take my phone from my bag and we switch, me programming mine into his enormous and pristine iPhone X and him programming his into my scratched iPhone 5. "Here you go."

We trade again.

"I'm leaving tomorrow," he says. "I only came here to make things right. To apologize for being such an ass to you when I didn't have all the facts."

I laugh under my breath. "You couldn't be an ass if you tried."

"Maybe reserve your judgement until you get to know the real me," he says. "I can be a dick when I need to be. Or when I think my cousin knocked up my girlfriend and didn't tell me for ten years ..."

"To be fair, had that been the case, your reaction would've been completely justified."

He laughs.

"Thanks for coming all this way just for this," I say before drawing in a deep breath. "Get a hold of me when you get back and we'll talk about visitation." I glance down into my lap, my fingers practically knitting a sweater. "As far as the other thing ... I'm dealing with a lot right now. I need to find a job and a place for MJ and I to live. And I need to figure out how I'm going to pay for Grandpa's nursing home. I have nothing to offer you, Thayer. I'm so sorry."

"Still as pessimistic, I see."

"You'll be happy to know that our daughter inherited your eternal optimism."

"I'd say the Ainsworth genes are strong, but she looks like a dark-haired version of you."

"I know, right?"

"She's beautiful, Lila," he says. "I can't wait to get to know her."

"You're going to love her."

"Already do." He glances away, gaze fixed straight ahead at the emblem on his steering wheel, like he's lost in thought.

I wish things could be different. I wish that with my whole heart. But my entire life, the other shoe has always fallen and I can't handle that happening with him another time.

"Goodbye, Thayer. Have a safe flight back." I climb out of the car and close the door with a soft click. He rolls the passenger window down, like he's not ready to let me go yet. "We'll figure out everything with MJ soon, but right now ... this is a lot for me to take in and I've got a lot on my plate, so if you could give me some space ..."

"Goodbye, Lila."

I back away and stand in the driveway, arms hugging my sides as his headlights illuminate the garage behind me. A moment later, his black SUV disappears into the dark night.

For the better part of a decade I've loved, missed, lost, and feared. I've fallen apart and put myself back together. I've laughed and cried and everything in between.

I head inside Ms. Beauchamp's house, emotionally exhausted and wondering if I had just made the biggest mistake of my life.

CHAPTER 55

THAYER

I'M in the back of a cab from JFK airport to the Upper East Side Wednesday when my mother calls.

"Are you at work, lovey?" The nasally tenor of her voice tells me she hasn't stopped crying since she got the news about Granddad.

"Just finishing up with something." I can't tell her about Lila and MJ with all of this going on. "I've got a few things to take care of in the city, but I'll be home tonight."

I'm not exactly thrilled about going to the funeral tomorrow, but I'm doing it for my mother.

"Are you staying through the weekend?"

"Didn't plan on it."

"Didn't Westley tell you about the reading of the will on

Saturday? You might as well stick around. What's one more day? And there's so much family in town ..."

"Granddad cut me out of the will," I say.

There's silence on the other line.

"We had an argument Saturday night, after Whitley's wedding," I say. "He told me I was no longer welcome at Rose Crossing, and I left."

"I don't understand ... the two of you were so close ... he would never ..."

"It's a long story, Mom. And I'll tell you everything when the time is right."

"Thayer, you have me worried now. Are you sure this is something that can wait?" she asks.

"Absolutely. I'll see you tonight, Mom." I end the call as the cab drops me off outside my building. I swipe my credit card, leave a tip, and head inside, giving the doorman a nod on the way to the elevator.

A pianist plays Chopin on a baby grand piano in the lobby. It was donated by one of our former residents, a concert pianist, who passed away, and ever since we get volunteers from all over the city who want to come and play for a few hours just for fun. It's a nice way to be welcomed home, and the co-op insists this little quirk would be great for resale value.

I try to imagine Lila and MJ here, traipsing through the marble-tiled lobby and squeezing between snotty older women with their purebred pooches under their arms.

Everything about Lila's life in Summerton is easy and simple, laidback and unfussy. My life moves at the speed of light. I'm constantly jetting off to meet with clients, working fourteen-hour days, buzzing across town and back for dinners and luncheons and speaking engagements, guest lectures at NYU and Columbia, and dropping by thousand-dollars-a-plate charity events.

Lila would hate this.

And I would never expect MJ to be uprooted from the only home she's ever known to be transplanted in the chaos that is the Manhattan school system. I didn't even go to school in the city, and just hearing about how hard it is for parents to get their kids into freaking preschool stresses me out. That's too much pressure to put on a child, and I would never do that to mine.

I shoot Lila a text, letting her know I landed and I'll be in touch soon. She didn't ask me to text her when I got back, but I think it's a good idea to open up a casual dialogue between us.

We talked last night over coffee, and when I suggested the idea of revisiting what we once had, she damn near recoiled at the thought. Her reaction stung, and honestly, I have to say I didn't see it coming. She sat there and claimed she still loved me and always would, and then she went on to say she had nothing to offer me.

I imagine she drew comparisons between us, our lives, and the people we grew up to be and convinced herself that there was no way the twenty-nine-year-old me would want to be with the twenty-eight-year-old her.

But she couldn't be more wrong.

And I'm going to prove it to her, even if it takes a lifetime.

CHAPTER 56

Lila

"HOW'S THE MILKSHAKE?" I ask MJ after school on
Wednesday.

She dunks a diner French fry into the top of her glass.
"Amazing."

"So I brought you here today because I wanted to tell you
something," I say, swiping a fry from her plate. This may be
a huge bombshell I'm dropping on her, but I want to keep it
casual and lighthearted. I've learned with kids, if you make
something a big deal, they will too.

"Did you find us a house?"

"Not yet. I'm looking," I say. I've spent every waking school
hour this week searching for jobs and housing, but I kind of
need one before I can get the other ... so until the job thing
happens, we're going to have to stay put. "Do you remember

the man who came to our house last week? With the dark hair?"

"Yeah. Your friend. The one who liked my necklace at the coffee shop." She sips her shake, her cheeks sucked in like a vacuum.

"So his name is Thayer Ainsworth," I say.

She wrinkles her nose. "What kind of name is that?"

If she only knew ...

I laugh because the first time I heard his name I had the exact same reaction, but I don't dare tell her that.

"Let's not get sidetracked here," I say. "MJ ... that man who came to visit? That's your father."

She finishes chewing her latest fry, swallows, and then stops, staring blankly ahead at me. I expected a bigger reaction out of her than this, but I'll go with it.

"How do you know?" she asks.

I bite my lip to keep from laughing at her innocent question. "Because I do. You're just going to have to trust me on that."

MJ pushes her food and shake away and leans against the back of her seat, uncharacteristically quiet.

"I'm sure you have a million questions, sweetheart, but right now all you need to know is that he would really love to get to know you and be a big part of your life," I say. "What do you think about that?"

She shrugs. "Okay."

MJ reaches for another fry, and a minute later she's blabbing on about some game she played at recess today.

I adore her resiliency.

And I'm beyond relieved at how well she took this news. The thought that MJ will get to know her father and have a relationship with him is more than I could have ever hoped for at this point in our lives.

I spent a significant part of my younger years feeling like a piece of me was missing, feeling like I wasn't worthy enough to be loved by a man because my father didn't love me enough to stick around. And after learning about Ari Caldecott being my biological father and spending an entire summer in his presence and being treated as if I were invisible, I can only say that my "unworthiness complex" has only intensified.

Just last night, Thayer was practically begging for us to try to be together again, and I realize now that I shut him down because I didn't feel worthy.

How could I have not realized?

"Where does he live?" MJ asks. "My dad."

"New York City."

"Can we go there sometime and visit him?"

"Of course."

"This summer?" she asks.

"I think so." I'm sure Thayer can make that happen, but I'll let him make the offer first. I'm not about to go to him with my hand out. I'm far too proud, and that's never been my style. "He'll come here, too."

"Where does he work?"

"He's a constitutional lawyer," I say. "I'm sure he'd love to tell you all about it when you see him again."

"Do you think he knows how to play Chinese checkers?" she asks, referring to the game Grandpa used to play with her almost every night after dinner before his condition got worse.

"If he doesn't, you can teach him."

"What's his favorite kind of ice cream?" she asks next.

"You're asking all the important questions, aren't you?" I swear she's destined to be an investigative reporter.

"I just want to know how alike we are." She sips her milk-shake until air rattles through the straw.

"Believe me, MJ, there are a hundred things about you that are just like him."

"Like my hair?" She tugs on a pigtail that hangs on her left shoulder.

"Like your inquisitiveness. He was always asking questions, always trying to get to know people. And he was so good at making people feel welcome. I know you're the same way at school, always making sure everyone's included. And he's persistent. Remember how many times you fell off your bike when Grandpa took the training wheels off? You never gave up once. You kept trying until you nailed it," I say. "And you're always looking on the bright side. Your dad was like that. I would assume the worst, he would assume the best. You definitely take after him."

She smiles and for a fraction of a second, I see him.

And I see us.

And I see an entire life together.

CHAPTER 57

THAYER

"ARE you sure that's the most current version?" I ask Granddad's attorney Saturday morning. I had no intention of attending the reading of the will, but when my teary-eyed mother begged me to come, I didn't have the heart to say no.

I'm seated between my parents in a small conference room. Aunt Lorelai sits beside my mother, their hands clasped as Uncle Ari massages Lorelai's shoulders. Ever since learning about Uncle Ari fathering Lila with Ed and Junie's daughter, I can't look at him the same. I've lost all respect. And it kills me that my aunt is none the wiser. I can't imagine being married to someone for almost thirty years and never knowing that he fathered a child with someone else and carried on like that child never existed.

"This is the most recent version we have on file, yes," Hageman says. "Signed and notarized in 2014."

"He didn't call you last Sunday?" I ask.

Westley shoots me a look, probably hoping I'll shut the hell up before he loses the five million Granddad designated for him. According to this guy, my mother and her sister will each receive twenty-two million dollars, a laundry list of various valuables and collectors' items, and will share ownership of the family home in Bridgeport. Westley and Whitley will each receive five million dollars placed in a trust they can access once they reach thirty-five years of age.

But me? According to Howard Bertram's last will and testament, I'm to receive a lump sum of eleven million dollars and Rose Crossing Island.

"I didn't know," I say to all of them, palms in the air. "I swear to you. I have no idea why he divvied things up the way he did."

Or why he didn't call his attorney Sunday like he claimed he was going to do ...

Perhaps his threat was empty and only hurled at me as an attempt to scare me into changing my mind, and maybe he was going to wait a day or so to see if I'd come crawling back to bend to his will.

Or maybe he meant to do it first thing Monday but his heart gave out first.

Honestly, I don't even want the island.

The rest of the family is quiet and stoic, eyes glassy and red and averted, everyone except for Westley and me.

"That concludes the reading," Granddad's attorney says, rising from his chair. "I'll have my assistant give you each my card. My personal cell is listed there and you can contact me any time night or day if you have questions. Howard was a long-time client of mine, and I promised everything would be handled in a timely manner with the utmost care."

Collectively, we stand and stretch and gather our things and make our way to the hall. Mr. Hageman's assistant hands me one of his cards, and I tuck it into the interior pocket of my jacket.

"I need to take off," I tell my parents.

"So soon, lovey?" Mom asks. "We were going to grab lunch, all of us. I'd love for you to join us."

"Tippi, let him do what he needs to do," my father says, his hand on the small of her back. If I know my dad, and I do, he probably thinks this is my way of mourning, that I need alone time and space.

I hug my parents before heading to the elevator and order a ride home to grab my things before heading back to the city.

On the way, I make a call to an old friend.

"Rose Crossing Ferry and Charter, this is Leon," he says when he answers.

"Leon," I say. "Thayer Ainsworth."

"Oh, hey," he says, his tone losing the cheery disposition it had a second ago. "I heard about your grandfather. I'm so sorry for your loss."

"Appreciate that," I say before cutting to the chase. "Anyway, I'm calling because I have a favor to ask of you ..."

CHAPTER 58

Lila

I HOLD a check for ten thousand dollars and run my fingertip along the blue signature at the bottom. It's the second check Thayer's sent, and while I know he's only trying to help, I'm having the hardest time bringing myself to cash it. We need it. But we don't *need it* need it. Not yet.

We're coming up on a month now living with Ms. Beauchamp, and while she seems to enjoy the extra company (especially at dinnertime), it's only a matter of time before we outstay our welcome.

By the grace of God, I managed to find a hygienist job at a new dental office opening up. I don't start for another couple of weeks, but it's thirty flexible hours a week with full-time benefits. I almost squealed and dropped the phone when they called and made me the offer last week.

Once I get a few paychecks under my belt, I'm going to find

us the perfect home. MJ requested a place with a big back yard on a street with lots of kids and a park. I told her I'd do my best.

Thayer and MJ talk on the phone constantly. I think they've racked up dozens of hours, or maybe it just seems that way. He was planning to fly us out to the city this summer for a couple of weeks, but now that I'm starting a new job, I told him we should hold off. I thought he'd be disappointed, but he took it well, and he said he'd see about rearranging his schedule so he could spend a few weeks out here for the summer.

I get the feeling co-parenting with him will be a breeze. He's so sanguine and easy-going about everything. We still haven't talked through any custody details, but he isn't pressuring me. We both agreed that we need to focus on the two of them getting to know one another before we worry about that.

The two of us have been texting more. At least a few times a day. Sometimes silly pictures, other times little notes to say hi. A little friendly banter here and there. A few times a week we'll talk on the phone—mostly about MJ and what she's up to. But it's strange ... not once has he brought up "us" again.

Ever since I shut him down at the diner that night, it's like he accepted my answer as final—which has never been his style. I've never known him to give up on something once he decides he wants it.

Clearly he had a change of heart.

I try not to think about it for too long. It tends to put me in a funk, and I don't want MJ to see me like that. Besides, I'm grateful that he's back in my life, even if it's in a platonic capacity.

"Lila?" Ms. Beauchamp calls for me from down the hall. "Lila, there's something here for you."

I follow her voice to the living room where she's by the La-Z-Boy with a white envelope in her hands.

"Someone just stuck this in the door," she says. "I don't know when they did it, but I went out to water my begonias and there it was."

On the front of the envelope, in familiar blue handwriting are the words:

For Lila, forever.

"WHAT IS IT?" Ms. Beauchamp asks.

"I think it's a letter?" My heart is sprinting, blood whooshing in my ear.

He's in town.

Why didn't he say something?

"You going to open it or are you going to stand there and stare at it all day?" She chuckles.

I almost don't want to open it until later, until after I pick MJ up from her last day of school and after I put her to bed and the house is quiet and I can be truly alone for the first time all day. If this letter is nothing more than a tender, well-worded explanation for his absence of relentlessness over the past month, it'll only bring me to tears, and I don't want my daughter to worry and ask questions because she's much too young to understand.

"I think I'm going to save it for later," I say.

She scoffs. "That's ridiculous. It's just a letter."

I check the time. I don't have to get MJ from school for another ninety-minutes, so I suppose I could open it now and get it over with ...

I think about all the phone calls and text messages we've had over the past month and how not once has he brought up the two of us being together again. For that reason alone, the odds of this letter being some profession of his undying love and devotion are slim to none. It wouldn't make sense for him to be so indifferent and then leave a letter on my door out of the blue.

I rip the seal of the envelope and slip my fingers in to retrieve the letter ... only there's no paper inside.

There's no letter.

There's only a small key attached to a thin leather keychain embossed with an address:

377 Wildflower Lane

"WHAT IN THE WORLD ..." Ms. Beauchamp stares at the key in my hand.

Sliding my phone from my back pocket, I Google the address and get a hit.

"What a strange thing to leave somebody. What are you going to do now?" she asks.

"Guess I'm going to Wildflower Lane."

CHAPTER 59

THAYER

I STAND on the front porch at 377 Wildflower Lane and keep an eye on the road. Any minute she'll be pulling up, and this is going to go one of either two ways. At this point, it's anyone's guess as to how she'll react when she sees this, but I'm hopeful.

I check my Apple Watch as a text comes through from Ms. Beauchamp, letting me know Lila's en route and should be here any minute.

Every part of me is buzzing with anticipation, head to toe, inside and out.

A blue car passes a moment later, but it speeds up and disappears over the hill.

A dusty silver minivan coasts past next.

And finally ... I spot Lila's little white SUV in the distance.

I give a wave when she gets closer, and I meet her in the driveway.

"Oh my god," she says as she flies out of the driver's side and forgets to shut the door behind her. "Is this real? How did you ...?"

Last month after discovering Granddad left me the island, I wasted no time drafting up paperwork transferring ownership to my mother, my aunt, and my cousins equally—but with one caveat.

I wanted The Lila Cottage.

A hundred phone calls and logistical nightmares later, and with a little help from my friend Leon who owns a ferry operation in Rose Crossing and has an impressive amount of connections, we were able to have the cottage moved from the island, ferried to the mainland, and then hauled over three thousand miles to this little acre of land I bought in Summerton for Lila and MJ.

But all the permits and paperwork and setbacks and headaches were worth it for this view ...

Lila stands on the newly poured concrete walkway that leads up to the front door. With tears in her eyes and the biggest smile I've ever seen, she makes her way inside, and I follow behind.

Once inside, she stops just past the front door and gasps.

I took great care in making sure the place was delivered unchanged. I wanted her to see it exactly as it was when it was ours. Truly, it's like stepping into a time machine.

FOR LILA, FOREVER   315

"I told you it was yours," I say as I follow her into the kitchen.

She traces her fingers along the decade-old writing on the wall:

For Lila, forever.

And then she traces her fingers along my signature below.

"This is too much," she says when she turns to me, her amber-green eyes gleaming.

"This is *your home*," I correct her. "The deed is on the kitchen counter. This house and this land are yours now. No one will ever be able to take this away."

"I can't believe you did this," she says, breathless as she sails down the hall and moves from room to room. "Everything looks exactly the same. This is insane. I can't believe I'm standing in *the* cottage ..."

She takes a seat on the edge of the very bed MJ was conceived, her hands cupped over the lower half of her face as she lets this sink in.

"Also, these are for you." I hand her a stack of bundled letters. "I hid them all over the cottage before I left for college that fall. Just little notes for you to find when you were missing me ..." She begins to read the first one. "Lila, there's something I need to run by you."

She rests the first letter on top of the stack and gives me her attention.

Her eyes are wide and bright, which gives me hope that

she's going to be receptive to my next proposal. A month ago she asked for space, so I backed off. I kept things cordial and friendly and platonic despite the fact that I still very much wanted for us to be together again. It took everything in my power not to give her the full Thayer Ainsworth treatment, but it helped knowing I had this little ace up my sleeve.

I planned on buying them a house regardless, one less thing for Lila to worry about so she could focus on MJ and not on how she's going to keep a roof over their head. But when I remembered the cottage and how much she loved it and how it was the beginning of *us* ... it gave me this idea.

"So what did you want to run by me?" she asks.

"How would you feel about me moving to Summerton?"

She sits straight, her exuberant expression vanishing. "You're not serious, are you? I mean, not that I don't want you to, but life here is ... night and day from Manhattan. What if you hate it?"

"My daughter is here," I say. "And so are you. I assure you I won't hate it here. Anyway, I have a few connections in the area, and it sounds like I should have no problem lining something up."

Lila rises off the bed and heads down the hall. I trail behind. A moment later she's on the back porch, marveling at the red hammock from the summer of '09.

"MJ's going to love this yard," she says as she gazes at the tree-filled open space that surrounds the home. "So many trees to climb ... so much room to run around."

"Thought maybe I'd build her a treehouse this summer," I say. "Also, I know this place looks like it's straight out of the nineties, so if you want to remodel or redecorate, just let me know and we'll make it happen."

Lila slips her hand in mine and leads me back into the house. We stop in the living room, in front of the sofa.

"Do you remember the first time we made out? Right here on this couch?" She begins to say something else, but the words get stuck as she chokes up. "I'm sorry. I'm feeling everything right now, and it's a little overwhelming."

"That's the way I used to feel every time I looked at you," I say. "Still do."

She glances up at me through dark, damp lashes. "Really?"

"You act like you're surprised."

"It's just ... after that night at the diner ... you never brought it up again ... I just assumed you'd changed your mind about us."

"Change my mind? About us? Never."

A private investigator asked me once what made this girl so special that I was willing to invest all my time and money and emotional resources into finding her. I didn't have an answer for him at the time, but I went home that night and thought about it.

Sure, I could've cataloged her best features, listed all the things I loved about her, from her contagious laugh to the smell of her peach body lotion to the dimples above her perfect ass. But those were never the things that kept me going.

From the moment I saw her, something called to me.

I believe now that it was her soul calling to mine.

She's my soulmate.

I love her because there's no one else on this earth my soul longs to be with.

"I did," Lila says. "I changed my mind about us. Right after you left, I knew I made a mistake pushing you away like that. But you never brought it up again, so I assumed I missed my chance. I thought it was too late."

I take her hands in mine, bringing them to my lips. "It will *never* be too late for us."

Circling her waist with my hands, I pull her against me.

"I've waited so long to hold you again," I say. Our noses brush and our lips graze, but I want to savor this moment. "I love you, Lila."

"I love you too."

I claim her soft mouth with mine, and a moment later we stumble backwards, collapsing onto the sofa. I tug at her shirt, she tugs at my zipper. Her lips are warm against my skin, my hands greedy against her curves.

And just like that she's mine again, only this time it's going to be forever.

CHAPTER 60

Lila

"HI, MOM." MJ climbs into the backseat, flinging her backpack to the empty spot beside her before buckling up.

I maneuver out of the school pick up lane, hardly able to contain my excitement as I steal a glance at her in the rearview. "I have a surprise for you, MJ."

"What kind of surprise?" she asks. "Like ice cream?"

"Better than ice cream."

"A puppy?" She sits up taller.

"Not a puppy." I chuckle. She's been asking for one since first grade, when her friend Lucy got a Boston Terrier from "Santa."

"What is it?"

"You'll see in about seven minutes ..."

I drive to the north side of town and pull onto Wildflower Lane before parking in our new driveway.

I still can't believe Thayer pulled this off. I can't imagine it was easy and I'm sure there were times he wished he would've bought a pre-existing structure and saved himself the hassle, but that's the thing about him—he's never met a challenge he couldn't accept.

And there's nothing he won't do for the ones he loves.

"What's this?" MJ asks as she peers out the rear passenger side window. "Is this someone's house?"

"Yes it is, MJ," I say. "It's our house."

"What? No way!" She unclicks her seatbelt buckle and climbs out before running to the front door. I scramble to chase after her because I want to see the look on her face when she walks in and finds Thayer waiting for her.

I catch up to her just in time, and Thayer rises from a living room chair to greet her.

"You came! You came!" MJ runs to him and he embraces her. With all of their phone calls the last month, they've really become close, and I can tell they're going to have a special bond.

He hugs her tight and she buries her head against his stomach, her arms wrapped around him as far as they'll go.

"MJ, you want a tour?" I ask.

"Remember what you promised?" she asks Thayer. She's so caught up in her excitement she doesn't hear me.

"I do," he says.

"What did you promise?" I ask.

"Thayer said he'd take me out for ice cream the next time he saw me," she says. "We both love mint chip, so we're going to see who can eat the most without getting sick."

I chuckle. That sounds like something she probably saw on YouTube ...

"MJ, don't you want to see your new room?" I ask.

"I will later, Mom." She hasn't taken her eyes off her father once.

Thayer shoots me a look accompanied by a shrug.

"A promise is a promise," I say. "Go on ahead, you two."

MJ jumps up and down before grabbing Thayer's hand. "Bye, Mom!"

Thayer gives me a wave as he lets her yank him out the front door, and I watch them climb into his rental car.

Warmth blankets me and a fullness blooms in my chest as I watch them together, and I quiet the voice inside that tells me the other shoe's going to drop when I least expect it to.

It won't drop this time.

I refuse to let it.

I'll triple knot the laces if I have to.

I'll quiet all my doubts and fears and I'll hold onto him with everything I've got, forever.

CHAPTER 61

THAYER

"SHE'S OUT COLD." I stand in the doorway of Lila's room as she unpacks another cardboard box of clothes.

"How was ice cream?" she asks.

It's the first chance we've had to sit together and talk since MJ came home from school. After our ice cream eating competition, we rolled ourselves to a park where we played for a solid hour, and on the way home, she asked if we could stop at the dollar store to grab some new coloring books and see if they had any Chinese checkers games. Five coloring books, a jumbo pack of crayons, a box of markers, and one board game later, we finally made it home, only then MJ decided she'd rather chase me around the back yard.

"Exhausting," I say. Lila laughs through her nose. "You know that book If You Give A Mouse A Cookie?"

"Yeah."

"It was like that." I take a seat on the bed, the mattress springier than I remember. I make a mental note to have a new one delivered ASAP.

"That's our daughter," Lila says, folding a sweater and placing it in a dresser drawer.

"I should probably get back," I say, yawning. I've been in town four days now, overseeing all the final details, and I've got a room at the Marriott on the square. Despite what transpired between us this afternoon, I don't want to be presumptive.

"Get back where?"

"I've got a room in town," I say.

"What? No. You're not sleeping in a hotel. This house is just as much yours as it is mine."

"The house is yours," I say. "Just so we're clear."

"I want you to stay," she says as she crawls across the bed and curls into my arms, resting her arm across my chest as she nestles against me.

The springs squeak with each movement.

I vow to make the new bed agenda priority one first thing in the morning.

"Tell me everything I've missed the last ten years," she says, voice low as she stifles a yawn.

I close my eyes for just a moment, and suddenly I'm transported all over again. She's the eighteen-year-old girl with pinwheel eyes who can't stop playing with my hair and I'm the nineteen-year-old boy who can't take his eyes off her for more than a minute at a time.

When I open my eyes and look down, I find her sound asleep. Her breathing is steady and her beautiful face wears the most peaceful expression, like she doesn't have a care in the world.

And she shouldn't.

As long as we have each other, we've got everything we'll ever need.

CHAPTER 62

Lila

I WAKE to the smell of bacon and eggs Saturday morning, the other half of the mattress vacant. Sliding my phone off the nightstand, I check the time.

Holy shit.

I don't remember the last time I slept in until ten o'clock.

Crawling out of bed, I make my way to the kitchen, following the savory scents wafting in the air along with the sound of MJ's cherubic giggles.

"And that's your Ancient Egypt Fact of the Day," Thayer says as he flips a pancake.

"That's disgusting. I can't believe they ate moldy bread," MJ says, pinching her nose and sticking out her tongue as she colors in a coloring book I've never seen before.

"You should try it. Maybe you'll like it," Thayer says, though I know he's messing with her.

"Only if you try it first," she says.

Touché.

"Hey, Mom," MJ says.

Thayer turns around, a spatula in his hand. "How'd you sleep?"

"Like a rock," I say.

"How do you sleep like a rock?" MJ asks.

"Figure of speech," I say, ruffling her messy dark hair.

Thayer carries a plate of pancakes to the table, and I notice they're filled with an abundance of chocolate chips and covered in powdered sugar, but I let it slide because this is a momentous occasion, and momentous occasions deserve chocolate chips and powdered sugar.

"Mom, why is there writing on that wall over there?" MJ asks, pointing.

"Thayer did that," I say, winking at him.

"Okay, I wrote on the wall one time and I got in huge trouble. You took my markers for a week!" She spears a piece of pancake on her fork.

"It wasn't a week. More like three days," I say. "Not that it matters. You were four when you did that. I'm surprised you even remember."

"How old was Thayer when he wrote on the wall?" she asks.

"Nineteen," he answers. "Old enough to know better."

"Then why'd you do it?" she asks.

"Because I wanted to impress this girl I liked ..." He carries two breakfast plates to the table and places one in front of me. "She liked this cottage and I liked her, so I promised it to her and I wrote it on the wall so she knew I was serious."

"Who was the girl?" she asks.

Thayer and I laugh, exchanging looks.

"Me, silly," I say.

"Ohhhhh." MJ perks up, as if it all makes sense now.

Under the table, Thayer's fingertips graze the top of my knee until I slide my hand into his.

Thank God he's persistent. It kind of equals out my stubbornness.

Ten years and a rollercoaster ride later, I'm finally realizing that all of our differences were a good thing. His strengths and weaknesses balanced my strengths and weaknesses.

It turns out all of those opposites I was so worried about were the very things that made us perfect for each other.

EPILOGUE

5 years later

THAYER

"THE TWINS ARE *EN ROUTE*," I say to Lila as she pushes our two-year-old, Benjamin, in the swing that hangs from an oak tree in the backyard. "They just called. Landed a little bit ago and finally got their luggage. Said they should be here within the hour."

Shortly before I moved to Summerton, I sat my parents down and explained why I was moving and filled them in on every last detail. My mother was, of course, in disbelief. I think it took her a solid week to come around and start asking questions. She didn't want to believe that the father she knew was capable of orchestrating such a despicable arrangement, but in the end she chose to focus on her newly-minted status as a grandmother and started asking when they could come visit.

By the end of the summer that followed, Lila and I were married. It was a small ceremony, no more than twenty of our closest friends and family gathered in our backyard as we said our vows with MJ at our side and her best friend, Taylor, officiating.

Lila wore a simple white dress and a marigold wreath in her hair as a nod to the first picnic date we had on the island. When it was over, I took my bride to Italy for two full weeks while my parents stayed with MJ.

I fire up the grill on the back patio and head inside to grab the meat. As soon as Westley, Whitley, and Whitley's husband arrive, we'll have a barbeque dinner and do some catching up. Lila doesn't quite have that brother-sister dynamic with the two of them yet. It took my mother three years before finally deciding to tell her sister what she knew about Ari.

She struggled with knowing it would destroy Lorelai's life as she knew it, but she also felt Lorelai deserved to know and that Ari needed to be held accountable for his transgression.

It was hard on them at first, they did couples counseling for over a year, but in the end, Aunt Lorelai couldn't forgive him. The hurt was too devastating and it ran too deep. It was a scab on their marriage that was never going to heal.

I head back outside to prep the grill. The sound of Benjamin's giggles fill the air along with the chirp of birds and sunset crickets. To my left, MJ has her nose buried in a book, lying in her mom's hammock. We ended up replacing the old one years ago for safety reasons, and I swear MJ hasn't left it alone since. If ever we can't find her, we know where to look.

My gorgeous wife turns to give me another wave and then she cradles her growing belly. Without a doubt, Lila is the most stunning pregnant woman I've seen in my life. Everything about her glows, and she radiates a sense of calm like I've never seen.

We'll be welcoming a little girl this August that we plan to call Emilia, but the way everyone's acting, you'd think we were expecting the future Queen of England. The whole reason the twins are in town is because Whitley insisted on throwing a "baby sprinkle." She threw Benjamin's baby shower two years back and suddenly realized she had a knack for party planning, and she's trying to build her portfolio.

Once Emilia's here, I plan on taking at least a month off from the law firm to bask in those first few newborn weeks and help out with MJ and Ben.

The cottage is feeling smaller by the day and a few times I've broached the topic of looking for something a little bigger, but Lila won't hear it. The cottage is her favorite home, she says. The only one she ever needs. The only one she ever wants.

But I don't mind. Home is wherever I'm with her.

THE END

PAGE AHEAD for a sample of PRICKED, which is available now!

Chapter One

Brighton

"I can't help but notice you don't have any tattoos." At least none that I can see beyond his white tank top and ripped jeans. I scan the smooth, tanned arms and the arch of his muscled shoulders as he concentrates on my bare flesh. "Why is that? If you don't mind my asking?"

"I'm going to need you to stop shaking." The raven-haired man with bronze skin ignores my questions and quiets the buzz of his tattoo machine. He forces a hard breath through his nostrils like he doesn't have time for this, resting his forearms on the tops of his thighs as he studies me. "You want this to be crooked?"

"It's a little chilly in here." And I might be the tiniest bit anxious. If I could stop myself from shaking, believe me, I'd have done it by now.

A cool draft of air from the AC kisses the bare skin of my exposed abdomen, and a rush of goose bumps spray across my flesh.

His full lips press together as he studies the custom drawing he sketched and stenciled on me a little while ago, and I can't help but wonder if he always looks this serious. I figured the owner of a tattoo parlor would be more on the laidback side, but Madden Ransom hasn't so much as smiled since I got here, and every time our eyes meet—little bursts at a time here and there—there's a kind of heaviness in his stare that I've never seen on anyone else before.

"A lot of people come in here saying they don't have a thing about needles, and then as soon I get started—"

"—I *don't* have a thing about needles." I clear my throat, my fingertips tucked under the hem of my shirt, which is lifted just enough to cover the lowermost part of my bra. "I'm pre-med actually."

I offer a nervous chuckle and, in this moment, I detest how much I sound like my mother, casually and nonchalantly working humble brags into conversations. Only despite the way it might seem, I'm not bragging, I'm simply trying to prove a point.

"Good for you." He doesn't look up, doesn't seem to care in the slightest. His needle returns to my skin, the buzz filling my ear, and my body tenses. "The pain okay?" His voice is monotone, disingenuous. I suppose if a person does this job long enough, their sympathy eventually wears off. "You need a break?"

Madden stops.

"No ... keep going." Dragging in a hard breath, I let it linger in my chest as I brace myself against the hard bed beneath me.

He readjusts his black latex gloves before switching the machine on again. And that's what it's called—a machine. According to the research I did before coming here, tattooists hate when you call it a "gun." I wanted to make sure I knew the vernacular before I wandered in here like a lost child off the street (or an overprotected, naive, Park Terrace princess who's rarely allowed to venture outside her castle).

"So, why don't you have any tattoos?" Once more I ask the question that's been bothering me since I walked through the doors of Madd Inkk a half hour ago. A ribbed tank top made of bleached cotton hugs his sinewy torso, and I couldn't help but notice when he took me back to his station that there wasn't so much as a hint of ink on his perfect skin.

The man at the next station over gives a puff of a laugh, his full chest rising as he shakes his head.

"Madd's got commitment issues for days," he says, turning his crystalline blue focus back to his client and filling in a geometric pattern with ink the color of midnight.

The sturdy-shouldered man in his chair doesn't so much as flinch as the needle pricks his skin. He just keeps scrolling his thumb along his phone like it doesn't feel like a thousand tiny kittens are scratching his flesh.

"Can't commit to a woman, a car, or a tat," the artist adds.

"Fuck off, Pierce." Madden returns a gloved hand to my

ribcage and starts the machine once more. A moment later, the needle peppers tiny specks of ink into my skin. Every so often, he wipes the area clean and starts again. "About half done."

He said it would only hurt a little, and that it wouldn't take long, but the past eight minutes have all but dripped by, like morphine into saline, tiny drop by tiny drop.

"Seriously though, why don't you have any?" I ask.

I'm not letting this go because it's a valid question given his profession as both an artist and the sole proprietor of this shop.

Plus, I'm curious.

And I need a distraction to get me through the rest of this. The front of the shop is covered in wall to wall "flash." Drawings and renderings. Hundreds if not thousands of them. Back here the walls are less interesting. There are certificates. State licenses. A few framed photos. And a privacy curtain.

I don't expect some lengthy, personal response. I've spent maybe a half hour with this man and he's said all of fifty words to me. A simple answer would suffice.

The needle drags against my ribcage and his mouth flattens into a hard line. "Guess I haven't found the right one yet."

I don't buy it. And I'm pretty sure he's giving me an answer just to shut me up, but it's not like I can call him a liar. I don't even know him.

"It's ink, bro. Not a woman." The artist at the next chair—Pierce—says without so much as glancing in our direction.

"No fucking shit, *bro*," Madden snaps back at him, and I can't tell if he's joking or not. His expression hasn't changed since the moment I first laid eyes on him.

I lift my gaze to a hand-written sign across the room, hanging behind the cash register.

NO INFINITY SYMBOLS
NO TRAMP STAMPS
NO TRIBALS
NO CHINESE SYMBOLS

The distractingly pretty, lavender-haired girl working the front snaps her gum as she hunches over the glass counter, her face colored with boredom as she thumbs through her phone. The shop isn't as busy as I thought it would be, but then again, it's the middle of the day on a Wednesday. It's not exactly peak hours around here.

"I think you're going to like this." He wipes a damp rag across my stinging flesh, his inky brown eyes resting on his work. Madden sniffs, though it isn't quite a laugh. "Shit. You better. It's forever."

He looked at me sideways when I told him I wanted *him* to choose the design. I didn't come prepared. I didn't bring screenshots or Pinterest pins or any other kind of inspiration. To be perfectly honest, this isn't about the tattoo so much as it is about *getting* the tattoo.

"I trust you," I told him as his dark brows knitted together, and then I added, *"I just want it somewhere hidden."*

A moment later, I was handed a clipboard and a small stack of forms to complete, trying my hardest to steady my breathing as he prepped his station.

When he brought me back, Madden suggested the side of my ribcage, in an area easily hidden by bras and bikini tops, and he didn't once ask me why I'd take the time to have this done if I wasn't going to show it to anyone. His one and only caveat was that I never ask him what it means.

Ever.

He was adamant.

"*Not even on your deathbed,*" he said. One of his colleagues overheard him and called him a "heartless bastard," offering a laugh that was more amusement than anything else, and for a split moment, I felt like the butt of some inside joke.

And then I wondered if he was gaslighting me. I know what people see when they look at me.

Privileged.

Naive.

Innocent.

Gullible.

Easily had.

"Still doing all right?" he asks, not glancing up.

I nod even if he isn't looking at me right now. "Yes."

The muscles of his forearm flex as his left palm splays across my skin. A moment later, our fingers brush when he pushes the fallen hem of my top out of the way.

In the strangest way, this feels like a dream.

The icy-cold air on my bare flesh ...

The sterile scent of alcohol wipes and powdered gloves ...

The vibrating sting of the needle against my skin ...

The heavy metal playing on speakers in the back ...

The shaved heads, "sleeved" arms, Harleys parked out front, and the girls in half-shirts and mini-skirts all work together to form an ambience foreign to any I've ever known ...

I try not to stare too much, but this must be what Alice felt like when she first arrived in Wonderland.

"There." Madden shuts off the machine when he's finished, and then he cleans the tattoo one more time before dabbing on a finger-sized scoop of ointment.

"Can I see it first?" I ask when he reaches for a bandage.

He stops, turning to face me, his shoulders slumping like I'm asking the world of him. "Right. Go ahead."

Sitting up, I contort myself until I can almost see the beginning of a black and blue outline against warm pink skin.

"Here." Madden shoves a handheld mirror toward me.

It's a butterfly. Small. Not much bigger than a silver dollar. Brilliant blue with black veining.

"You done now? We good?"

I place the mirror aside and let him patch me up. Tattoos are flesh wounds, I know that. And I've already read up on the aftercare. I say nothing as he hands me a set of instructions printed on yellow paper.

Madden cleans up his station before yanking off his gloves and tossing them in the trash. "Missy will check you out up front."

"Oh." I'm not sure why I expected him to walk me up. He's not a hairstylist or aesthetician. People don't come here because of the service.

Sliding off the client bed, I tug my shirt into place and locate my bag. My skin throbs from beneath the bandage, but it's tolerable and not as bad as I expected.

"Thank you," I say, turning to him before I make my way to the front. My gaze falls to his right hand for some reason—as if my subconscious was expecting a freaking handshake—and he definitely notices.

Awkward.

I can't get out of there fast enough, and as I trot to the front in my pink Chanel flats, I'm not sure if all eyes are actually on me or if I'm imagining it. I'm sure to them, I'm an alien—a strange sight. I even heard one of them say, "They don't make 'em like that in Olwine," when I first arrived.

If they only knew how much I'd rather be like them than like ... me.

I envy their freedom more than they could ever know.

As soon as I pay—$150 cash plus a twenty-five percent tip—
I step lightly toward the door and eye my little white Volvo
parked on the corner, but the closer I get, the more I realize
something looks ... off.

"Oh, my God." I clap my hand over my mouth when I see it
—the boot. "No. No, no, no."

A sign a few feet back says: NO PARKING 4-6 PM
MONDAY THROUGH FRIDAY, and I check the time on
my phone.

4:07 PM.

"Seriously?" I talk under my breath, a habit my mother
detests. But if she knew I drove to Olwine today to get a
tattoo, she'd detest that even more.

I grab the ticket off the window and dial the number on
back, which goes to voicemail after a few rings.

Great.

Taking a seat on the curb, I hold the ticket in one hand and
my phone in the other and try, try again.

And again.

And again.

I just need the jerk who did this to take it off so I can get
home before my mother marches down to the police station
and tries to file a Missing Persons' report—which she's done
before when I was forty minutes late coming home from the
library once.

True story.

"You, uh, need help?"

Following the sound of a man's voice, I twist around and shield my eyes from the afternoon sun.

Madden.

Rising, I tug my shirt into place and exhale. "Seven minutes past and they put a boot on my car."

"Probably just did it to be a dick." He almost smiles. Almost. It's more of a smirk.

"Really?"

"Probably thought you were some yuppie, suburban soccer mom with that Volvo."

I wish I could tell him that I didn't choose that car, that I didn't even want it, but my parents insisted because they wanted the safest, most reliable car they could find for their "precious cargo."

Digging into his pocket, he retrieves his phone and thumbs through his contacts. A moment later, he lifts it to his ear and paces a few steps away. The sound of traffic and revving motorcycles drowns out his words, but when he returns, he slides his phone away and rests his hands on his hips, studying me.

"He's on his way," Madden says.

"Who's on their way?"

"Dusty. Works for the city. You're lucky he owes me a huge fucking favor." His gaze grazes over my shoulder before returning. "You can wait inside if you want."

"Thank you," I say, taking careful measures not to look at his hand this time. "I really appreciate this. This has never happened before. I don't know what I'd have done if—"

Madden gives a nod before strutting off while I'm still mid-sentence, almost like a silent way of telling me to shut it.

No one's ever done that to me—walked away while I was speaking to them.

I watch him stride down the block, stopping next to a black muscle car with two white racing stripes—I think my brother had a model of something like that many years ago—and when he climbs inside, I catch him glancing at me for a single fleeting second.

Fumbling with my keys, I get into my own car and crank the air. It was kind of him—at least I think he was being kind—to offer for me to hang out and wait in his shop, but I think I'm going to ride out the storm in my own little UFO, counting down the minutes until I'm en route to my home planet of Park Terrace.

I kill some time on my phone and pretend not to notice when Madden drives by, his engine rumbling with the kind of contradictory unruffled intensity that almost matches his personality perfectly.

Twenty-six minutes later, a white-and-yellow City of Olwine truck pulls up behind me and a little gold light on its roof begins to flash. A minute later, a man in a gray uniform steps out, grabbing an oversized wrench of some kind from the back and waddling toward me.

I roll my window down. "Thanks for coming. I tried calling the number on the ticket, but I couldn't reach anyone."

Dusty, as the name on his shirt reads, doesn't look up from what he's doing, crouched next to the front tire on my side.

"You're lucky you're friends with Ransom," he says when he stands, his face red and his breaths shallow. The wrench hangs in one hand, the boot in the other.

Free at last.

"Ransom?" I ask before remembering that it's Madden's last name.

"Madden," he says. "I was on break. You're lucky I answered for the bastard."

An elaborate "piece" runs down his left arm, intricate and filled with bold greens and reds and purples, and barely hidden by the cuffed, long-sleeved button down the city forces him to wear even in June.

"Oh. Right. He was just helping me out. We're not actually friends."

Dusty snorts, his squinting eyes scanning the length of my car. "Yeah. Of course you're not."

"I didn't mean it like that."

"Right." He begins to walk away.

Climbing out of the car, I yell for him to wait. "Do I need to pay the ticket?"

He hoists the wrench in the back of his truck, the metal hitting metal with a hard clunk, and then he waves his hand.

"So is that a 'no'?" I ask, just to be sure.

Dusty gives me a thumb's up before squeezing back into his truck.

I swear, it's like I don't even speak the language here.

The tattoo hidden beneath layers of bandages begins to throb just enough to grab my attention, and I return to my idling five-star-safety-rated princess carriage. Pressing the "home" button on my GPS, I head back to Park Terrace, back to Charles and Temple Karrington's castle-like manse complete with iron gates, a staff of seven, and a million security cameras.

You can make a prison beautiful but at the end of the day, that doesn't make it any less of a prison.

But I'm making plans to break out.

And this tattoo? It's only the beginning.

Chapter Two

Madden

"Who was that kid you were talking to?" I give my sister side eye before checking my rearview and pulling out of the Olwine Junior High pickup lane.

Devanie rolls her eyes as she situates her faded denim backpack between her dirty Converses before yanking at the seatbelt.

"You going to answer me or what?" I ask. I check my side mirrors. These little shits love to think they're invincible around two-ton killing machines.

She releases a sigh from her overly-glossed lips and twirls her curly blonde hair around one finger. When I pull onto

Whitehead Avenue, she spots a pack of middle school acne factories and sinks back into the seat.

I remember that feeling. Wanting to be invisible. Wanting to disappear into my own world the second the school bell rang.

"Who are those assholes?" I ask when I notice one of them staring in our direction.

"Nobody you'd know." She speaks. Finally. And then she reaches for the radio.

I swat her hand away and kill the volume completely. "Obviously, smart ass."

Dev almost breaks into a smile, but it's gone before I get the chance to appreciate it. They're far and few between these days.

"You should be lucky someone gives a shit about you." I say, turning onto Givens Road. Two more blocks. "And I say that with you know ... nothing but ..."

"Yeah, yeah."

I know damn well that it's overkill, me insisting I take her to and from school every day, but someone needs to be there for her.

Someone needs to make sure she doesn't get yanked off the street by some pot-bellied man in a rusted minivan with out-of-state plates.

Someone needs to make sure she's actually going home after school and not climbing into the back of some sixteen-year-old pencil dick's Mazda and handed a joint and a bottle of stolen beer from their dad's garage fridge.

Someone's got to make up for all the worrying, caring, and shit-giving our mother can't be bothered to do.

"*So* lucky." She mumbles under her breath as she picks at a thread on the hem of her cutoff shorts. They're way too tight on her, way too short. She's long-legged, like our mom, and I see the way the boys already stare, all gap-mouthed and bug-eyed, hiding their pathetic little boners with their Trapper Keepers.

"Hey, I need you to actually be on time tomorrow," I remind her. "I've got a client flying in from Seattle, so I need to prep the shop as soon as I drop you off."

"Idiot."

"What?" I pull into the driveway of the paint-chipped bungalow with the leaning porch that I once called home.

"Today's the last day of school."

"Shit. You're right," I say, killing the engine.

She climbs out of the passenger side, swinging her holey backpack over her right shoulder as she trots up the front steps. Before I have a chance to so much as lock my car, she's already inside, raiding the kitchen.

"Did Mom finally get bread?" I ask once I make it in.

I drop my keys in a metallic clunk on the kitchen counter and head for the fridge. I don't help myself to anything here like I used to. There's barely enough for my sister as it is. I'm just making sure she's not going to go to bed hungry tonight.

"Nope," Devanie says, reaching into a cupboard. "But I did."

I clench my jaw, but keep my back to her so she doesn't see.

Examining the minimal contents of the almond-colored Kenmore, I inventory an expired carton of eggs and a near-empty half-gallon of orange juice. Ketchup, mustard, and a partial stick of butter haphazardly wrapped in its waxy paper are all that remain otherwise. If I didn't have an appointment at four, I'd grab some groceries for her my own damn self.

Wouldn't be the first time.

Or the second.

Or the hundredth.

And it won't be the last either.

When I turn around, I find Dev fixing a peanut butter sandwich on cheap bread that tears with each spread of the butter knife. Scraping the knife against the insides of the plastic jar, she excavates every last bit.

"Wipe the crumbs when you're done," I say.

She looks at me with one eyebrow bent, and I know what she's thinking. This place is a shithole. A literal shithole. It smells like cat piss despite the fact that we've never had one. The carpet is a hundred years old. The ceiling is stained yellow, thick with nicotine from our mother's pack-a-day Virginia Slims habit, and laundry is only ever done on an as-needed basis and always left in baskets to wrinkle, never folded or put away.

But that's not the point.

I want to do everything in my power to make sure she doesn't end up as the second incarnation of our mother because this life ... this latchkey, slob-village life, is all my sister knows to be normal, and it's anything but normal.

Most people don't live like this.

She's not even thirteen years old and already her life is a flea-infested sundae. The rotten cherry on top? A father who's lived the entirety of her life in prison.

I've never asked for much in my life, and I don't believe in wishes or any of that hope-wasting bullshit, but I'll spend my dying breath making damn sure my sister never ends up on an episode of Jerry or Maury.

"Don't you have somewhere to be?" she asks, mouth gummed with cheap bread and store brand peanut butter. "Like ... I don't know ... work or something?"

"Why are you in such a hurry to get rid of me?"

She chews, the sandwich balling in her left cheek, and then she swallows hard before glaring. "You're so annoying."

Good. Means I'm doing something right, which is impressive given the fact that there was never a precedent to go off of.

"Not having any boys over later, are you?" I ask. Not like she'd tell me the truth if she were, but I have to let her know that I'm one step ahead of her at all times. I was thirteen once. And girls like Devanie were low-hanging fruit: zero parental supervision, pretty but doesn't really know it yet, attention-starved, and desperate to belong.

"Oh my God, Madd." Dev slams the last piece of her sandwich on the counter. "You really think I'd bring someone here? And if I did, do you really think it would be a boy ... that I want to *impress*?!"

I mean ... valid point.

"What's his name?" I ask, referring to the one who put that giant grin on her face in the moments before I rolled up outside her school and rained on her seventh-grade parade.

She's quiet, sucking a dab of peanut butter off the side of her pinky.

"His name," I remind her.

My sister exhales, her wide, ocean-blue eyes lifting onto mine. "Kyler."

"Kyler what?"

"Kyler Riggs."

"Sounds like a douche." I fold my arms against my chest and lean against the counter, giving her a good, firm stare, one that hopefully reminds her that I've got my eye on her at all times – even if that's not possible. "Stay away from him."

"Oh my *gawwwd*," she groans before twisting away and wiping the crumbs off the counter ... proof that she does hear what I say and she does listen. "Stop it, Madden. I'm not a baby."

"Exactly. You're a teenager, which means you're not safe from the world and the world is not safe from you. Some-one's got to keep you in check."

"You act like I'm not capable of making good decisions when I've never been in trouble," she says, voice reaching whiny-girl intensity. "I get almost all A's. I've never had detention. I've never smoked a cigarette or snuck out at night like some of the other kids at my school. Maybe you should give me more credit?"

"I know you're a good girl, Dev." But I know from experience a kid can go from goody-two-shoes to juvie hall regular in under a semester if the conditions are right.

"Then maybe you should act like it." Her back is still to me and her voice is soft and low.

"What time does Mom get home tonight?" I ask one last question before I go.

She careens around, shooting me a dead-eyed look, one that implies we both know the answer to that: Mom comes home whenever she damn well pleases.

I wonder if she ever misses Dev, ever thinks about her when she's going into work at three, getting off at eleven, and hitting the bars until close. She sleeps through breakfast ... sleeps through most of the day actually ... then does it all over again.

The weekends are for her boyfriend-of-the-whatever. Day. Week. Month. She hasn't quite made it to a year with any of them. They tend to crash and burn once they get past the first ninety days and the men realize my mother is a batshit crazy narcissist whose emotional maturity is permanently stunted at the age of seventeen—when she became a mother for the first time and was forced to grow up overnight.

"I talked to Mom last week," I say. "About not going out so much."

"Why?" Devanie's nose scrunches.

I don't think she cares so much that Mom's always gone. In fact, I think she prefers it that way. It's not like they'd spend much time together when Mom is home, but still. Someday Dev's going to be an adult and she's going to look back on her childhood and wonder why her mom was never there, and then she's going to be angry. And then she's going to turn to drugs or food or sex or gambling or God knows what to fill that gaping hole in her chest that won't go away no matter how much she tells herself she's over it.

"Because I give a shit. And because you need more supervision."

"No, I mean why do you waste your time even talking to her about that?" she asks.

Valid question.

"All right. I'm out." I ruffle her pale curls before swiping my keys off the counter and heading for the front door.

The screen door slams behind me, and I turn to pull it all the way shut. Glancing through the tear in the storm door's screen, I watch my sister stand in the middle of the kitchen where I left her, arms folded across her chest as she stares at the ground. She's still as a statue, and I wonder if she's waiting for me to leave or if she's just lost in thought.

I'm sure all the other kids her age are texting each other on their phones - something Devanie has never been able to experience - making plans for summer or meeting up at the pool. I need to cave and get her a phone ... mostly for safety reasons ... but no good has ever come from a teenager having a cell phone, especially an unsupervised teenager having a cell phone.

Dev still hasn't moved, and I realize now that I recognize that look on her face.

She's lonely.

And of course she is.

She's alone. Constantly. And while I'm more than familiar with the feeling, at least I'm alone by choice. Devanie isn't.

I force myself to turn away, to go, to leave her behind the way I've done hundreds of times before. One of these days, I just might take her with me. But it won't be that simple. Or that easy. Mom won't allow it. Dev is her meal ticket. Her tax refund. Her extra little bit of food stamps that she trades for who the hell knows what.

Cranking the radio, I head back to the south side and pull into my reserved parking spot in front of Madd Inkk.

The white Volvo with the boot is already gone by the time I get back. Good to know Dustin was able to make that happen. I'd never seen a girl so antsy to get out of here, like she was late for a flight to the Maldives or wherever rich assholes go.

Not that *she* was an asshole.

Quite the contrary.

She was polite. All "pleases" and "thank yous." Proper grammar and all of that. I'm willing to bet she's fluent in French and takes tennis lessons, and judging by her dainty, nimble fingers, I'm sure she plays piano – classically trained by European dignitaries or something. The kind of shit her parents can brag about to their friends over dinner at "the club."

I've seen a lot of shit in my day, and in all the years I've run Madd Inkk, I've met all kinds.

But today? Some preppy little thing with a sugar-spun voice and honey gold eyes telling me to put anything I want on her body as long as it's hidden?

Definitely a first.

Definitely something I couldn't forget if I tried.

I head inside, smirking to myself and shaking my head as I shove my keys in my pocket and consider the irony in the fact that she cared so little about the ink I was permanently embedding into the side of her ribcage and cared so much about the fact that I don't have any tattoos myself.

Three times she asked.

And in three different ways, like she thought she could trick me into giving her an answer. She finally stopped prying when Pierce told her I was "commitment phobic."

Little will she ever know, commitment phobic doesn't even touch it.

Chapter Three

Brighton

"Ah, there she is! Happy Birth-"

I lift my finger to my lips, pleading with my eyes for Eloise, my family's loyal and beloved housemaid, to be quiet.

Her hazel eyes crinkle at the corners, followed by a wash of confusion over her porcelain complexion, and finally, the smallest of winks.

The number of times I've snuck in through the service entrance, I can count on one hand.

My parents made dinner reservations at my favorite restaurant tonight, and I should've been ready by now. If I could make it to my room unseen, I could throw on a quick dress, pull my hair up, and they'll be none the wiser.

With a sweaty palm wrapped around my purse strap and my heart inching into my throat, I round the corner past the kitchen, trek through the carpeted dining room, and poke my head through the double doors leading into the foyer to ensure the coast is clear. I make it to the foot of the stairs when my mother clears her throat.

Glancing up, I see her standing at the top, her lithe arms folded and worry lines etched across her forehead, deep and furrowed as ever.

"Where have you been, Brighton?" she asks.

"Library," I answer, just like I practiced in the car on the drive home. "I lost track of time."

I climb the stairs, slow and easy, hoping she doesn't notice the slight, square-shaped protrusion along the left side of my ribcage. Holding her eyes like my life depends on it, I offer a smile. Casual. The confidence of a skilled liar, not that I speak from experience. This is all very new to me.

"Where are your books?" Her cool gaze moves to my small purse.

I glance down, pausing mid-step. "Oh. Must have left them in the car. That's what I get for being in a hurry."

My mother's gaze warms and she reaches for my cheek when I approach the top landing. A smile tinted with relief spreads across her thin lips.

"Well, you're home now. That's all that matters. Get cleaned up and meet us downstairs," she says. "Happy twenty-second birthday, my sweet girl."

"Thanks, Mom." I slip away from her and duck into my room at the end of the hall. As soon as I close the door and listen for the sound of her footsteps trailing down the stairs, I tear off my blouse and pad into the bathroom to examine my new "piece."

That's what they call it in the industry.

Peeling back the taped gauze, I study the small drawing sketched in black and blue ink, permanently drawn into my skin, the simple yet beautifully drawn butterfly.

I don't even know what it means—if it's symbolic or it's nothing more than a butterfly. Madden, the artist, made me promise not to ask what it meant, which I thought was strange. But stranger yet is the fact that I agreed.

Had I said no, I would've been left to my own devices, and I probably would've walked out of there with some cliché quote or word or worse ... nothing at all.

Peeling out of today's clothes, I slip into a dimpled seer-sucker dress, white with pale blue stripes, and I twist my pale hair into a summery bun at my crown. I finish with earrings - platinum and diamond studs my parents got me on my tenth birthday - after "the incident." The family tragedy that marred our family history and sent my parents into a frenzied state of overprotection that's yet to show any signs of letting up.

It's truly a miracle they let me attend a college forty-five minutes away. I'm convinced that had to have been divine intervention.

I check my earrings, ensuring they're secure. I'm typically selective about when I wear these, and I'm careful never to wear them around my mother, but tiptoeing around the past has done nothing but enslaved us to it. We can't free ourselves from that heinous night if we keep pretending we're over it. And we'll never get over it when we haven't even processed it a decade later despite years of therapy.

I don't want to hurt my mother. I don't. I love her.

And I know she does everything with love in her heart ... but she has to let me go.

She can't keep treating me like a china doll, keeping me out of reach from anything and anyone who might possibly break me.

I'd love a good break.

Something to snap me in two.

Something that floods my veins with so much emotion, I become physically ill.

I'd love to step out of this protective bubble where I never have to worry about a thing, never have to want. Never have to need or worry or fear or miss out on any of life's grand opportunities.

That's not real life.

I want heartbreak.

I want a good cry.

I want to know what it feels like to miss somebody so hard my chest tightens and I can't breathe.

I want the head rush of falling deeply and irrevocably in love with someone and the titillating fear of knowing you could lose them if you're not careful.

There is beauty in those things. There's beauty in joy and hope and fear and sadness. I learned that from one of my philosophy professors my freshman year at college. He said that none of them work properly without their opposite counterparts and you can't fully experience one without the other.

Can we ever truly know joy if we've never experienced sadness? I think not, but I have no way of knowing for sure since my parents treat me like I'm sixteen and not twenty-two.

They don't see a young woman when they look at me. They see their only daughter, their youngest child who was almost taken from them in an unimaginably tragic crime years ago.

I grab a pair of white linen flats from my closet and change out purses. A moment later, I'm gliding down the stairs, my palm slicking against the polished, antique walnut banister, as my mother is waiting by the door. Her eyes light when she sees me, which means she hasn't yet noticed the earrings.

"You look beautiful, Brighton," she says, placing her hand on the small of my back and guiding me outside. "Radiant as ever."

My father's driver, Edward, stands outside the rear passenger door of our Petra gold Rolls-Royce. He tips his hat to us, lifting his white-gloved hand to the brim and nodding, and then gets the door.

"Happy birthday, Birdie-girl." My father looks up from his phone and offers a giant grin. He hasn't called me Birdie-girl in forever and it makes me laugh, makes me forget about this moment for a while. "How does it feel to be twenty-two?" He asks me the way a parent would ask their small child how it feels to turn six. "You measure yourself today? You grow at all?" he teases me.

Same jokes.

Different year.

I laugh to appease him.

Mom climbs in next, the two of them sandwiching me, which almost feels like a metaphor for my life these last twelve years.

The sting from my fresh tattoo zings me when my father shifts in his seat and his suited arm brushes against my side.

A moment later, the Rolls-Royce shifts gears and Edward leads us away from the Iron Palace - my secret nickname for the Karrington Estate, and off to L'Azule we go.

"I wish your brothers were here," Mom says as we ride in the quiet backseat. The scent of new leather fills my lungs, and I realize Dad must have traded this in recently. He only ever keeps a vehicle for six months. Maybe seven. He loves everything to be new and still scented like it was driven off the showroom floor that day.

It's a frivolous habit if you ask me.

"Me too," I say.

"Did they call you today to wish you a happy birthday?" she asks.

"Of course." I don't tell her they texted me instead of calling because that's what people do these days. She still insists a phone call is proper protocol and all in good taste.

Edward slows us to a stop at a red light, and when I glance out the window, I spot bumper-to-bumper rush hour traffic.

Mom pushes a breath through her nose as she makes the same discovery, but my father's attention has been redirected back to his phone, making him none the wiser. Always working, that one. He doesn't care for the concept of after hours.

Digging through my purse for something to do, I finger through the cards in my wallet in search of my license.

I'm going to order a drink tonight. It won't be my first, but it'll be my first time drinking in front of my parents. I don't imagine it'll thrill either of them, but it isn't either of their styles to cause a scene.

And besides, I intend on ordering a glass of champagne, and champagne is for celebrating. It's not like I'll be knocking back Jack and Cokes like I did with the guys at college. Turns out pre-med students at Rothschild University party just as hard as they study.

This is weird ...

I go through my cards two more times. My navy-blue debit card is there. My campus health club card. The access card to the pool at my parents' country club.

But no license.

Panic in the form of a cold sweat blankets me like a sheet of ice, but a moment later, the prickle of sweat dots the top of my forehead and I'm finding it absolutely stifling in here.

"Dad, can you get your window, please?" I ask, fanning myself.

"Brighton, what is it?" Mom's words are rushed, as if she expects the worst, and she reaches for the back of the seat in front of her, bracing herself as if she's going to ask Edward to pull over.

"Nothing," I lie. "Just got hot all of a sudden. But I'm fine."

"You sure?" Dad asks.

I give them both smiles and enthusiastic nods. My entire life I've been responsible, prepared. I never lose things. I always have what I need—especially important things like proper identification. But I can't help feeling like a part of me is missing.

Because it is.

And I remember now that it must be on the other side of town—at Madd Inkk.

I must have left it there earlier today when I was filling out paperwork. The girl at the desk needed to compare it to the information on the forms, and she must have forgotten to give it back after Madden called for me.

Sucking in a deep breath, I decide to stop mentally chastising myself for being so forgetful, and I remind myself I can head over there first thing in the morning and get it back. I'm not sure when they open, but I remember the owner saying he lived in the apartment above the studio. I'll stop by on my way to barre and grab it.

No big deal.

I'm panicking for nothing.

But the unsettled swirls in my stomach linger, and when I picture the striking features of the brooding Adonis who tattooed me today, they only intensify.

My heart skips - literally skips - when I sense the ghost of his fingertips against my ribcage, as if they've imprinted there. The way he touched me as he worked, so gentle, so careful and tender, was unexpected.

I'm not normally a fan of being treated with proverbial kid gloves, but for some crazy reason, when Madden was so delicate with me, I didn't mind at all. And it's funny. My father has always preached to me about staying away from "boys with fast cars and wicked glints in their eyes" and all of that. He always said those were the heartbreakers. And maybe he's right. A man like Madden could smash my heart into a million tiny shards until it's impossible to piece back together again.

My stomach flips at the thought.

As crazy as it seems, I kind of think it'd be magical.

END OF SAMPLE.

Available now! mybook.to/pricked

Also, if you're into psychological thrillers, check out my newest Minka Kent release, THE STILLWATER GIRLS at amazon.com/thestillwatergirls ! Three sisters raised in off-the-grid isolation are about to find out why ...

Reckless
Priceless

The Montgomery Brothers Duet
Dark Paradise
Dark Promises

The P.S. Series
P.S. I Hate You
P.S. I Miss You
P.S. I Dare You

Standalones
Vegas Baby
Cold Hearted
The Perfect Illusion
Country Nights
Absinthe
The Rebound
War and Love
The Executive
Pricked

View the complete Amazon/Kindle Unlimited catalog by
clicking here: author.to/winterrenshaw

ABOUT THE AUTHOR

Wall Street Journal and #1 Amazon bestselling author Winter Renshaw is a bona fide daydream believer. She lives somewhere in the middle of the USA and can rarely be seen without her trusty Mead notebook and ultra-portable laptop. When she's not writing, she's living the American Dream with her husband, three kids, the laziest puggle this side of the Mississippi, and a busy pug pup that officially owes her three pairs of shoes, one lamp cord, and an office chair (don't ask).

Winter also writes psychological suspense under the name Minka Kent. Her debut novel, THE MEMORY WATCHER, was optioned by NBC Universal in January 2018.

Winter is represented by Jill Marsal of Marsal Lyon Literary Agency.

Like Winter on Facebook.

Join the private mailing list.

Join Winter's Facebook reader group/discussion group/street team, CAMP WINTER.